TRAVELER

S. E. ANDERSON

BOLIDE
PUBLISHING LIMITED

TRAVELER

Cover Art by S.E. Anderson
Edited by Michelle Dunbar, Cayleigh Stickler and Anna Johnstone.

First published in 2018 by Bolide Publishing Limited

http://bolidepublishing.com

ISBN 978-1-9999529-6-9

For Hugo,
My Spaceman

TITTLES BY S.E. ANDERSON:

Starstruck Saga

Starstruck

Alienation

Novellas

Miss Planet Earth

The Horrible Habits of Humans (Pew! Pew! - Bite My Shiny Metal Pew!)

Miss Planet Earth and the Amulet of Beb-Sheb-Na (Pew! Pew! Volume 4: Bad versus Worse)

Dark Star (From the Stars, Torment Publishing)

CONTENTS

TRAVELER

BOOK 3 OF THE STARSTRUCK SAGA

CHAPTER ONE
THE MOST INTERESTING CLOSET IN THE UNIVERSE

When you hear knocking at the door in the middle of the night, you may be inclined to answer it; if you're in an alien space hotel, it's probably a bad idea.

My first instinct was to ignore it. For a few blissful minutes, I half-believed I was back on Earth waking from a bad dream—a dream in which my best friend had gotten me lost in some forgotten corner of the universe with no way of knowing how to get back to Earth. But that was a lie. The more aware I became, the more certainly I knew I was anywhere but home.

That might have had something to do with the giant window to my left, past which alien fish were swimming and paying a pretty penny to see what was unofficially an alien zoo. They stopped when they realized I was awake, probably hoping to glimpse some cool "alien" tricks. I groaned and tossed a pillow at them. It bounced off the glass, landing on the floor.

I sat up, groggy, letting my eyes become accustomed to the gloom. The room was dimly bathed in gentle waves of light, cast by the immense ocean outside. It would have been nice to watch, if it wasn't for the pounding on the door.

"Coming, coming," I grumbled, pulling myself from the warm sheets and shuffling to the door. It was probably Zander, back with an exciting story of Blayde's exploits at the hoverpool table.

Before I could reach the lock, the door flew off its hinges, slamming into the window across the room. Three men shoved inside, their weapons glinting in the ocean's blue glow. They pushed past the shattered doorframe toward me.

I didn't have time to move. They lifted me off my feet and shoved into the wall before I could make a sound. The gloved hand was sticky against my neck, the grip was hella strong. My breathing was ragged against his palm, and pain radiated through my body.

Oh, shit. This was not good.

One of them flipped the light switch, illuminating not only the room but themselves. Finally, I saw their faces: definitely not human. Bald and green, with pointed ears and squashed noses, and taller than any human I knew. My first thought was of a goblin or an orc.

This really wasn't Earth, but I still hoped it was a dream, the same way I'd hoped this whole disaster was a dream. I especially hoped this part wasn't real because

I had no intention of dying.

"Who … what …?" I hissed through my constricted windpipe. Bad idea. My mouth tasted metal, burning fire. Stars flickered in front of my vision, and not the pretty space kind.

I swung a foot forward and was rewarded with a grunt of pain. The hand around my throat loosened, and I crumbled to the floor, panting heavily. But there was no time to catch my breath. I psyched myself up to hop on my feet, take a fighting stance, and defend myself against the intruders.

Which I would have done, had I been someone with even a minute of training. Middle school karate club didn't count. I didn't have the strength to even get off the floor. All I could do was breathe as I struggled to get air into my lungs. Dark and bright spots flickered before my eyes, blinding out everything else.

Only three days had passed since I had survived my ordeal on Da-Duhui, falling miles down the chasm of their highways and taking a pounding from robot-zombie-aliens. The bruises had barely healed, yet here I was, being attacked once again.

"J'quad, that's not her," said one of the attackers. I was too busy staring at the ground to know which one.

"What do you mean that's not her?" said the one closest to me, wheezing. Apparently, I had struck gold with my swinging feet. Maybe luck would go my way tonight after all.

"It's human, though."

"How would I know? They all look the same!"

"Woah, man, that's specist," said the third guy. "It might be true, but you don't say that!"

"The human can't understand me. Chill, bud," said the wheezing one.

I could have pointed out that the universal translator sitting behind my ear did a great job of conveying what they were saying, though my lips stayed sealed. I might have been a survival novice, but I knew better than to throw away an advantage.

"Human," hissed the one behind me. The tone of his voice changed.

I heard the words coming from his mouth but understood them as English. I was still getting used to the device, but it was probably the best thing to come out of this whole ordeal. Maybe after all this was done and I was home, I could watch anime without subs *or* dubs.

"Are you the human they call Blayde?" he asked, his sense of urgency clear.

Well of course they were after Blayde. The woman was unhinged. As an immortal, it seemed she had no limits; when she wasn't off saving the world, she was cutting deals with shady lowlifes. There was no in-between with her. What she had done this time, I couldn't even begin to imagine.

"No. I'm Sally Webber," I said, pulling my legs under me and easing myself into a seat. It wasn't a good position to be in. They had the upper hand on me, and I knew it. The one who had pinned me against the wall was wincing, still in pain from my kick. Go, me.

"She's lying," said the one closest to the door–or, more accurately, to where the door had been before they'd busted it. "Humans lie to get their own way."

"The Blayde one has different colored hair, though,

more…"—the middle one waved his gnarled green fingers around his head—"explody. Red, orange. This one doesn't."

"She might have changed"—*wheeze*—"before we got here. An alien camouflage," said the one I had kicked.

"We know she's with them! They're the only humans in this place." The third one stormed over to me, lowering his weapon so it pointed between my eyes. I strained to stare down the barrel, trembling. Good Lord, please let this be a dream. "Give us our *falushing* money!"

"I don't have your money, please, I—"

They hit the floor simultaneously, and there, standing above them, was Zander, looking dapper in a trim crimson suit. He shot me a look, his brows furrowed.

Zander, one of my closest friends and interstellar… something. I still wasn't sure if he was a mythical hero or an outer space outlaw, but I didn't think he knew either. Like his sister, he was immortal and had lived so long his own home planet was lost to him. He was my best friend and the person who had stranded me on the far side of the universe rolled up into one, a paradox I was still trying to work out.

"Sally," he said, eyes wide, reaching a hand to help me up. "Are you hurt? What did they do?"

"Nothing." I rubbed my neck and took his hand. A few seconds was all it took to ruin a perfectly good throat. "They were looking for Blayde, but they didn't have time to hurt me."

"That's a relief." Zander helped me up, glanced me over, and nodded. "Look, Sally, I'm—"

"*This* is why we don't let anyone come with us."

Blayde stood in the doorway, her rainbow hair

flowing in an invisible breeze. She wore a tight, silver cocktail dress, the kind a Bond girl would be comfortable in.

Zander's sister and only other immortal in the room, perhaps in the entire universe, made me anxious simply by existing. The woman didn't like me all that much, despite the fact I had proved myself to her at least twice. I had helped save my own planet then Da-Duhui. That had to count for something. She had been polite enough during our stay in this hotel, but only when she had to. Any other time, she avoided me like the plague–though maybe not the plague, seeing as how catching it wouldn't phase her one way or another.

"Sally was sleeping and *still* managed to get in trouble." She stepped over an unconscious alien. An incredible feat in those insanely high heels of hers. "I keep telling you bringing her along was a big mistake."

"Excuse me?" I said. "I didn't have anything to do with this, they were after *you*. It's not like I asked to be stuck here. So, what did you do this time?"

"I was trying to pay our bill."

"Our number one priority is getting her home," said Zander and turned to me. "Sally, this won't happen again. I promise."

"Stop making promises you can't keep," said Blayde.

"Only when you stop hustling hoverpool."

"It got us the money for the hotel, didn't it?" She reached down to pick up a gun, sniffed it, shrugged, and hung on to it. "Sally, pack your things. We're leaving."

"What, now?"

"Yes, now," she said, glaring at Zander. Whatever problems she had with me seemed to emanate from him.

And so, I packed. I didn't ask questions; I knew better than that. I had enough information to understand that she had been running a scam in the game lounge and had conned the wrong people. It was odd that the woman who had saved billions of people on Da-Duhui was also playing hoverpool schemes to get an easy buck.

Then again, it wasn't like anybody paid her to save the world. A girl has to eat somehow.

The hotel was empty enough that no one had heard the commotion in my room. Zander dragged the bodies away (just unconscious, I hoped) as I packed. I stuffed all my earthly belongings into my duffel bag. IPod, dwindling prescription bottle, clothes, toothbrush, towel. I decided to keep the silky pajamas the hotel staff had given me, in case I'd be sleeping somewhere strange tomorrow night. I changed into jeans and a t-shirt, laced up my chucks, and was ready for the next jump.

Ready to go home, if indeed we were lucky enough to get there on the next try. The way jumping worked was randomized. You could only go back to the last place you visited. With Earth a few jumps behind us, finding it again would be nearly impossible.

But a girl can dream.

Zander came in next, changed from his bright red suit to something less conspicuous: a silver-gray pair of pants and a lighter gray shirt, hair standing tall and reaching for the heavens. Blayde followed in the same colorless clothes, tight leggings whereas Zander had loose pants.

"Let's go," she said, without asking if either of us

were ready. She was ready, so we must be, too. I took their hands, and my atoms scattered across the tide of space.

For a few nauseating seconds, the only thing left in the universe was the dark. The dread. A cold nothing. It clung to me, seeping into my bones and freezing me to the core.

I felt like this would be my lot in life, forever. Like I would be stuck in this in-between, the backstage of the universe. But the darkness flickered, wavering like a candle's flame.

Somehow, I felt the intensity of the universe, its size, its *scale*, but it was like there was a curtain between me and it. I felt part of the whole; part of the everything, and yet I was nothing.

And then, as quickly as it had struck, the darkness pulled away. *Whoosh.* The blindfold was ripped off, the universe snatched away—and I was in a broom closet.

The hair on my arms prickled as I was met with an unpleasant cold, the kind that nipped at your skin and made you regret not bringing a sweater. Not that I could do anything about that. Unless we had hit Earth on our first attempt, my closest sweater was a few light years away, along with all my other clothes, personal belongings, family, and friends. Which left me in a broom closet with two aliens, neither of whom seemed bothered by our being here.

I inhaled a deep gulp of stale air. It tasted processed, recycled. There was a hint of metal in the aftertaste, iron coating the back of my tongue. But it was real; not fresh, but real, and I forced the oxygen into my lungs.

My heart beat again. When had it stopped? The jolt

surprised me, like a harsh reminder that, yes, it was supposed to pump blood through my veins. Warmth trickled through my body, silently re-acquainting itself with my limbs.

Or not so silently. My stretch smacked one of the mop handles, knocking over the carefully stacked brooms and whacked Zander on the head. He put them back in order like it was the most natural thing in the world to do after making it through vast distances in space.

Odd to think we were breaking the laws of physics. Maybe if we acted casual enough, science wouldn't catch up with us.

"Arms-fingers-toes-shoulders-head-feet, all here," said Blayde. She was close enough for her breath to make the hair on my neck stiffen. "All in one piece."

"Arms-fingers-toes-shoulders-head-feet-Sally, all here," Zander replied, composed and as calm as his sister.

There was a pause, and Zander finally made eye contact with me, his head twisting at an uncomfortable angle. The room was small, and I suddenly realized that his leg was touching mine.

"Um, I'm in one piece, too," I said, awkwardly, pulling my foot away. I wasn't sure what the protocol was after a jump, seeing as the only times I had traveled this way I had passed out or gone a little loopy.

"Not going to throw up this time, then?" asked Blayde.

I didn't have to answer. Jumping randomly through space could do that to a person, sometimes, but the fact I was standing there in one piece, holding back the bile in the back of my throat, was enough to show I wasn't going to. I nodded at her, head held high.

"Where are we now?" Blayde asked, trying to turn around. I let out a grunt as her elbow jabbed my back, and, per usual, she ignored me. I shot her a glare, not that she noticed.

"Broom cupboard," Zander said, scanning the walls. "One unit long by one unit wide, maybe three high. Five brooms and a mop. And—"

"I can see that, you egg salad croissant," Blayde snapped, reaching over me to smack his head. He pushed her back, jolting me around, and I pulled my arms close to my chest to get out of their way. Brooms shimmied and rattled in their wake.

"But, in all seriousness," he said, lifting his arms as far above his head as they could go, "not quite three high." He put his arms down and bumped the brooms again. They fell over, as was to be expected, and it was my turn to catch them, right in the shoulder.

"So, um, where is this broom closet exactly?" I asked, shoving the brooms against the wall and edging out of the way. Blayde's shoulder in my back was starting to hurt. Zander lifted a corner of his mouth to give me a sly half-grin that his sister couldn't see. I smiled back, a little shaky still.

"Want to make an educated guess?" he asked, gesturing to the room with arms as wide as they could go.

I snorted. "How am I supposed to tell where we are? You two are the space travelers. I'm fairly sure I don't have the experience or know-how."

"Go with your gut," said Zander. "Use your senses.

Smell, sight, touch. Tell me where we are."

Well, I couldn't see much; that was for sure. Nothing beyond the confines of the closet. I closed my eyes, trying to take in everything around me. I tasted the stale air, feeling the taste of metal on my tongue. But there was also a rumble: a small hum that I could hear if I listened hard enough; faint, but present.

Stale air, rumbling. Could it be true, or was I just projecting?

"Are we on a—"

"A spaceship, yes," Blayde finished for me, shoving Zander against the wall to clear the floor.

“Hey, I was about to say that!” I snapped, but she was engrossed by the floor. She dropped to her knees and pressed her ear against the metal at our feet. Zander and I were smooshed against opposite walls, watching her work.

"We've heard these before. The engines sound like they belong to an interstellar ship, so I'd say… storm class. Possibly military but incredibly smooth, so they must be new."

"We're on a spaceship," I muttered. Or, at least, the broom closet of a spaceship. Sure, I was lost in space, but this was Christmas.

"Isn't that what I just said?" Blayde hopped back on her feet and brushed herself off, not that there was much dust in the closet.

"Does that mean we're stowaways?"

"Not for long." She reached out to grab my hand, none too gently. "Seeing as this isn't Earth, let's try again. On my mark—"

"No!" I ripped my hand back from hers, maybe a

little too quickly. I might have made the jump vomit-free, but who knew what two jumps in a row would do to me. "Sorry, Blayde, it's just… my stomach isn't up to jumping any time soon. And you owe me for letting those creeps attack me."

"Wimp," she scoffed, but stopped as she made eye contact with Zander. There was a brief second in which they exchanged a collection of glares and eyebrow movements, further convincing me they had some kind of sibling telepathy going on. She rolled her eyes and looked back at me. "Fine, let's give the earthling a tour."

"Awesome!" Zander was practically jumping for joy. "We'll be off in an hour, tops, okay? Just enough time to see the ship and not get spotted by the crew."

Blayde rolled her eyes again, letting out a heavy sigh. She reminded me of my mother when I'd asked her if I could go to a convention: *Why would you want to do such a thing?*

"One hour. Not a minute more. One hour, and we're gone, you hear?"

Zander nodded enthusiastically. He seemed just as excited as I was, maybe even more so, since he was furiously fumbling with the door.

"Oh, thank you! Thank you so much!" I smiled at her, but she didn't even look at me. Instead, she took out her laser pointer and aimed it at the door. The red beam sliced through it like it was butter. Seconds later, it slid open to reveal a plain, white hallway.

"One hour," she repeated, and I nodded again. How much trouble could we get into in an hour?

CHAPTER TWO
YOU CAN ACTUALLY GET INTO A LOT OF TROUBLE IN AN HOUR

I followed Zander into the hallway, taking it all in. The corridor, stark white and laced with utilitarian chrome, stretched in both directions. It was what I'd always imagined one of these would look like.

First jump and bam—spaceship. For me, jackpot. Not home yet, but I didn't want to jump anytime soon and I wanted to explore in the meantime.

Both of the times I had been on a ship, I had been abducted, never having time to inspect the alien technology. It was the price I had paid for freedom. And those ships sucked, anyway. This one was much better. A little more… glossy. Not some falling apart piece of garbage. Not some aliens trying to burn down the world. No, this was a *real* spaceship, one that gleamed and traveled the stars.

Blayde grunted and stretched, staring down the corridor.

"Ta-daa, spaceship," she said. "You've seen it. Happy? Now, let's go."

She tugged on Zander's arm, but he didn't seem to notice, or care for that matter. I imagined Blayde had strong upper-body strength, yet she wasn't swaying him one bit.

"I'm not trying to be mean, Sally," said Blayde, looking at me this time. "And I know I agreed to an hour, but I didn't realize this ship was Alliance. Every minute we stay here could get us deeper in trouble. They don't take kindly to stowaways."

The only Alliance I knew was close to Earth, which meant we couldn't be too far away.

She spread her arms wide. "They're the only union I know that makes their walls so insufferably white."

"We promised her an hour," said Zander, "and an hour is exactly what Sally's going to get."

My heart skipped a beat. He looked so… excited. Like this shared experience was making him giddy. And I had to admit this was the pinnacle of astrolust for me; I was actually seeing a spaceship, a *real* one.

"Can we look out a window?" I begged.

"There's really nothing to see," Blayde muttered.

"If the ship is in interplanetary mode, sure," Zander said. "If this *is* an Alliance ship, they black out the windows for interstellar travel. Faster-than-light travel isn't pretty to look at. There's a theory that you're not supposed to know how fast you're going on these things.

The second you do, poof, no one knows where you are. Others say it induces space madness."

"Space madness?"

"She asked if we were going to look around," Blayde said, "and the answer is no. We're leaving. Now."

"If Sally wants a window, then we're finding a window!"

"Fine!" she said, though it was obvious she was not fine. She threw her hands in the air, defeated and scowling. "Sally gets what she wants, right?"

"We owe her that much."

"You're putting her in danger. She could get hurt!"

"I thought I proved I can handle myself," I said. "What's with the cold shoulder all of a sudden? I thought you were getting used to me."

"That's when I thought you were staying five minutes," she said. "Everything we do could get you killed. And while I don't know you enough to care, I'm pretty sure it'll make Zander mopey for a few centuries, and who wants to travel with a wet blanket?"

"Come on, Sally." Zander shot a glare at his sister then grinned at me. I smiled back and trotted to keep up with his stride.

"Is she going to be okay?" I asked, lowering my voice so she couldn't hear me. Or, at least, I hoped she couldn't hear me. I would pretend I didn't hear the certainty in Blayde's voice when she said I could end up dead just by traveling with them.

"She's fine. She's just fussy. She can't stop our sense of adventure."

There was something in the way he said "our" that made my heart stop for a second. Or maybe that was the aftereffects of jumping. In any case, I was excited. Being around Zander was enough to make me forget that visiting this ship could end in total disaster.

We came to an intersection and to the dilemma of not knowing where to go next. Both ways looked identical: a row of brightly lit hallways with doors on either side and no markings anywhere. We still didn't see any windows, or people for that matter. It was like a poorly designed set that went on forever.

Zander took the left, putting his hands in his pockets and striding confidently. Blayde, on the other hand, was bringing up the rear with her lips curled over her teeth, checking behind as if we were being stalked.

"This is definitely an Alliance ship," she said. "If they catch us... if they recognize us..."

"Spaceships are great," Zander talked over her, still with that excitement in his voice that made him sound like an eager puppy. "I've always wanted one. Not something on this scale, of course. Something small that I can fly around in and be badass."

"You can travel the universe in the blink of an eye," I said. "Why in the stars would you want a spaceship?"

"I'm immortal, Sally. A little extra time between planets would never harm anyone. Plus, I could keep track of where I went. I could keep my things in the same place—"

"Quiet down up there," Blayde hissed. "You're going to draw atten—"

"Hold it right there," called a voice.

"What did I tell you?"

I spun on my heels so fast it made me dizzy. Zander and Blayde, however, obviously used to this type of situation, didn't seem at all nervous about the small man with the gun pointed straight at us. They put their hands behind their heads with a look of sheer boredom, turning slowly to face the stranger.

The man that stood there wasn't human, but he was humanoid. He was short, up to my hip, maybe the size of a child, though I had recently learned not to assume anything based on size. His short hair was jet-black, and his skin the color of tea, wrinkled like there was too much of it for his face. He looked rather young, though. He stared us down individually with eyes of the purest ebony, trying to look intimidating but failing.

"Are you stowaways?" he asked, surprised. Dumbfounded, even. The simplicity of his question gave away his lack of experience, and I felt Zander relax beside me. He reached for his sister's hand, slowly, so as not to test how trigger happy the stranger was. He reached for mine too, his hand edging closer.

Which is when the alarm went off.

I threw my hands over my ears. Daggers stabbed at my mind, the sound so shrill and sharp that I could imagine my brain bursting under the impact. The hallway pulsed with red light, which was enough to make anyone nauseated.

"What's happening?" asked Blayde, her voice one demanding authority. Her hands shook before her.

"It is of no consequence to you. You're coming with me to the captain."

What an odd title for a captain. Then again, this wasn't *Star Trek*. Who knew how they did it in space.

"Kid, this ship's in danger," Blayde said, arms akimbo. "And by the Code of Space Law, I'm sworn to help. So, consequence or not, you're taking me to the bridge."

It took all my willpower to keep my jaw from falling to the ground. We were under arrest for trespassing, and Blayde was dishing out orders? The stranger's expression didn't change.

And what the heck? The bridge was the last place we wanted to be. What happened to being inconspicuous?

"Listen, ma'am, you're not the one in charge here."

"And you are?" Blayde asked. "What is that alert for? What's happening?"

"Nothing you should concern yourself with. Now, if you will follow—"

Blayde spun her leg in a wide arc, kicking the gun out of the stranger's hand. Before she even hit the floor, she reached up and grabbed the weapon from midair, aiming it directly at the alien's face. She didn't shoot, instead flipping the weapon over and offering it back to our captor.

"Take us to the bridge," she said as he struggled to take the gun from her outstretched hand. "I need to see your captain and offer my aid. Space Law."

"Fine," he said, avoiding eye contact by looking at his gun. "We'll go to the bridge, but there's nothing to see."

"I can recognize a red alert when I hear one," she said.

"It's just… Whatever. I don't have time for this."

The alarms were still going strong as we followed Blayde and the alien down the hallway. It was hard to tell who was leading our little procession, the stranger or Blayde, but it gave me all the more reason to hang back.

"We're actually going to the bridge?" I asked Zander, keeping my voice low.

"Yup."

"As in *Star Trek*, the bridge?"

"Hey, I liked watching those shows when I was on Earth. They were pretty damn accurate. Got most of the big ideas right."

"And they call it the *bridge* too?"

He tapped the side of his head, right behind his ear, where the little translator chip was implanted. "You're hearing what you want to hear, Sally."

We rounded a corner, and Blayde increased her speed. The alarms were still blaring, but the shrillness was gone.

"So, how are we getting out of this one?" I asked. "Being a stowaway on a military vessel would probably have some pretty dire consequences."

"Don't worry about it," he replied, his usual cheerful self. Actually, he seemed more cheerful than usual. "Blayde and I have spent a large amount of time on ships like this. Though, admittedly, never as fancy." He brushed his finger along one of the walls then brought it up to eye level, visibly impressed. "Not always because we wanted to, mind you. There was this one time we were captured by space pirates, and they sold us to some jerks as slaves. Our minds were wiped, and for the whole trip we had no idea that we knew each other until the ship was attacked by something else. Our instincts kicked in, jolting back our memories. We saved the ship with the information we had absorbed in the months of working there and jumped away before they could crown us heroes."

"All this to tell me ...?"

"I've got this."

"Ah, good, just what I wanted to hear," I said, shuddering. Mind wipes? It's all good and well on immortal space travelers, but a human wouldn't enjoy it all that much. "So, what about me?"

"Sit back, relax, watch and learn, and enjoy the show," Blayde said. Per usual, she was listening in without me knowing. "Trust me, this will be much more interesting than your little Space Tour."

"You mean *Star Trek*?"

"Same diff." She shrugged me off and turned around. The guard was still avoiding her gaze.

"And you're not worried about them"—I dropped my voice—"recognizing you?"

"Don't fret," said Zander. "No one's knows what we look like anymore. We're just random stowaways to them."

"Unless… the whole Da-Duhui incident…" Blayde looked back and frowned. "Take a different name. Play dumb. If they recognize us, we get right out of here. Whether they need us, or not. Understood?"

Zander nodded. I walked closer to him, in case we needed to make a quick getaway.

"In any case, they're probably going to toss us in the brig, and then we can leave when no one's looking. So long as this captain doesn't get in the way."

So, basically, the full starship experience. Bridge, brig, broom closet, and all.

We reached the end of the hallway, arriving in front

of what looked like an elevator. The stainless-steel doors slid open to reveal a white, shiny wall with hundreds of buttons on it, for hundreds of floors in probably more than one direction. It was a tight fit, and yet, somehow, we all squeezed inside, our captor guiding us with the barrel of his weapon.

Blayde crossed her arms and leaned back against the wall as the doors slid shut. Her hands were twitching, itching to move. Our captor seemed jittery too, probably because Blayde loomed over him, even without trying. He fiddled with his gun's settings, looking up to catch our gaze every few seconds, like we would disappear when he wasn't looking.

Which, I had to admit, seemed like a good idea right about now. But no, Blayde had decided she wanted to stay.

I was terrified and excited, per usual. I was going to the bridge of a spaceship. There was nothing less thrilling than that; although, the alarm blaring in my ears told me there might be a little something to worry about. Plus, if it kept going any longer, I might go deaf.

The elevator stopped with a ping, but the doors didn't open. No, our captor held down the button that kept them shut.

"From here on out," he said, trying his hardest to look intimidating with his eyes scrunched together, "you must not say a word unless you are spoken to. You will not step over the white line. You do, and you're dead. Do you understand?"

We all nodded. That much seemed to relieve him, but he still looked tense.

The doors slid open, and I couldn't help but let out

a gasp. The sight was incredible, so much so that my knees buckled and I clutched Blayde for support. She shrugged me off, but I wasn't paying attention to her.

My entire focus was wrapped around the bridge—the command deck, the control room, whatever you want to call it; words did not do it justice. It was majestic, more like an IMAX theater than a spaceship. In front of me, a huge wall of glass extended upward over the crew then downward as well. It went so deep I would have to walk to the railing to get an idea of how far down it went.

Desks were set up to face this monstrous window, all polished surfaces with lights above them. Behind them all sat a chair on a raised dais, throne-like. If TV had taught me anything, it was that that chair was the captain's, and he was busy commanding this vessel.

This was exactly how I imagined a ship would be. It was perfect. It was breathtaking. I pinched myself to see if I was dreaming. Ouch. I shouldn't have pinched over that bruise. This was definitely real.

I gazed beyond the huge window, trying to take it all in. The stars had never felt so close before. There was a fantastic pink nebula in the distance, just off starboard—ha, I was already thinking in nautical terms—and right off port, there was the rustiest bucket of a ship I had ever seen.

I was relieved at that moment that I was on the gorgeous, gleaming ship, even if I was a captive.

Though that confidence did get a little shaken when the other ship started firing at us.

CHAPTER THREE
FIFTEEN WAYS TO LOOK COOL ON TV

"Shields!"

The ship shuddered as the beam of light smacked into us, making the interior lighting flicker. Voices yelled out reports to the captain, who took in everything while throwing back simple replies and orders. The crew stayed steady at their posts, focused on the job at hand.

"They're at eighty percent and holding, Captain," said one.

"Their weapons are recharging, sir," said another. "Almost at maximum."

Screens rose up in front of some desks, completely see-through, with glowing lettering scrolling from nowhere to nowhere. Data glowed turquoise and reflected ominously against the faces of the aliens there, turning as they turned, following the motions of their heads. They were all in uniform, a tight grayish-black bodysuit with differently colored trims at their wrists and neck.

While I could only see the back of the captain's dark, bald head, I could tell he was imposing. He was fully in control, calling out commands with a calm demeanor. He extended a hand out of the side of the chair, and I saw that his own uniform was fringed with gold.

Blayde had rushed onto the deck the second the doors had opened, only for the twitchiness she'd had before to melt away. Something about the well-oiled activity of the bridge and crew had calmed her nerves. She stood as close to the white line as she could without stepping over it.

The pulse hit again, throwing everyone sideways. I hadn't felt it this time, but one of the panels near the window exploded in a rain of sparks. My heart was now entirely off the rails.

"Shields at seventy-three percent and holding, Captain."

"Close off the unoccupied decks, Xacrelf. Direct the energy from their life support to those shields. We'll let them tire themselves out until they're ready to talk."

And there was Zander, calmly scanning the bridge as if we were not under fire. He slipped along the wall while our captor wasn't looking, waving me forward and pointing at a plaque.

The small being who had found us seemed more intent on the goings-on of the crew than us. He kept glancing over at Blayde, who was standing tall with her hands clasped behind her back, almost as if she were a part of the crew.

"Check it out," Zander whispered, pointing to the etching on the plaque. "The UPAF *Traveler.* I don't believe it."

"We're under attack," I sputtered, "and you're taking a tour of the bridge?"

"Just look at the sign, Sally."

"Why?" I ran my fingers over the dents and groves that spelled out the name, marveling at how the alien words made sense to me. I would never get used to this translator. "What does it mean?"

Zander grinned. "It means we have nothing to worry about. We're on the best of the best. The *Traveler* is a legend, not just within the Alliance. It's shown on every news channel, screen, and hologram across the galaxy. You can't go anywhere without hearing about it."

"Well, I haven't heard of it."

"Yeah, how do I put this? Earth is… special," he said, throwing an idle wink in my direction. "This crew is elite. The top ranking officers of the entire Alliance. And we get to see them in action."

"Wait a second." I glanced at Zander, then at the bridge, then at Zander again. I wasn't mistaken; his look was of pure awe." You're actually impressed by a ship? There's something in this universe that the incredible *Zander* looks up to?"

"You don't understand," he said, running a hand through his hair. "This is the *Traveler.* I might not always like what the Alliance gets up to, but this ship has done some mighty fine work. They stand for justice. I've seen the captain defy direct orders to do what was morally right. I have a lot of respect for this crew."

But it wasn't respect making Zander bounce up and down; it was excitement. There was a gleam in his eye, like Santa had come early. It was a dream come true, a child's thrill.

Damn, this captain must be good.

Small orbs whizzed around the room—white spheres with a large black eye hovering near the crew members, sometimes right in their faces. The crew seemed not to notice, despite how distracting they must have been.

"What are those… flying things?" I whispered. I grabbed the back of a chair for support, terrified that we'd be hit again.

"Cameras," Zander replied. "This is being televised. People have a right to see their flagship in action."

I gulped. If this ended badly, I wouldn't want to see it on TV. And if we were being streamed across the galaxy, there was no telling who would recognize Zander or Blayde.

The absence of the alarm drew me back to the situation at hand. My eyes went straight for the front window, riveted on the brown ship. It had drawn closer in the last minutes. There was a new alarm, like a bad cellphone ringtone.

"You going to get that?" asked Xacrelf, and the tension eased on the bridge as everyone chuckled.

The captain pressed a button on the arm of his chair, and a face appeared on the window, a garish, green face. He looked more insect than man, his many gleaming eyes set on a bed of matted brown hair.

"Captain Praedo, so we meet again," the captain of

the *Traveler* said as two orbs bobbed to him. Zander's face was bliss, lighting up in eager anticipation.

"For the last time, I hope," Praedo answered, sneering. His voice was strange and interrupted by sharp clicks. I still couldn't see the captain's face and wondered if it bore the same intense hatred.

"As do I," the captain replied coolly. "The last time I saw your face, you were trying to take over our outpost on Strayar IV. I stopped you then, and I will stop you now."

"Foolish captain," said Praedo. "You and your... Alliance... are weak. They will fall to my torpedoes as easily as butter under my thumb."

"I'm authorized to give you one last chance, Praedo. Stop now, and the war will end. You and your people can return to your planet. We will not harm you in any way."

Praedo laughed. "As if you could harm me! I will not rest until the Planetary Alliance is torn apart! With your sense of entitlement to this arm of the galaxy, trying to control how I rule my people, expand my civilization. No more! I will rid the universe of your meddling."

"Then I will make you rest early," said our captain, "Because if we burn, you burn with us!"

I looked up at Zander, wondering if he had heard the same words I had. They sounded awfully familiar. The entire conversation sounded oddly contrived, more scripted than reality. I had assumed that special negotiations would be more civilized than two macho captains having a pissing contest and throwing one-liners at each other. And, yet, Zander sucked it all in.

Praedo's laugh became more demonic, the laughs and the sharp, insect-like clicks weaving together, each snap tightening my heart.

"Will you now?" Praedo said. "Because I have something that you do not. I have the Alpha Box."

"No!" The captain stood, enough to give me a better glimpse of the back of his head, but there was nothing much to see. No feathers or reptilian skin or anything out of the ordinary. It has been said that many things can be told by the back of one's head, but the only thing I could be sure of was that this man had no hair.

"Oh yes!" Praedo said between guffaws. "And I will use it to bring you down—you and your puny Alliance!" The screen turned off mid-laugh, and the captain growled.

"The Alpha Box?" said a woman sitting to his right—his first mate, I presumed from the golden edging on her uniform. She was human in appearance and barely looked older than I was. A stunning blonde whose facial expression resembled a video game character in need of saving rather than an officer in a military fleet. "How can he have the Alpha Box?"

"Why does everyone seem scared now?" I asked Zander.

"The Alpha Box is one of the most dangerous weapons in existence, capable of imploding its target, forcing it into a singularity… but it should be a myth," he replied. "Now, shush, I'm trying to watch!"

Up on the bridge, the blonde woman was still speaking. "Captain, I believe he is bluffing—the Alpha Box was presumed destroyed decades ago. It was the only weapon of its kind in existence."

"We cannot take that risk," said the captain. "Finch!

Bring us under them. Crandle, launch missiles one, two, and three on their helm."

"What of the Alpha Box?" she argued. "If he has it—"

"Better no Alpha Box than in his hands." He sighed, sitting down, his hands rigid at the controls of his chair. "Crandle, this is our last hope of destroying him once and for all. Praedo has been terrorizing this corner of the cluster for far too long. We must bring his reign of terror to an end. We gave him the option to retreat, and he did not. We must do what we can to stop him."

"But there will always be rebels, pirates, and criminals to catch. Will it never end?" she said, with the air of someone presenting a well-rehearsed speech. She gazed into the distance, which was a little weird considering that she was addressing the captain. One of the floating orbs whizzed closer to her face.

"As long as I have my ship, and this fine crew, it will not matter how many law breakers and destroyers of justice there are. We will never let them stay! We will always stop them! Isn't that, right?" The crew cheered in approval.

"Now," he said, rubbing his palms together, "let's stop him before he can cause any more destruction."

"But, sir," a crew member piped up in the front, "the explosion could trigger the Alpha Box. It'll destroy us and anything else nearby!"

"There are no other planets in the vicinity nor any ships other than this one. If we die, then so be it. Our plan's not one hundred percent effective, but, of course, nothing in the universe ever truly is."

What the hell? I knew those words. An old memory

of a *Star Trek* episode flickered before my mind. Captain Kirk had used them in an episode I couldn't pinpoint, but the odds of hearing these words from the mouth of an alien entity were astronomical.

Maybe I was being silly. Maybe the words were something I had heard on YouTube. A TED talk, maybe? But it was practically word-for-word.

Maybe my translator was acting up.

"What do you think, Crandle?" the captain continued.

"I think we should listen to his demands. Then we can try to make peace."

"You know, Lieutenant," he said, almost flirtatiously, "the greatest thing about being captain is that you can ask for an opinion without having to follow it."

There. That was *almost* an exact quote! There was absolutely no denying it; something fishy was going on here. The captain of a ship that had never been to, or had probably never even heard of Earth, was quoting *Star Trek*.

I had to be hallucinating.

"We're going in!" he said, his voice echoing around the bridge as if we were in a cathedral.

I wasn't at all scared by his words. I was too distracted trying to pinpoint how he'd managed to say, almost word-for-word, quotes from an Earth TV show. I hadn't occurred to me that we were in a life-or-death situation.

It was very possible I was about to die, yet I was too focused on *Star Trek* to care.

Zander held his hands up to his face, hiding his excitement, while the crew looked only slightly worried, maybe even not at all. This man must be amazing for them to put their trust in him so readily.

The next few minutes happened in slow motion: the ship coming underneath the enemy's, the missiles going off, blowing Praedo's bucket sky high. It was a blooming flower of red and orange, a beautiful light show, more stunning than scary, the entire front window afire.

"No one could have survived that, Captain," said Crandle, a strange air of serenity in her voice.

"Now, Mr. Finch!" the captain said from his chair. His hands clutched the armrest tightly, his knuckles white. "Step on it."

Finch tapped the touch screen in front of him, and the ship shot off into space. Or at least, it seemed like it did. The crew acted as if the velocity was impossibly fast, the screen a hyper-speed blur, but I felt nothing, not even the slightest feeling of forward propulsion. The orbs spun wildly, getting close to the crew's faces before zipping away again.

Blayde and Zander's faces tensed in confusion until our captor motioned for us to follow his lead. Blayde was the first to catch on, falling against the nearby wall and clutching a chair for support. Zander and I followed her example, and we spent the next few minutes acting like we were affected by g force, crashing into walls, and holding on for dear life to everything and anything we could.

Finally, the ship appeared to slow down, the stars on the screen grinding to a halt, the crew members relaxing and straightening in their chairs. Relief exploded from the crowd, and spontaneous applause ruptured all around for a good day's work. Some of the crew gave each other high fives with elbows as they whooped, cheered and shouted. The captain waited patiently for them to calm down and cleared his throat a few times. It was only when the crew was back in place that he started his speech.

"Crew," he said, "you truly deserve the title of Defenders of the Alliance. What we did back there was amazing, exemplary for those who sit at home, safe on their planets, ready to take their leap and join the fleet. You are the true heroes for today, and without you, Praedo would still be out there. I salute you!" He raised his arm in a three-fingered salute, and the crew saluted him back. It was a moment of pride, of relief, a moment that felt perfect, eternal—

A buzzer resonated across the deck, and the saluting arms dropped. Their perfect postures fell, and the crew let out a collective breath of relief. The orbs flew into mounts on the wall and were swallowed by the ship. The men and women left their screens and chatted amongst each other, forgetting about how close they had come to death. One of the men near the window was unfastening his uniform, panting heavily and airing himself as I watched in confusion.

"What's happening?" I asked Zander. "Are they going to throw us in the brig now? Or—"

"I don't know." His voice cracked slightly, "This is a little… weird."

"This isn't normal starship stuff, then?"

"Not at all," Blayde interjected. "There's something strange going on here. And we've overstayed our welcome, so let's hope they find us a cozy cell soon, or things might get a little tricky."

The captain rose from his chair, stretching his arms high, then bent over to talk to the small alien who had caught us. Our captor nodded rapidly, pointing at us with a short stubby finger.

"I think it's happening?" I said. "Looks like the captain's about to decide."

"Don't say anything, and if you have to, just play along," Blayde hissed. "We want to get out of here as quietly as possible. I don't like being around the Alliance any longer than I have to, even if this is the *Traveler*."

Finally, the captain turned around, and it felt like my jaw dropped all the way to the floor. He looked completely human, but more handsome than any human I had ever seen. He was tall and well built, like an actor in a spy film, his tight uniform enhancing his muscles and giving him the look of a professional—much too young to be a captain on such a stunning ship.

"Does he look more like Idris Elba or Terry Crews?" I whispered as quietly as I could manage.

"Huh?" Zander answered, taken aback.

I shrunk. There was no Marcy to chat with now. A stray thought crossed my mind, a thought I extinguished as soon as I became aware of it: Would I even see Marcy again? Would I be able to share what was happening with her?

No, I insisted. *I will see her again.* But she wouldn't believe me if I told her ... or would she?

The captain strode to us, his stern expression melting into a smile. I was melting, too. Blayde stood next to me in pure shock, her eyes wide and unfocused, her hands trembling. Zander and I stared at the man, fully transfixed, though—hopefully—for different reasons. And I only say "hopefully" because being in competition with Zander over anyone would be a surefire loss.

"Are you three our stowaways?" he asked, beaming. Not quite the reaction I had expected.

Zander was the first to reply, his excitement palpable.

"Oh, Captain, it's an honor!" He blurted, his mouth tripping over his words. "You've truly been an inspiration in my life. It's incredible to finally meet you in person."

The captain's eyebrows knitted, but his smile never wavered, even when Zander's gaze became so intense that the captain had to turn away. His eyes fell next on Blayde, lighting up instantly. Blayde wasn't drooling like Zander but still gave him a polite, "It's a pleasure to meet you, sir," as he looked her over.

"And you are?" he asked her. He didn't seem to mind that we were stowaways, even seeming pleased we were there.

"I'm Thratra, and this is my brother Haln." She pointed to Zander, who seemed ecstatic the captain was looking at him again. "And our traveling ancillary, Sally. If she says something stupid, don't blame her. She's from a level-five planet. She barely even knew ships existed until about ten minutes ago." She gestured toward me without giving me a second glance.

The captain did a double take. He scanned me over quickly, lingering on my shirt. At first, I thought he had wandering eyes and was about to tell him off, until I remembered what I had put on today: my shirt had a picture of the *Starship Enterprise*. It was rather plain, a dark blue with the words *To boldly go* printed in large on the front. It was the oddest of coincidences that I had decided to put it on today. It had been the first thing I could grab out of my duffel bag when Blayde shouted that I had to be quicker about getting ready.

"Which planet?" he asked, his words expelled in a single breath.

"We call it Earth."

The captain's face twisted up, staring at me like he had seen a ghost. I knew that some of the Alliance knew about my planet, a tourist destination for some, but I was not expecting that kind of reaction.

Up until that moment, I'd seen the look only twice before: the first being the moment Zander learned he could stay at my place, and the second when Matt had handed me those flowers in the elevator. But this was much, much more intense. It was like he wasn't just seeing me, but my life, my planet, and all that I stood for. He wasn't looking *at* me, but through me.

"I'm sorry," I said, trying to find an excuse for him to stop looking. "But I haven't gotten your name yet?"

The room fell silent, all eyes falling on me. The urge to hide in a corner was growing exponentially. Everyone seemed shocked by my question, their eyes wide, almost as wide as the captain's, yet they said nothing. If we were not on a spaceship, I would expect I could hear crickets chirping.

"Sally," Zander whispered, awestruck, "this is the man—no, more than a man—the Planetary Alliance's greatest asset, the defeater of the Hillons, protector of justice and our most basic rights, a true hero, Captain James T. Kork."

CHAPTER FOUR
THE UNIVERSE'S MOST EXCITED FANGIRL

"Captain… Kork?"

I openly stared at the man before me—the tall, handsome starship captain with a name a mere vowel away from the Captain on TV, ignoring the looks from those around me.

But he couldn't *be* him; there was no possible way. For starters, *he* was a TV character. He was a man in costume. He was fictional. Not to mention that he was from Earth, and hardly anyone here had ever heard of that lonely planet.

The man before me was very real. His skin was so dark, so perfect. He had the physique of a man who ran half marathons every day and could probably lift me one-handed into the air.

Which I found myself wanting him to do.

And yet, as I gaped at him with feelings making somersaults in my stomach, he looked bashful, like he was somehow embarrassed by Zander's shower of compliments and list of accomplishments. Our eyes connected, and that's when I knew that he knew that I knew that he knew, but what he knew I knew, I wasn't sure. It was as if we were sharing an intimate secret, and yet, I had no idea what it was.

"Kork? Really? As in, *Space, the Final Frontier*?" I asked, pulling my eyes away. I had to look anywhere but at him to cool the rising heat in my chest. More like the *Fine Frontier.*

"Yes, that's him," Blayde whispered, her face reddening. Crap, now I was embarrassing her in front of her hero. Or crush. Not too sure what she was feeling toward this majestic mountain of a man, but I was somehow making her look bad. "I-I," I stammered, only making it worse. This had to be a prank.

His name was the same—almost—yet he had no connection to Earth. He was spouting out one-liners that just happened to have been on the show. But if he was Kirk, then how was he on a ship, fighting wars on planets our world had never heard of? Why had he picked such an obvious name? And if he was a real live Captain Kirk, was everyone else just as real?

Was Ohura here? Did Klingons exist?

Don't tell him I was more of a Picard girl. Wait, was he real too? Is there some kind of space France?

Blayde nudged me in the ribs. Right, I was making her look bad. I bowed at the midriff, the only piece of etiquette I had picked up from my trip to Da-Duhui.

"I am an admirer of your work, Captain," I said. "I never imagined I would actually meet ..."

"Oh, well then, both of us have had a bit of a surprise today." He beamed. And then—then—he winked at me. That small movement made my heart leap inside my chest, much higher than I expected it to.

Shit.

What was going on in his head? What was that expression that made him look so embarrassed and proud all at once?

Why was it filling me with warm fuzzies?

A sharp buzz came over the coms, just like the one that had followed the end of the attack. Everyone on the bridge froze, turning to the window as a face appeared.

It was just a man. A *human* man, with gray hair that curled around his temples. Huge, thick glasses wrapped around his eyes in a wide band, the neck of his gray turtleneck extended all the way to his ears. Not the kind of alien attack I would have expected unless one of the *Star Trek* writers had returned for revenge.

"Could Crew Beta get down here, please?" he asked, dully. "Crew Beta, we have a lot to discuss. Thank *you*."

With that, almost everyone from the fight, and some who had lingered behind the white line with us, simply got up and left. They filed out through the elevators on both sides of the bridge, chatting happily together, including the man striping off his uniform. He was now half out of it, his jacket slung over his shoulder, hopping as he tried to put a pant leg back on.

Yet the captain stayed.

There were very few who remained, including our

captor, who was the shortest person in the room by far. None of them seemed too concerned by the guy in the turtleneck.

"Oh, you haven't been formally introduced yet." The captain reached for the woman at his side. "This is my first mate, Lieutenant Nolla Crandle."

Zander bowed so low I was worried his hair would sweep the floor. This woman must have been famous as well; even Blayde looked stoked to see her. I followed their lead and bowed, not knowing who exactly she was, but relatively certain I should be impressed.

"Jezeal, there you are!" Kork waved at the elevator.

The second the doors opened, I bit down on my lip, hard, doing everything to hold back a scream. Because there, standing in the little chamber, was a three-meter tall spider with all eight eyes and eight legs, thick gray-brown fur, and ebony mandibles. His head was at an angle to fit inside the elevator, but he seemed twice as impressive as he stepped into the bridge and straightened.

He stood on his four hind legs, two to a pant leg each and two arms per sleeve, so he almost looked like any other member of the crew, except hairier. He wore the same uniform as everyone else, though his cuffs and neckline were a light turquoise. He stepped forward, taking a large bite of a snack bar as he approached.

Maybe a cousin of Tchilla, back on Da-Duhui? He looked like a Meegran, the only species I had met so far that was so… spidery. But her clothes allowed her multiple legs to flow. They were not constricted as Jezeal's were here.

"Ahoy, Captain," he said, between bites, crumbs

sticking to his mandibles. "Who's this now?"

"Ah, well, we have a small case of stowaways on the ship," Kork joked, slapping Jezeal on the back playfully, seemingly not intimidated by the *huge freaking spider.* "Don't worry, I don't think it's catching. Thratra, Haln, Sally, meet our trusted doctor, Ter Jezeal."

"Oh, cool." Jezeal offered a bow of greeting, one which brought his hands almost to the floor. "Has Finch met them yet? He was complaining about the same faces around here. New blood will cheer him up."

"What's going to cheer me up?" asked a man, exiting the lift behind Jezeal. He was a plain-looking human, clean shaven with trimmed hair. He gave an awkward smile as he saw us. "Ah, stowaways. Fun."

"Oh my stars, that's Finch," said Zander, incapable of containing his excitement, nodding in the man's direction as he went to his chair without paying any further mind to us. "He's the chief engineer, insanely talented. A child prodigy."

"Wait, hold on a second," I said, confused, trying not to mention the giant spider in the room. "I shouldn't be saying this, but shouldn't you be, I don't know, arresting us? We shouldn't be here. Isn't being a stowaway illegal?"

"Oh god, Sally," Blayde hissed. "Know when to keep your mouth shut."

"Oh, it's perfectly fine," said Kork.

"It is?"

"Yeah, we're used to it." he said, He nudged his lieutenant for her to back him up. Crandle rolled her eyes and walked away, much to his disappointment. "Seriously, though, you have no idea the lengths fans go to when they want to meet us."

"You'll be dealt with as soon as the crew meeting is over," Crandle said from her desk, where she was now starting a game on her screen. Or, at least, I thought it was a game. She could have been fighting a real war on that thing. "They're probably talking about you right this minute."

"Damn, you're grim," said the man sitting a row ahead of her, spinning his chair around to get a look at us.

"What part of that was grim?" said Crandle, glaring at him.

"The voice part."

"I meant nothing by it."

Like most of the crew here, he was a human, which was weird. Even in Da-Duhui, I hadn't seen a concentration of humans like this in one place. Everyone here had the usual number of eyes and limbs. It almost felt like home.

Minus the eight eyed, eight-legged spider man. And the spaceship.

“I'm missing all the fun, aren't I?” said Xacrelf, stepping forward, grinning widely. The man looked straight out of a comic book. With his broad shoulders and picture-perfect bowl haircut, he could have been He-Man if he showed more chest. Still, the Alliance uniform was tight across his muscular physique, which didn't seem humanly possible—and probably wasn't. Human, that is.

“Stowaways, meet our head of security, Ualph Xacrelf,” said Kork, throwing an arm over his buddy. “Ualph, meet some fans of ours.”

“Of yours, you mean.” He patted the captain on the

shoulder before peeling away. “Nice to meet you. Regular viewers, I take it? Impressive move, slipping on board and avoiding our scans for so long. Not many can pull it off.”

“Oh please,” said a woman, gliding past him and joining Finch at one of the posts. “It happens, like, once a month. Security is slipping around here.”

“That's actually her!” said Zander, beaming. “The human translating machine, Cara Doesso! They say she’s written half the code of the Alliance translators. Astounding.”

“Don’t feed her ego too much,” said Xacrelf, “or it’s going to develop an appetite and eat you next.”

“Says the man who keeps pictures of himself hidden around his quarters,” said Doesso, spinning around on the chair just long enough to shoot him a glare. Her straight-cut hair moved as one piece, like a chocolate fountain.

“That’s my sister!” Xacrelf spat.

“The looks run in the family, then.”

"Anybody care for a drink?" Kork interrupted, sliding a wooden panel on the wall to reveal a mini fridge, "Non-alcoholic, I'm afraid, but our selection is pretty good. Remind me to give catering a huge tip for the *Traveler*-versary. Crandle?"

"Computer, remind Kork to tip catering before the anniversary."

"Captain," came an electronic voice from above, "don't forget to ..."

"I got it, computer." He grimaced. "Sorry about that. This morning was trying for us all."

"Oh, we can understand that," said Zander.

Kork handed us what looked like juice boxes—rectangular, unmarked silver bars that sloshed when I took it. I watched Zander as he pulled back the tab, which made a spout pop up, and he sipped it with relish.

The snacks soon followed. Nuts, crackers, and fruits I had never seen before were passed from person to person, and suddenly, there was a small party happening. Kork congratulated his crew on their performance while subtly avoiding my gaze. And Zander's, for that matter, mainly because the immortal warrior still foamed at the mouth having talked with his hero.

Kork seemed more a regular guy than a celebrity. He had a natural charm about him and looked so, well, human. Zander, on the other hand, was acting like an eight-year-old, overflowing with excitement. I had never seen so besotted before, but Kork put up with it, talking with him like an old friend. Blayde, on the other hand, was having a nice conversation with our host on one of his most remarkable exploits, though it had never turned up on *Star Trek* back at home.

She was treating him like an equal. That might have been her version of flirting.

I slipped away, excited to explore the bridge, trying not to think about the group of people somewhere out there determining my fate. I might not get another chance like this. I let my fingers trail over the sleek desks, over the library lights, and through holographic screens. I was in science-fiction heaven.

The window was larger than just this deck, and it went pretty far down, too. I leaned on the railing. If I stuck my head out far enough, the curve of the window enveloped me, and I was surrounded by stars. It was almost like hanging in space, basking in interstellar emptiness in my own oxygen-soaked bubble.

"Pretty amazing, isn't it?"

The voice made me jump, and for a second I thought I was going to fly off the railing. But there was his hand on my shoulder, helping me back to Earth, so to speak.

Kork. Captain Kork.

"Oh!" I said. "Yes, yes, it is. I've never seen anything like it."

"No, I wouldn't suspect you get views like this on your Earth." He grinned.

"You know Earth?"

"I—no, I don't. You said you were pre-contact. I wouldn't think you have civilian space stations yet."

"And you would be right," I said, turning back to stare at the stars. If I looked at him any longer, the butterflies in my stomach would become too much to handle. "Well, we have… never mind."

"First time in interstellar space?"

"Oh boy, yes."

"So, space is black, empty, dangerous, cold, and out to kill you in any way possible," he said. We gazed quietly off the bow together. His voice dropped to a whisper, like he would disturb the universe merely by uttering a word. "How do you like it?"

I stared straight ahead, taking it all in. There was only one possible answer.

"I love it." And in that moment, I was completely and utterly content.

"I like your shirt," he said, but then looked away, as if making a statement that he *wasn't* looking.

"Thanks?"

"You know, that's my catchphrase—and seeing as how you don't have a clue who I am, I find it incredibly surprising to see it on your shirt."

"I think someone back home might have stolen it from you, you know." Though as the words came out of my mouth, I realized that our *Star Trek* would have been older than this Kork. But before I could think any more about it, the captain distracted me again.

"Ah, figures," he said. "People can make a bundle selling alien wares to unsuspecting pre-contact civilizations. You won't believe how much concert swag gets passed off as high art on those worlds. Sometimes they include quotes from interstellar celebrities. I get that."

"It kind of sounds like someone on Earth is rebroadcasting your show with different actors. The captain has your name, too—sort of," I said, trying not to think too hard about how, timewise, as it should be the other way around. Any way you put it, Earth's *Star Trek* came first. "It's pretty popular back home—the show, not your name."

He laughed so hard it almost sounded ridiculous. His crew stared at him—him, not me, for once—as if he had just sprouted a second head. It was only then that he met my gaze.

His eyes were a beautiful green. And deep. And just for a second, I was back home, on Earth, looking into the eyes of a fellow Terran, a random earthling. And then I was transported somewhere else, somewhere that was neither Earth nor the bridge of the UPAF *Traveler*. Somewhere above and beyond it all.

"James T. Kork." He extended a hand to shake.

"I know," I said, then stopped myself. Rude much? "I'm Sally. Sally Webber."

We shook hands. I wondered what this gesture meant to people of the Alliance. I hoped I hadn't sold my hand in marriage.

At that moment, though, I probably would not have cared.

"Let me savor this," he said, taking back his hand. "Sally, have I finally met the first person not to bombard me with questions?"

That made me laugh, and he joined in, causing some more heads to turn. Zander lifted his eyebrows quizzically then rolled his eyes and returned to talking to Doesso, the language girl.

"Maybe," I said, ignoring my friend's dismissive look, "Though, maybe one ... do you know better than to always go on away missions?"

"Now *that*"—Kork winked again—"is not what I expected."

He was looking at me, and I was looking at him. I had a million questions, yet at the same time, just one. My mind raced, and I leaned closer to him, taking in this interstellar hero I had never heard of and yet suddenly falling into his orbit. He smelled, surprisingly, of peaches and marigolds.

And in that minute, the universe threw another smack into my face.

"Alert, alert," the computer said, an electronic voice devoid of emotion. "An error has occurred. Error. Error. Going offline."

The lights extinguished, all at once.

There was a scream.

Kork grabbed my hand. It felt like a shot of adrenaline was injected into me through his touch, and my heart skipped a beat—either out of excitement, or from terror, or being on a dark and drifting spaceship.

"Um, I've got this, I think," Jezeal said. I could only guess it was Jezeal, seeing as how I couldn't see a thing. But why the doctor would be the one fixing the ship, I would not know.

The lights came back on but it was emergency power, and everything was basked in an awful orange glow, like a pumpkin had vomited all over the bridge.

"Ejecting sections forty-three through eighty-eight," the computer continued, in a hacked-off drawl. "In ninety-nine, ninety-eight ..."

Suddenly, every console on the bridge lit up, the countdown flashing in bright red digital figures. The room filled with the same blaring alarm. My ears rang as the noise echoed from wall to wall. The crew was instantly on their feet, all composure gone, replaced by full and complete terror.

"No, stop that. No!" Crandle slammed her hands on the desk, tapping wildly at the touchscreen. "Anybody have any idea how to work this thing? Oh, Veesh, this does not sound good!"

"What the hell did you do, Jezeal?" Finch shoved the man-spider against the captain's chair. Jezeal's mandibles shuddered, and he jumped away from the engineer, who was practically foaming at the mouth. Doesso grabbed Finch's arm and pulled him back.

"The conference room is on deck fifty-seven," Finch snarled. "If we lose the crew, so help me, Jezeal."

"The computers are locked down!" Crandle's voice

was barely audible over the roar of alarm. "What do we do? If we don't shut off that alarm soon, I'll get tinnitus."

Everyone stared at Kork. He released my hand; he had still been holding it, and I had forgotten. Funny how a panicking spaceship crew does that to you.

"You should be able to manually override the command," Zander said, cool under pressure, shooting a look at the captain. "From your chair?"

"Yes, yes, I should," Kork replied, looking increasingly worried. That was understandable; the lives of those people were in his hands.

Kork walked to his command chair. He sat. We stared at him as he pulled up his screen and typed in strings of commands. Even from the outside, we could see it wasn't working. A warning flashed backward on his screen: *Error. Error. Error.*

It was echoed by the computer's ominous voice.

Doesso shouted obscenities while holding back Finch as he tried to take another swipe at Jezeal. The doctor was trying not to run, struggling to stand his ground, but the engineer's arms were getting closer to his face. All the while, the captain typed, sweat building at his brow.

Zander and Blayde stood to the side, together, watching with sinking faces.

And I watched as their awe of this man drained out of them.

"Zero," the computer said, cold. "Levels ... ejecting."

We felt nothing. We could have been moving, but there was no reference point out the window to make heads or tails of our speed. But the loud, reverberating sound that filled the bridge was proof enough that a huge portion of the ship had just ... vanished.

"Conference room! Can you hear me?" the captain bellowed into his armrest. He hailed them again, but there was only static. No one was answering on their end.

It was too late.

"The crew is… gone," Kork said, as if he couldn't believe his own words.

Gasps echoed around the room. Crandle put her hand over her mouth, looking like a young girl and not a war-stricken lieutenant. The captain continued nonetheless.

"The entire section detached," he said, "though luckily enough, they have all the storerooms. They have food, and they can signal for help. They'll be fine, but we're on our own from here on out. And it's not them I'm worried about," He paused to let the news sink in. All eyes were intent on him, and he shut his lids, as if trying to block them out. "The ship abandoned them without any of us controlling it. I'm calling sabotage, though it was more likely on their end than ours. And while they have enough food to last them years, we have the minibar and whatever you've snuck to your quarters. We're screwed, to say the least. And we're ... seven, plus the three stowaways. We're going to have to ration."

Instantly, voices rose, yelling, calling out accusations. Mainly at us. If I were in their shoes, I'd blame the strangers first.

"The trouble only started when they got here," said Doesso, shoving Finch back once and for all, a scowl on her flawless face.

"Yeah!" agreed Finch, forgetting about Jezeal.

"They're to blame."

"Arrest them!" Doesso grabbed the gun at her waist. "If you don't, I will."

"They couldn't have done anything." Kork stood up, stepping before her, coaxing Doesso to release her grip on the gun, and calmly spoke again. "The crew has a security perimeter set up. They must have been hiding in a cupboard since the launch. If not, the crew would have intercepted them beforehand. They could not have done anything." His words calmed the crew. It was clear they believed every syllable out of their leader's mouth.

"Has anybody seen Xacrelf?"

The question seemed to come from nowhere, but it was Jezeal, looking around the bridge with his eight large eyes, his fuzzy face scrunched in confusion.

"I refuse to believe he's responsible for this," said Kork. "He's probably gone to fix what he can."

"Come to think of it, I haven't seen him since we passed out drinks," said Crandle. "Has anyone?"

We all looked at each other, trading glances. In that moment, every look was accusatory.

"Computer, locate Xacrelf," said Crandle, staring at the ceiling.

"The computer's voice command is offline," said Doesso, "but I know the basics of the manual panels. They're saying Xacrelf is on the observation deck."

"What on Pyrina could he be doing there?" asked Kork. "Finch, you're the closest. Call for him, will you?"

Finch grabbed the railing and looked over. He said nothing, instead turning back to us with wide, blank eyes.

"Xacrelf is… no longer with us," he said, shaking.

"What do you mean?"

"It seems… he must have—Captain, I don't know how, but in the confusion, I think he fell. His neck, he—"

"You're saying…"

A silence fell over us all. We didn't need Finch to use words; the look on his face said it all.

"Murder," Kork said, solemnly. "First, sabotage. Now, murder. Someone on this ship is a traitor." Tears streamed down his Kork's face in strong and even streaks. His friend had just been murdered, and he could not scream or shout. He had to remain in control.

"It's them," hissed Doesso, pointing a steady finger at me. "They came here. They broke the *Traveler*. They *killed* Xacrelf. Kork, if you don't take them down, so help me."

"It's easy to point fingers," said Kork, glaring at his crew in turn. "It's harder to find the truth. We had our eyes on the newcomers the whole time. It's hard to believe they could have pulled this off with no one noticing."

"And yet the fact remains, Captain," said Crandle, wiping her eyes with a corner of her sleeve, "the fact remains that someone here did manage to… *kill* our friend, without anyone even noticing he was gone. We're all suspect."

"Then we must get in touch with the crew," the captain responded, nodding, "and contact the correct authorities."

"I see a simple solution for that," Zander said, finally losing the eight-year-old attitude and maturing a good thousand. "We regain control of the ship and reconnect.

Manually. It's tricky maneuvering, but Kork's been known to pull off worse. Isn't that right, Captain?"

"It's true; we saw what happened at Stone Hovel." Blayde smirked, like she was in on some big secret.

"Not to mention the incident with the *T'k'lr*," added Zander. "Plus, you have your crew! You have the team together, and what is it you always say? With this fine ship and this fine crew ..."

Crandle glanced at Kork, who nodded hastily. The crew was suddenly preoccupied with their own feet. The lieutenant walked towards us in slow motion, as if making up her mind whether to let us in on some big secret. The room's silence was so extreme that I could hear my own rapid heartbeat.

"Technically," she whispered, "we're not the crew. We're not even soldiers."

"What then?" Blayde glared at her, scowling.

"We're—well, if they're the crew, we, urm, we're the cast."

"I don't understand." Zander's face dropped. "The cast of what?"

"We're actors, Haln. We're just actors. And this is the greatest show of all time."

CHAPTER FIVE

ZANDER AND THE REAL WORLD: SPACE EDITION

Santa was dead, and Crandle had murdered him.

Zander and Blayde glared at her like she was the worst person who had ever lived. The expression "murder in their eyes" was an understatement. Never mind Kork, who they ignored completely. They were back to being children now, and children could hold very strong grudges.

I would too, if I'd learned my hero was just an actor. And when you're an immortal with a man crush, heartbreak is freaking awful. I did not envy Zander right now, not one bit.

"Well, Kork is a real captain," Crandle continued, her words spilling out fast, like vomit. It brought some relief to the siblings, but not enough to wipe the obvious disgust from their faces. "We're part of a team that makes propaganda videos to, you know, keep people united. The Alliance needs support, and this show keeps the soldiers coming. We were just filming the end of a two-parter, actually. I guess Marcoli's real too; he's a child-hire. The writers thought bringing one of them into the cast would help viewers be more accepting of the child-hire program. Not that he's in the main cast. Actually, the only reason he's here is because he found you. Finch, though, while I bet he could fix this baby, he wouldn't do it very well. No offense, Finch. He was kicked out of Basic Training because of some— *ahem*—disciplinary issues and was given the choice of prison or working here. Perks of a handsome face."

"Disciplinary, my ass," he scoffed, trying to edge closer to Doesso, who was visibly upset and having none of it. "Not just anyone can build an EM pulse emitter. I should have been commended."

Crandle ignored him. "We needed someone to replace Jofa, after that interdimensional unicorn sex scandal almost went viral."

"So, the battles, the war ...?" Zander's eyebrows furrowed. He didn't need to finish his sentence.

"If you're asking if the war is real, well, of course it is," she said. "We're just not on the front lines. The Alliance has been fighting the Consortium over this arm of the Milky Way for years. We sweep in afterward, so the people back home can see how glorious battles can be. Our fight scenes are scheduled and scripted, for the most part. It's better for morale on the home front to see us winning. Even this bridge is just a set. The director overrides everything. He controls this ship's every move from down below. Or could, before we split."

"They get everything on camera," Jezeal said, stuffing his multiple hairy hands—were they hands?—into the pockets of his uniform, "edit it together for flow, and the glory of war is shown on screens back home. The youngsters beg to join, the parents feel safe, and the criminals feel afraid and give up their evil ways." He didn't sound proud.

"You lied to us," Zander said, stepping forward past Crandle to glare at Kork, who was sitting in his command chair, head in his hands. "This is all some fucking joke to you? I admired you! All of you!"

"We were doing our jobs, okay?" Crandle reached for his arm, hesitated, then drew back. Zander was like a mad dog on a short leash, and if I were her, I would have moved further away. Maybe even off the ship.

"Do you realize how surreal this sounds?" Blayde piped up, shooting Zander a stern look. *Stop it; get your act together*, it said. "This ship is real, isn't it? And they gave the best ship in the fleet to a bunch of actors? The *Traveler* isn't a ship you can fight off with missiles and witticisms. It's the most powerful arsenal in your fleet."

"Oh, the ship is real," the woman continued, "but it's more beautiful than deadly. We don't pack real ammo. Wouldn't stand a chance in a real space battle. It's all flash, you know. Make the potential recruits feel good about joining and all. Plus, we have to look good for the reward ceremonies."

"If you pay us enough, we'll even do your kid's

birthday," Finch added.

"Shut up!" said Doesso, slamming her hands on the desk. "Look, we have bigger problems to deal with than our shitty jobs. We need to reconnect with the other half of the ship before anything bad happens!"

"Like what, Doesso?" asked Finch.

"We're sitting ducks out here: weaponless, no communications, and we're the flagship of the fucking Alliance. This would be the perfect opportunity for the Consortium to strike a massive blow. It's all about the show, and if we go down, the people won't be able to handle it. Whoever split this ship has made us the biggest, easiest target in the galaxy."

The crew—or, should I say, the cast—fell silent. They avoided looking at us, looking at each other. Zander glared like he could light them on fire with his gaze if he tried hard enough. Blayde, however, was already recovering. She stepped up to the command chair and placed a hand on the seat back.

"She's right. Let's get this over with," she said. "Kork. If we were to return control to the chair, would you be able to re-attach both sections of the ship?"

"I should be able to," he nodded. "The Astrogator will do the bulk of the job."

"The Astrogator?" I asked, glancing around the room. No one had been introduced as an Astrogator. Zander shuffled uncomfortably, leaning down to my level.

"It's the piloting system," he explained, "the real brain of the ship."

"Ah, so it's not a person, then?"

"Not exactly."

"What's that supposed to mean?"

"Exactly what I said," he replied. "Kork here is a captain, and you only reach that rank if you're able to take on any and every role on the ship. If need be, he can communicate directly with the Astrogator, with the ship itself, and take on every crew role at once. It's mentally and emotionally taxing, so not everyone is capable of doing it. I've met some incredible people who were never able to rise through the ranks because they simply could not fuse with the Astrogator."

"As serious as you sound, I can't help but think of a celestial alligator."

"Sally, come on," he said, "not now. Come on."

I shut my mouth. He was right; timing was all wrong. Getting a look like that from a usually jovial Zander was chilling. Further proof this wasn't a game.

A man had died, and I was making jokes. Cue the self-loathing.

"I'll need to meditate beforehand," Kork said to Blayde, rising from his chair. She nodded in understanding.

"Of course," she replied. "In the meantime, we need to regain control of the ship. Move back to regular power, if we can. Orange is not the right color for any of this."

"Finch, Jezeal, take care of Xacrelf, please. Take him to the med bay until we can figure out what needs to be done. Anyone with actual computer experience, work on getting the guidance systems back online. And will someone get these people uniforms?" Kork said, addressing that last part to Marcoli, the child-hire. "They're with us now. Oh, and Marcoli? Stay away from red, all right?"

And with that, our not-so fearless leader strode out of the room, leaving everyone in silent contemplation. Marcoli didn't waste any time, though. He approached us without a word, hand resting on the weapon at his hip. The young man grunted.

"Come on, let me get you sorted," he said. As if on cue, the rest of the crew began to talk to each other again, ignoring us, as if none of this had happened. I liked them better this way, anyway. They had very good reason to be embarrassed, but we had bigger fish to fry.

More like bigger ships to fly. I was proud of that one. Too bad Zander was right, and this wasn't the time for jokes.

We followed Marcoli off the bridge and down a short flight of stairs near the elevator. We were now in a hallway, cramped and tight and completely unlike the wide corridors we had seen upon arrival. The orange strip lighting only made everything feel even more suffocating.

"Temporary crew quarters," Zander explained, not even waiting for me to ask this time, "for on-staff duty on deck. People with long shifts who need a nap and a shower during their breaks. Except that no one here actually works around the clock, do they?"

"When the ship acts like an actual ship and not a flying film set, they do," Marcoli said coolly.

He opened a closet in the hall and pulled out a rack of identical uniforms. He tossed us the dark ones trimmed with blue, like Doctor Jezeal had been wearing, trying to approximate our sizes at a glance. There was the Alliance's symbol on it, a three-pointed silver star embroidered over the right breast.

"You can change in here," Marcoli offered, pushing open a door to a small cabin with four stacked bunks in it. "I'll be right here."

True to his word, he leaned against the wall, crossing his arms in front of his chest. The sagging skin around his lips wobbled as he tried to force a commanding expression. It didn't fit him well.

I slipped into the small room behind the siblings, who wasted no time stripping off their gray clothes. I turned away quickly. I didn't want to see anything new there. It's called being polite, right, folks?

After all, nobody cared. But there was something about being in the presence of someone as intimidating as Blayde that made me seriously regret not working out more.

My duffel bag was missing, I realized with a start. I must have dropped it in the broom closet we arrived. I wondered when I would get a chance to get it back. I would need to take my meds sometime soon, and I was already missing my iPod.

I wanted to take pictures of this, dammit! Television set or not, it was still a ship in outer-freaking-space. One day I would get a chance to brag about this, and I wanted the pics to prove it happened.

I wanted to prove it to myself, mostly. One day when I'm back on Earth and in a mental institution recovering from all this, I want proof in my hands that I was not imagining it all.

"Is it me, or do the zippers stick a little too low?" Blayde said, her voice bringing me back to the present. I turned to look back at her, clutching my own uniform against my bra-covered chest.

Blayde's bust was sticking out. A look that suited her, if she were in an action flick maybe, but was not to her own liking. This wasn't *Tomb Raider*. Her cleavage was impressive, and I'm not afraid to admit that I was sweating just looking at her. That muscled figure in that tight-fitting uniform, her hands clutching her chest as she tried to fight the zipper. Enough to make any girl feel fluttery.

"Mine's fine," Zander said, zipping his up all the way to his neck to underline his point. The zipper faded into invisibility.

Blayde tried to force hers again, but she ended up breaking the toggle. Her face flamed red with fury.

I slipped mine on, surprised at how soft the material felt against my skin. It was like wearing a wetsuit, only one made of the softest silk, which hugged my features close and made me feel trimmer in an instant. I pulled the zipper up, enclosing the belly, the chest and—

And it stuck, right there, right between my breasts, refusing to climb any higher.

"Um, Blayde, I think you're right," I muttered, trying to pull it up. But it was stuck. I tried not to imagine what I looked like right now.

Probably killer impressive, but, hey, still not what I was going for.

"I fucking hate propaganda," Blayde said, the words coming out as a snarl. She pinched the two sides of her collar together, trying for a quick fix.

"I think my ass has padding," said Zander, turning to inspect his rear, "and I doubt it's for comfort."

"Well, screw them," Blayde spat. "I'm not playing by their rules. If they want us here, we're doing it on our own terms."

"We don't have to stay, do we?"

The two of them stared at me like I had suggested we murder a puppy. But the three of us *were* together, and I'm pretty sure my hour of exploring was up by now. Why Blayde wasn't grabbing our hands and jumping us right here and now, I did not know. I had seen the ship, but this was going too far.

They were actors, after all. They didn't deserve the siblings' help. And like Blayde said, the longer we stayed, the more chances there were of them recognizing us—them—and making matters worse.

I was tired. I just wanted to go home. It was still the middle of the night for me, after all.

"You don't owe these people anything," I pointed out. "Just because you once admired them doesn't mean you have to be here for them. They're in their own mess. Let's let them dig themselves out."

"Damn, girl." Blayde let out a soft laugh, like the tinkling of a bell. "I didn't think you had that much backbone!"

"Oh, so where were you when I was making deals with alien races to save my own skin?" I quipped, surprising even myself. "Look, I'm not the one who should be angry here. You two should be furious. Your heroes let you down. So, let's get out of their way and let them screw things up on their own."

"I'm going to look for a mirror," said Blayde, waving her hand as if she was leaving for quite a while. "Going to fix this zipper. Bro, you handle the Terran."

She made her way to the back of the cabin and pressed on the wall, which popped back to reveal a small bathroom hidden behind a fake wooden panel. This left Zander and me alone together, but something was off.

"As much as we'd like to," Zander spoke, looking at me with that same cold gaze that had snuck onto his features in the past hour or so, "there is a certain code out here. In space, we look out for each other. It's Space Law. They're in trouble, so we can't leave them stranded, whether we like it or not."

"Says who?"

"Says ... I don't know, the universe." He waved his arms widely. "Morality? Human decency? I don't know, Sally. It's just a jerk thing to do, leaving people out in space to die like that."

Did he just call me a jerk? I hadn't meant to be selfish; I just wanted to get home in one piece.

"But they won't die," I pointed out. "They're smart, right? Resourceful?"

"They're actors," he replied. "They're just actors."

With that, he sank onto one of the cots. He looked weary, drained. I had never seen him this empty before.

He was my friend, so I went to him. Something in his voice told me I should be there, even though his words told me I should go. I sat beside him, and, without thinking, put my arm around his shoulder. He leaned into me, accepting the awkward sideways hug.

"Are you going to be okay?" I asked, the words falling out of my mouth before I could think them. It was Marcy post-breakup all over again. I wish I had ice cream for him.

"Always," he replied, but his words did not carry the weight they usually did.

"They say to never meet your heroes," I quoted, a walking cliché. Zander laughed at that.

"Usually because they're different from what you've imagined," he said. "Not because they're actors pretending to be everything you wanted them to be."

"True."

"I can't believe it's all been a lie."

I just couldn't get it. Why a man who had lived long enough to forget his own home world even wanted a hero. Why one-half of the most powerful duo in the universe needed someone to look up to. Why Kork should matter to him at all.

"Maybe Kork should be looking up to you instead," I suggested.

"Me?" Zander scoffed. "Come on, Sally. I'm a criminal to them. Or a lab experiment. Kork needs me like he needs his secret to get out."

"Fine. So, maybe he doesn't need you, but you sure don't need him. You're incredible, Zander. He's a phony; you're the real deal."

"I'm not, though," he shrugged me off, sitting up straight and leaning his leg against mine. "I'm an immortal, Sally. My sense of life gets warped, and Kork, he ... he kept me grounded, you know? He always acted in the best interest of others. He was loyal to his crew and to doing the right thing, even if it might kill him. I've never had to make that decision. Watching him, it kept me human. But now, knowing it was scripted—"

"Isn't it liberating?" I suggested. "Isn't it better knowing there isn't actually someone who is always right? Who's always selfless and perfect? Trust me, Zander. You're sounding more human than he ever was, on screen or off."

The bathroom door flew open, and out Blayde, boasting her beautiful uniform, which now closed around her neck in a perfect fit. But her eyes, though. Her eyes were fire, glowing flames rising as she took me in. Her nose wrinkled as if reacting to a rotten smell, but this dropped quickly. The flames, however, did not.

"Sally? Can I have a minute with you alone in here, please?" she said, courteous to say the least. "Again, emphasis on alone?"

"What's up?"

"Oh, nothing." She shrugged. "It's just that you look like a space slut, and I've got to fix your zipper. Zander? Why don't you go upstairs and get a head start on the repairs? I would love for us to get some real light going here."

He turned to look at me, mouth opening just a tiny bit, but then I was grabbed by the shoulder so sharply that I yelped. Blayde dragged me, practically kicking and screaming, into the tiny bathroom. She took out her laser and pointed it right at my chest.

Where the zipper was, of course. Or, at least, I damn well hoped so.

"Is the door shut?" she asked.

"Yes." I nodded quickly. "Also, who are you calling a slut?"

"Not an actual slut, per se." She raised her shoulders in a tiny shrug. "Just a woman who's trying way too hard, and it's driving me crazy."

"What now?"

"You listen to me, and you listen to me well," she said, pressing the laser flush against the zipper. "You are a human. A Terran. An *earthling.* You're a tiny, insignificant mortal. My brother? He has a lot on his plate, and he doesn't need another heartbreak right now. Is that clear?"

The pointer pushed the zipper into my chest, and it was beginning to sting. That wasn't the only thing either; her hand wrapped around my wrist and started to squeeze.

"Stop that, you're ... you're hurting me!" I stammered, trying to pull back, but there wasn't any room to go. "Is that a threat?"

"No, I wouldn't do that." She shook her head. "You mean a lot to my brother, but that needs to end now. He doesn't need you in his life. He has me, and I have him. That's how it's always been, and it's fine just the way it is. Sally, you're sweet and all, but soon enough we're going to find your home, drop you off, and leave again. You'll live out the rest of your short human life and die on that insignificant little world of yours. And we'll keep living. We'll be the same people we are now when your grandkids tell their grandkids the bedtime stories about your time in outer space. Your entire planet will grow, and die out, without us aging a day. We. Are. Fucking. Immortal. And I don't want my brother moping about you for the rest of eternity. So, stay away from him, do you hear me?"

"In what ... manner?" I realized as soon as the words came out that I should not have said that. She pushed harder against my chest with the laser, and I felt the heat of it searing my skin.

Which is why I was surprised when she grabbed a bar of soap from the sink and started rubbing it up and down the treads of the zipper.

"You do realize I'm stuck with you *because* of you, right?" I sputtered. "*You* got me stuck out here. *You* offered for me to tag along."

"And if I had half a mind, I would leave you here with the crew and get them to put you on the first Alliance shuttle back to Earth once they put you through the wringer for being seen with us," she said. "But the promise I made to you is also a promise to Zander. I promised to keep him safe. Physical wounds are nothing to us, but mental ones ... don't put yourself in a position to even begin to break his heart, Sally. You're going to stop this now."

"Stop what?"

"You know perfectly well what." Blayde tossed the soap back onto the sink, keeping her voice calm, even though I could feel the heat behind her words. "Get your wandering paws off him. The flirting stops now."

"I'm not interested in him!" I shouted, losing my cool. I ripped my arm loose and pulled back, the recoil of my move practically shoving her against the sink. I toppled over, falling onto the toilet, but I sat there with pride, as if I had been meaning to do that all along. My arm was ripped from her grip. I was free–ish.

My legs were shaking as I stood, wiping the spittle from the corner of my lip with the edge of my classy blue sleeve.

"Make me believe it." And with one last grimace in my direction, Blayde reached forward and tugged the zipper up, pinching the tender skin at the base of my neck. She patted me lightly on the cheek.

"Now, run along," she ordered, throwing the door

CHAPTER SIX

PER USUAL, EVERYTHING GOES FROM BAD, TO WORSE

Marcoli was waiting in the hallway, just as he had promised he would. He eyed me wearily, like someone had put him on standby. It was unsettling.

My heart still pounded from my conversation with Blayde. There isn't anything like an immortal threatening your life to shut you up.

Was she right, though? I hadn't meant to flirt with Zander; I knew how impossible a relationship with him would be. He was my friend, nothing more. And he never would be. He never could be.

Why did that make me sad?

"Hey there, Marcoli," I said, trying to make a good impression. As far as rank went on this ship, I was definitely at the bottom, and this guy wasn't much higher. Seemed like those at the bottom of the barrel had to stick together.

His eyes lit up as I acknowledged him, making eye contact, bobbing his head in a curt nod.

"Fa Webber, I hope the uniform is to your satisfaction?" he asked, polite to a fault.

"Yeah, fits great," I replied, preparing to give him a thumbs up before remembering it could well be an insult here. I returned the little head bob.

"Fantastic. Is there anything else I can do for you?"

"Nah." I smiled, trying to make myself appear as friendly as possible. I *was* friendly, after all, "Though can you clear something up for me?"

"I can try."

"Great. "So, tell me, back there Crandle said you were a child-hire or something like that?"

He nodded.

"What is that, exactly?"

"It means I'm from an underdeveloped planet," he said, beaming proudly. "And I've had the remarkable opportunity to join the Alliance and pave a better life for myself."

"What does that mean?" Is that a bit like an exchange program? Aren't you a little ... young to be on a war vessel?"

"I am proud to make myself useful to the Alliance, even at my young age."

"Wow, that's some determination," I said, but internally, my stomach was knotting. Something was off about this fellow. He didn't deny his youth, so I had been right to assume he was a kid. But there was something shifty about this Marcoli kid.

"So, where are you from?" I asked, pressing for information, though it wasn't as if the name of his planet would mean anything to me.

"Where I am from no longer matters," he replied, almost robotically. "It's where I'm going that makes me who I am. And I am on a trajectory to greatness in the Alliance. I am a part of something bigger than myself."

"Still, you got a home world out there?"

"I ..." The boy froze. His eyes glazed over like he had been hit with some kind of freeze ray. "I can't ... I can't ..."

"Marcoli, what's wrong?" I urged, stepping forward but afraid to touch him. He lifted his hands in front of his face, staring at them in awe, like it was the first time he had seen them in his life.

"They took—" He shuddered. "They took me. My whole life ..."

A spasm traveled through his body, and he toppled forward. He jerked on the floor, practically foaming at the mouth.

"Marcoli!" I dropped to my knees to help him, but by the time I reacted, his episode had ended. He was already getting back up on his feet, smiling broadly as he stared straight ahead. Through me. His eyes were empty.

"Is there anything more I can get you, Fa Webber?" he asked.

"What the hell just happened?" I glanced up and down the hallway, checking to see if anyone else had seen, but, no, it was just me. And by the eager look on Marcoli's face, it was almost as if I had imagined the whole thing. "Are you all right?"

"Why wouldn't I be?" he asked me. "Are you quite right, Fa Webber?"

I nodded, slowly. Something was wrong with crewman Marcoli. I needed answers, and they weren't going to come from him.

"Ah, Webber, there you are," said someone who definitely had them. Crandle slipped her arm through mine and led me away from Marcoli without a glance in his direction.

"Lieutenant?" I said, my voice thinning to a squeak and turning it into a question. I looked back down the hall, but Marcoli was waiting, as if nothing had happened.

"Are you messing with the child-hire?" she asked, punctuating her question with a shrill laugh that almost sounded fake. "Darling, look, I know it's fun, but we need him to function. It looks like he's the only underling we have left and the only one here, except maybe Kork, who has a damn clue about how to fix this ship. So, don't re-route his nodes, all right?"

"What?" I sputtered. "I have no idea what that means."

"Oh, right," she laughed again, rolling her eyes. "I keep forgetting you're new to all this. I've never met a pre-contact. It's so *fun*. Honey, you're going to have to tell me everything!"

"Everything about what?"

We neared the end of the hallway, and Crandle steered us to the left, following the outer curve of the bridge. I wondered where she was leading me, but it was too late now to turn back.

Or maybe it wasn't. I could make an excuse, pull free, and try to find my way around here on my own.

Better not risk getting lost on a dead ship.

Not to mention that someone here was possibly the saboteur. I knew it wasn't me, and it probably wasn't Marcoli, not in his ... condition, whatever it was. So maybe it was smart to get in nice and cozy with everyone here, if things went further south than they already were.

Zander and Blayde had said there was a space code about helping people, so I guess we were here to help. And I would pull my weight, even if it made me follow strange women through strange ships.

"Crandle, right?" I said, giving her a wide, pageant queen smile. "Tell me about *you.* I haven't seen a single episode of your travels. How long have you been a lieutenant?"

"About five years now," Crandle replied. We walked down a set of stairs, and then around a large column—though what it was doing there, I did not know. It was probably just aesthetic. "Though I've been on the show about twenty years or so? I started when I was in my thirties."

I had thought interviewing these people would be easier. She looked about twenty, maybe thirty now, tops. I knew then that I was ill-equipped for this self-appointed job. She took my look of shock as a reaction about her age—rightfully so, in a way.

Throw all preconceived notions of humans out the window. Nothing is sacred.

"Medical miracles, the lot of us," she continued, patting my hand. "Since day one of the show, we've been under constant visual supervision. 'Not a hair out of place,' that's their motto. I can't tell you how many procedures I've had."

We were getting pretty far from the bridge now, and the hallways were widening again. They looked identical to the ones we had wandered when we arrived on the ship, all pristine and empty.

Where the heck was she taking me?

"I take it you've never seen any of my films." Crandle shook her head like this was some great shame. "I was quite famous before I got recruited. The government thought they could increase the viewership of their new show by enrolling a star in the army. I started off as the bridge linguist, like little Doesso, you know. Anyway, more viewers meant more enlistments. People liked seeing me running around on a spaceship."

This was a woman who liked the sound of her own voice. There was another sigh, more theatrical than the last, and she brushed her blonde hair behind her ear. She obviously had no problem with the low-cut suits, and the purple accents on her shoulders seemed picked just for her, matched perfectly with the golden emblems to bring out her beauty. She was radiant with manicured nails and pearly white teeth. It would be obvious to anyone she had never been in any real war.

"They were laughing a lot less when the last lieutenant died," she said, and there was a weird glee in her eye. "A tragic accident, so sad. I auditioned to get the role as his replacement. The fake tests they put me through filled three whole episodes and were some of the highest rated of the series, outside of the space battles. Those draw a crowd no matter what."

How many turns had we taken at this point? And why hadn't I been paying more attention? If I tried to leave now, I would never find my way out of this place.

I was royally screwed. I was stuck listening to this woman brag about her fake life while she led me who knows where.

Not to mention I thought she just admitted to murder. I shrunk into my uniform. What the hell was happening on this ship?

"Then they asked us to fake a love interest in each other, the captain and I, I mean. I don't know if we're still keeping up that pretense, anyway." This time when she sighed, she was deflated. Her shoulders slouched. Her voice dropped an octave. "Whenever I get to visit my home, I have to dress up so I don't get chased by a mob. My own parents don't know that we're faking the wars. Everywhere I look, I see my face on recruitment posters. They even have a toy in an effigy of me. Girls want to grow up like me." She looked to me, those bright purple eyes, a gaze older than the rest of her face. "You have no idea how much I hate myself for that."

I must have hit my head during the trip, because I could not have just heard that.

Crandle's grip on my arm tightened, and my heart raced in response. She pushed open the door and we were back on the bridge, having walked in a large circle for absolutely nothing.

"Why?" I asked. I tasted iron on my tongue, though that could have been from where I was biting my own tongue. "You might be a fake, but you make a good role model."

"Do I really?" Her gaze was intense. Her nails were sharp. "Girls throw themselves into the army as soon as they are allowed to. They sell away their lives because they think what I'm doing is glorious. That the war is righteous. We're not really in a war! We're fighting over territory. Lines on a hologram. And now look at me: I've worked on a ship for the best years of my life, and I can't even begin to think about flying it myself. Let alone repairing it."

"And, um, why are you telling me all this?"

"Because if you get out of here, you'll spend the rest of your life in an Alliance jail, so you won't have anyone to tell. Ah, here we are."

Crandle walked us to the railing in front of the window, but instead of looking at the view, she spun around.

"Haln, she's here."

I looked down, and lo and behold, there were legs. Zander's legs. He slid out from under whatever panel he had been working on, smiling up at the two of us. To my relief, the claws on my arm released their grip.

"Thanks, Crandle," Zander said, hopping up on his feet. "I haven't managed to find the problem yet, but this wasn't accidental."

"Veesh," she swore, crossing her arms over her chest. "No one here is capable of doing any of this. We're just actors. We've got fancy toys, sure, but we're still actors. And Kork, he ... well, he's the best of us. And he would never do this to us."

"I agree," said Zander, nodding slowly. "If he's anything like the man he portrays on screen, we can take him off our list of suspects."

"I still haven't taken you off my list," Crandle said, but there was something in her tone that was almost provocative. She gave Zander one of those looks that said a lot more than she was letting on.

"And yet, you trust me enough to leave me alone with your computer terminals," Zander replied, his voice smooth like ice cream. I glanced at him, then at Crandle, then back again. What the hell was going on here?

"I'm going back to the captain. It's the others I don't trust."

She spun on her heels and walked away, her stride long and elegant. Neither of us could take our eyes off her gait, and we realized this, exchanging knowing looks as we forced ourselves to look away.

"So, did she give you the talk?" he asked and winked. I rolled my eyes.

"Crandle? Yeah." I checked to make sure she was out of the room. "She gave me her whole life story. Did she seriously walk me all the way down here just to tell me about how hard it is to act in propaganda shows?"

Zander let out a small chuckle. "I meant Blayde, but don't worry, I got the sob story too. Pretty sure she confessed to murder. Anyway, don't worry about Blayde. She gave you the talk—means she likes you."

I must have looked confused, because damn, was I ever confused. Zander rolled his eyes before going back to work on the console. Standing, this time.

"She doesn't give the talk to just anyone, you know. It's not even you, not exactly. She thinks you're interesting enough that *I'm* going to be interested. But don't worry, it's not like I'm—"

"I told her I wasn't interested," I said quickly, "but, wait, does that mean you think I'm not worthy or something? Because, come on, I'm pretty awesome and you know it."

"I know it," he grinned, his face lighting up with a smile. "But you know how it is. Immortal, mortal. It wouldn't work out."

"Yup, not a good idea."

I watched him as he worked on the computer, inputting strings of commands to no avail. He looked up at the orange LED above his head, sighed, and dove back in, his nose pressed against the old-fashioned monitor.

"I know what you're thinking," he said suddenly.

"No, you don't."

"I was thinking the same thing." He shrugged. "Why don't we jump around, running their errands for them? Oh, what a marvelous, flowery world where people actually help each other and—"

"I wasn't thinking that. Well, you're right about the jumping thing. We could go right now, and we wouldn't have to deal with any of their crap. This isn't like the Downdwellers. These people are responsible for their own situation."

"Quite literally, as it's becoming more likely that the saboteur is on our end."

I felt myself go cold. "What?"

"I'm having trouble fixing the communications array, for starters. It looks like it was disabled from the bridge. Very crude, but someone here managed the ship separation while we were having drinks."

"But… who? Can you, I don't know, figure out which post the communications were severed on?"

"It's not that easy," he said, brows knitting together in concentration. "Anyone could have used any post while we were chatting. I wasn't paying attention—were you?"

I shook my head. I had been trying to work out if Kork was flirting with me.

"If there is a saboteur on board, can we trust anyone?" I shuddered. "Zander, why are we still here? This is a mess. Can we just—"

"We're in a lose-lose situation," he said, not peeling his eyes away from the screen. His hands flew over the small keyboard. "Why do you think we gave these people fake names in the first place? The Alliance doesn't need to know we were here. Leaving now will do nothing but get us unwanted attention. We can't stay here long enough for them to catch on to who we are, but if we leave now ..."

"Then they'll get the idea."

"Exactly." He nodded his head vigorously. "And no one wants that. And remember: We can't leave them here. Space Law. But we can't jump *them* out of here, either. You know what happens when we jump."

"You mean you could get them lost on the other side of the galaxy."

"Not the other side," he said, looking up glumly from his work, "but I'm not going to do to them what I did to you. I'm not making the same mistake twice."

"So, I'm a mistake?"

"I didn't mean that, Sally." He looked exhausted, and I felt bad for saying those words. Zander had tried to do something nice for me; a trip to space was what I wanted, after all.

It wasn't his fault he got me lost. Not exactly.

"Forget I said that," I sputtered. "Here, change the subject. What's the deal with Marcoli?"

"What about him?" asked Zander, looking confused, but going back to his rapid typing on the little alien keyboard.

"The whole child-hire thing. Isn't he too young to work on a spaceship?"

"You say that like he had a choice in the matter."

"He didn't?"

"Hell no. He was abducted."

"What?"

My mouth was suddenly dry. I looked back at the hallway where Marcoli was probably still waiting, standing like a robot.

"The Alliance abducted him?" I hissed, lowering my voice, trying not to draw the attention of the others. "To force him to work on a military ship?"

"Well, *they* didn't," Zander replied. "There's a huge black market for abductees. The Alliance breaks up a few xeno-trafficking rings from time to time, but they can't send any of the kids back to their families. Not after what they've been through, especially since their planets are ninety-nine percent of the time pre-contact worlds. The humane thing to do is wipe their memories and use them as extra hands. It's too dangerous to send them home. The wipes might fail and leave the child traumatized and ostracized. The Alliance sees it as a kindness after what the children have seen."

"But how is this any better?" I spat, disgusted. "Marcoli's a kid! He should be out playing with others his own age, not stuck on a spaceship where he could be killed."

"I'm telling you, there's a huge business of buying and selling child-hires as farm hands, as cheap labor, basically as slaves. But it's much better compared to what they go through before."

"How can you be okay with this?" I clasped my hands over my mouth. I was getting louder as I was getting more indignant.

"Oh, trust me, I'm not," he said, "but right now, I've more immediate concerns than driving a child-led revolution to break chipped indentured slaves of their bonds. Let's get this ship back in one piece, and then we can worry about abolishing the galactic slave trade."

"I'm going to hold you to that one," I insisted. "And Marcoli, he's—"

"Memory's been entirely wiped," Zander explained. "It helps them deal with the trauma. As I said before, Blayde and I went through that. It's not pleasant, but I would think working on the *Traveler* would be the best of a bad situation. Aha!"

His outburst made me jump. Let there be light! Everything turned back on at once, every console lighting up. The bridge turned a gleaming white again, the awful orange glow flickering out of existence. Even the little camera drones whirred out of their hidey holes, only to go right back inside and lock themselves away.

Blayde and Marcoli rushed up the stairs to join us just as the captain's chair came to life. Blayde was wearing her leather jacket over the uniform and was really pulling it off, though why I noticed this, of all things, was beyond me.

I shook my head and refocused on the situation at hand.

"Computer!" Zander called to the space above us all. "Computer, respond."

"Computer is ... offline, I think."

The voice was faint, uncertain. It hovered in the air like a thin mist and the promise of rain. We all looked up, knowing full well we wouldn't get our answers there but driven by confusion and nothing else. This was what we got.

"What the fuck is going on?" Crandle shouted, jumping up from her seat at her own console. "Is this some kind of joke?"

"Who is that?" I asked, and no one answered. Maybe no one knew the answer.

"Wha-what?" the voice continued over the com. Like it was waking from a long sleep, the woman's voice was disoriented yet calm, "Why were half of the floors ejected? I don't like that. No, no. That doesn't feel good. I think it hurts."

And then there was Blayde, staring at the ceiling like she had just seen a ghost. And there was Zander, looking like he believed she had.

"Will someone please tell me what's going on?" Crandle slapped the console, making the holograms jump. Blayde ignored her. She ignored everyone. She shoved Zander away from his interface and typed out a long stream of nonsense.

"No, this can't—no," the voice said.

Blayde looked up again. She was shaking now, glancing back at whatever result she had found before staring at the intercom speaker on the ceiling once more. And then back. And repeat.

"I have to get away from them," the computer said.

The second the voice said those words, the entirety of space lit up before us. Outside the window, lights flickered into existence. Dozens of bronze ships appeared, filling the view with a nightmare of metal.

"C-consortium s-ships!" Crandle stammered. "They're… everywhere."

The computers went haywire. Whereas a few seconds ago there was nothingness, the desks were now filling with red lights, alerts popping up everywhere at once. The entire bridge crew was frozen.

"Can't let them catch me," said the voice.

Which was when the ship decided it didn't want to stay here anymore. The stars outside the window turned to streaks, and space twisted around our ship for good.

CHAPTER SEVEN

THE SKY IS FALLING, SALLY WEBBER!

The ship bucked. We were riding a bull that had been stung by a bee, and the bull was charging. Without a sound, the ship surged forward; the stars stretched out in front of us, long blue streaks of white leading to an impossibly far, eternal horizon.

The entire crew jumped from petrified to frantic in an instant. Crandle grabbed her head and let out a blood-curdling scream as Jezeal threw himself onto his back and folded his legs over his torso, playing dead.

"This was not in my contract," said Crandle.

"Close your eyes!" Zander leaped over the pulsing, red desk and throwing himself at the big, red button on the wall. Sirens blared; blinds crashed to cover the window, shattering the rays of light.

But while Zander had stopped us from seeing it, we could still feel it. The *it* being what appeared to be a jump to light speed, or warp speed, or whatever these ships used to travel astronomical distances in short amounts of time. Unlike the little show the actors had given for the audience back home, this kind of flying wasn't mimed emotion and a few fake falls across the room. No, it was bone-shattering, muscle-liquefying force.

I fell into a chair and gripped the desk in front of me, clinging to life itself. In mere seconds, I had lost the ability to move my hands, or any other part of my body. I was pressed back into the seat, writhing as the ship bolted through the universe.

As suddenly as it had left, the ship now lurched to a stop, the deceleration throwing me forward. My head slammed into the table, smacking into my arm and narrowly avoiding a broken nose. I clenched my teeth as I pulled myself back up, listening to the groans rise from the rest of the cast. I inhaled deeply, trying to calm my breathing, but with my heart pounding the way it was, that was going to be a struggle.

"Are we ... can we ..." Doesso staggered to her feet, motioning to the red button.

"We'd better," Crandle replied, straightening her uniform, even though there wasn't a wrinkle. "What the Veesh just happened? Where did those Consortium ships come from? It was as if they knew where we were."

She aimed this question at Zander through a murderous look, and he shrugged awkwardly, looking down at the panel in front of him.

"Well, we definitely moved," he said, "and now the

computer's stopped responding. Everything's frozen."

He attempted to coax it to life vocally as the dark blinds slowly rose on the giant window and letting in a thick beam of bright blue light. Together, we squinted out into the unknown, Zander's calls to the computer going unanswered.

We were in front of a planet. A huge, blue, gas giant, a shade lighter than Neptune with stripes of white floating around the poles. It was beautiful.

It was glorious.

It was getting bigger.

"Orbit is failing!" Doesso shouted, throwing her hands into the air. "Gods help us all!"

"We never even had an orbit," Finch snapped.

"Fuck this, I'm getting out of here." Doesso grabbed Finch's hand and gave it a sharp tug, but Finch was so absorbed in staring at the planet that he paid no attention to her.

"With what? Escape pods?" Jezeal said, sounding tired and defeated. He sat on a chair and strapped himself in like this would be a nice drive to buy some ice cream, tapping the console in front of him as if that would make a difference. Nothing changed. "Those were on deck sixty. Gods-know how many light years away those are now."

"We have shuttles," Kork said, finally appearing from his quarters.

He looked much more like a captain now—stoic, put together. He marched to his chair and took a seat without waiting for a reply. A few taps on his arm rests either resulted in nothing or exactly what he wanted to know because he gave up on them quickly.

"For lower planetary orbits, yeah," Jezeal said, sinking lower into his chair. "They're not going to help us now."

"They will."

"In case you didn't notice, *Captain*, we're heading straight for old Bluey here. We'd get crushed by the pressure before we could find somewhere safe enough to linger."

"And I'm pretty sure none of you noticed the moon over there," he said, his voice carrying no judgment. "We can put ourselves down there. At least then we can send out an SOS."

"Well, I like that idea," Doesso insisted. She gave Finch another sharp tug, but he still wasn't responding to her. "Surviving sounds pretty good."

"We're not leaving this ship," said Blayde, appearing on the bridge from one of the small conduits.

"Thratra, don't you try and stop us." Kork rose to his feet, glaring at her. "You are not a part of this crew. You have no say in the matter."

"I speak on behalf of a member of your crew," she said, crossing her arms over her chest, "because, unless you haven't noticed, your astrogator is awake. And I'm pretty sure it's bad standard to have a *conscious,* disconnected astrogator go down with the ship."

Her words meant nothing to me, but they meant a whole lot to the rest of the people on the bridge. Everyone froze. Whoever, whatever this astrogator was, it was important.

"She'll land us safely," Blayde assured us, "even if her control of the ship is minimal. Everybody sit back, and let her do her job."

"And how do you know all this?" Finch was quick to retort, finally pulling out of his planetary revelry. "I'm sure no one cued you up with the ship's functions. How are you getting this information? Are you a spy?"

"No," she replied, gliding past him and taking a seat at a console. "I'm just smart. Sometimes I wonder if I'm the only one who pays attention."

"You're insane," said Doesso, but Kork was already strapping himself in. "You're all insane! This ship is going to crash, and what, we're all going to go along for the ride?"

"Sit down, Doesso," the captain said coolly. "If you want to survive this, you're going to have to sit."

"Need I remind you that a ship this size is not meant to break atmo'?" Doesso continued. "It was never built to go planet-side. If the fall doesn't kill us, the landing will."

Crandle was already sitting in her lieutenant's chair, saying nothing as she buckled her seatbelt and glared at her inferior. Doesso met her gaze, opened her mouth as if to say something, then snapped it shut again. She looked terrified.

The crew took their places for the final descent. Kork was in his command chair, looking calm through all this, with Crandle at his right, tapping idly at her console as if doing something useful would make her feel better.

"If the crash destroys my face," she said, "my bills are all coming out of your paychecks. It's in my contract."

Zander sat down next to me, and I heard the metal-on-metal sound of his seat belt clipping shut. Right, I should probably buckle mine too. I gulped, realizing it wouldn't help us all that much. It would probably only help to identify our bodies once we were all dead.

To my right, Doesso and Finch took their seats, the woman looking furious while Finch gave off the impression of being totally at ease with anything that was about to happen. Jezeal and Marcoli were in the back somewhere. The nine of us were about to crash onto the surface of a tiny moon, and the thought wasn't reassuring.

The moon itself looked nice, from a distance. All greens and blues like Earth. Of all the places we could crash-land on, finding one where we could breathe would be an amazing coincidence. The odds of that were astronomical, no pun intended.

As we drew closer, our slow crawl became a race toward our doom. I gripped the edge of my seat, pushing my nails into the cool metal, feeling the pain there and using that to distract me from my terror.

"Warning," the ship said in a pre-recorded voice. "Orbit deteriorating."

"We get it, computer," Doesso hissed, slamming her fist on the console in front of her. "Why is *that* the last bit of the computer that's still working?"

"Recommending a ten percent burst—"

She shut it off before it could say any more. No use getting advice we could not follow.

It's almost impossible to put into words what it's like to watch yourself approach a planet and have no control over the fall. First, it's the amazement, the wonder, when you see this tiny rock and realize it's a whole world. But then things speed up. Then you think, hey, that beautiful curvature isn't all that curvy anymore. And then you see clouds in front of you, and you're amazed at how detailed they are.

And then, you realize what was in front of you is a straight drop. It's like leaning out over the Empire State Building and realizing how high you are. But, in that instance, the realization isn't usually followed by, *Shit, I'll have to get down there one way or another. I'll have to fall.*

I hadn't realized the ship's engines had such a distant hum until they stopped entirely. There was silence for a second—a long, seemingly eternal second when we felt the drift, when we moved closer to the moon without the realization fully kicking in.

And then, all at once, gravity hit.

That's when we went from ambling around in space to plummeting toward the surface.

I hate to break it to you: I closed my eyes. Those of you with me since the beginning of my misfortunes know that I abhor heights, and yet you'd think I would be used to them by now, after all that shit they put me through. Falling from the Killian's ship. Falling through Da-Duhui—twice. All in a day's work.

But never had I fallen from outer space; that last time was lower Earth orbit. Learn the difference.

Why am I rambling about this? Because my eyes were entirely sewn shut. It felt like a roller coaster had dropped out from beneath me, and the ground was nowhere in sight. And, no, not because I had my eyes closed and couldn't see it. More like it was a long, long way down to reach it.

I realized one of my hands was no longer clutching my seat. Unconsciously, I had reached for Zander, and he had taken my hand, holding it tight, squeezing it for comfort. For his or mine? I didn't know, but I sure was thankful.

He would survive this, though.

It became very clear to me, right then, a thought that had been swimming in my mind these past few days—weeks?—and had popped back to the surface just now: I did not want to die. I wanted to make it home. I wanted to make it to Dany and Marcy's wedding. I wanted to be their maid of honor, dammit. I wanted to see my family again. To hug my mom, my dad, my dog, my friends.

I wouldn't let a small thing like a crashing spaceship take that away from me.

The screams made it worse. I couldn't tell them apart. Everyone and their mothers were screaming, shouting, swearing, cursing, pleading, anything but keeping quiet.

But there was one voice that stuck out; one voice was laughing.

I'll let you guess who that was.

The engines turned back on. All at once, I felt the ship rumble to life beneath me, and it pulled forward, breaking out of the nosedive. The sheer force of the move pushed me against the seat, pressing on every muscle, making me think I would be crushed to death rather than broken into a million bits on an alien moon.

For a second, I thought we were saved, that this would mean a smooth landing and everyone would get out and just walk about. But the fall was far from over. I forced my eyes open, begging the ship to just *please* pull out the landing gear and make things work.

But Doesso was right: This ship wasn't meant to land on a planet. We had no landing gear. As my eyes opened, I saw smoke billowing in front of the bridge's window, coming from who knew where and who knew what part of the ship. We were on fire. Or, at least, I think it was us. It could also be the forest we were crashing into.

The trees crumbled before us. They bowed as we flew above them, moving so fast they split rather than harm our ship. Out in the distance, I saw mountains, red, pink mountains topped with white, a large plume of smoke rising from somewhere beyond them.

Our ship was falling to pieces.

And then, touchdown.

The shock threw us all forward in our seats, pushing us hard against the little strap of fabric across our lap. Somehow, the small thing was enough to hold us back as the ship bounced then landed again, making my neck crack violently. If whiplash was the worst I would get, I could handle it.

Just let me survive this.

Finally, we bounced for the last time. The ship came down, hard, against the ground and slid forward until friction forced it to a halt. We hung, limp, in our seats, and we shook as we wondered if this was over.

I could smell urine. I didn't care whose it was. It could have been mine, for all I knew. I couldn't feel my legs.

"Everyone out," Blayde ordered, turning away from the bow, looking like she had just watched the best movie of her life. We were at an incline, but she had no trouble walking up the bridge to reach us. She ran up and past us, not waiting for a reply or even a grunt of agreement.

"Like she said"—Kork unbuckled his seat and stood tall—"this place could be unstable. We don't know if the core containment's been hit. So, up and out. Come on!"

We didn't need to be told twice. We only needed a minute to come to our senses. I unlatched my buckle, letting go of Zander's hand and realizing how sweaty I was, the stickiness making my hand slip a few times from the metal clasp, and stood, my legs wobbly. Zander reached out for my arm, and I let him guide me up the slant to the stairs at the back of the bridge.

Here's the thing about spaceships: They don't have a lot of emergency exits. They need to stay pretty darn closed in space, so any flaw in that perfect hull could mean death. And seeing as how that window had survived the crash, I was pretty sure that wasn't ordinary glass.

That stuff was more than shatterproof. It was space-proof.

Smoke billowed out of the corridors as we rushed to escape. Already, automatic fire extinguishers were going off, blowing foam in all directions. We narrowly avoided them, running with our hands over our eyes to keep the smoke at bay.

Finally, I emerged into the blinding sunlight, coughing as clear air filled my lungs. I toppled out of the breach, collapsing in the grass, panting. When I rolled over, it was to look up at a pastel pink sky, smoke the only cloud visible for miles.

I realized this was the first time I had seen the ship

from the outside. It was sleek and elongated, blisteringly white and cut a sharp contrast with the black dirt it had dug itself into. While the back end was missing, the rest looked ... surprisingly good, other than the massive cracks with steam billowing out of them.

She must have been the most beautiful ship of all time, and I wasn't just saying that because she was the first real ship I had seen. Her gleaming white exterior was polished and smooth, with a gunmetal finish accentuating the curves of the underbelly and the point of the nose. She was flat, her sleek design built for speed, which was odd, since aerodynamics didn't mean squat in space, yet it was a stunning feat of engineering. The front rose a little, like a whale almost, smooth and delicate as she rested in the dirt she had upturned as she crashed. The bridge sat on the topmost part, the glass window overlooking the empty sea of blackness that was space.

I pushed myself up. The crew was all around me, sitting, trying to catch their breaths. Kork was pacing, already steady. The only ones missing were Zander and Blayde.

"Screw you, assholes!" Marcoli flew out of the breach, smoke billowing out from behind him. He coughed into his arm. "I'm free!"

The kid leapt off the ship and dashed into the forest, the leaves hiding him within seconds. No one tried to go after him.

Zander appeared on top of the ship, in the exit I had toppled out of, surrounded by smoke. He held my duffel bag in the air above him.

My hero.

"Oh, thank you," I said, head still spinning, as he hopped out of the breach and made his way to me.

"You got it," he replied, sitting down next to me.

"And Blayde?" I asked.

He said nothing, at first. I watched his body tense, then relax, as if giving up trying to hold back a secret.

"She went back for something that means a lot to her." Always cryptic when I wanted clear answers. I didn't press him, though. The dizziness was getting stronger.

I must have been hallucinating what I saw next because when Blayde finally emerged from the ship, it was from a crack in the hull's underbelly. She was glowing blue, covered in gel, and she was not alone.

She carried a woman in her arms—a nude woman covered in bright blue slime.

And the woman was coughing.

CHAPTER EIGHT

THINGS WERE EASIER WHEN EVERYTHING WAS SCRIPTED

"Ow," I hissed. The pinch really did hurt; I was not dreaming. Blayde was tenderly—yes, there was some tenderness in her stone-cold heart—laying the woman down on the soft grassy knoll. She pushed the gel off her skin, revealing a pale, milky white underneath.

I must have died in that crash. All common sense had disappeared.

The stranger's head was entirely bare, as if it had just been shaved with the straightest razor. Her whole body was hairless, I noticed, before realizing I was staring, which was probably impolite.

Still, she was incredibly feminine. She was skinny, the kind of skinny you didn't see often, but despite this, she didn't give off an air of fragility. Every protruding muscle was taut and firm, like a gymnast's.

The ship's crew—or cast; I wasn't sure what to call them at this point—crowded around her. I guess I had followed them there, drawn to this unconscious stranger in an urge to know more about her. Blayde glanced up long enough to glare, saying nothing. It was Zander who raised his voice out of nowhere.

"Will someone get a ration pack?" he asked, then pointed at Finch. "You. Get this woman some water. She's been pulled out of stasis; she's going to be parched. And will you all step back and give her some room to breathe? She hasn't used her lungs in a while."

The coughing was slowing now. The woman was beginning to breathe on her own, but in wheezing, rasping breaths, like she had forgotten how. Finch was back in seconds, bringing her a canteen that looked far too small to hold water. Blayde snatched it from his outstretched hand and put a few drops on the woman's tongue, helping her drink with a nurturing look on her face that I had never seen there before.

I didn't think Blayde was capable of looking serene. It was almost motherly, the air of utter devotion. I could not wrap my head around it.

"Buh ... Blayde?" the woman sputtered, her eyes finally peeling open. She lifted her hand to touch Blayde's face, leaving gel on her cheek.

"Hey, stranger," Blayde answered, smiling warmly.

"Let's give them some space," Zander said, stepping forward and pushing everyone back. I guess I was part of the group because I stepped away too, leaving Blayde and the stranger alone on the ground near the foot of the crashed ship.

"Who's that woman?" Jezeal asked. "I mean ... I've been on this ship five years, and I ..."

Everyone stared at Kork, but he said nothing. His hands were stuffed down his pockets, his head focused on the ground as we walked. He looked like he was sulking, all signs of the strong leader had gone, replaced by an annoyed child.

"That's our astrogator," Doesso said, turning her back on the stage scene and leading the charge back up the hill, a safe distance from the ship and the weirdness that was a loving, caring Blayde.

"Wait, what?" I looked back at the stranger then took Crandle's lead and forged ahead. "She's ... the Astrogator's a *person*?"

"I mean, obviously?" Doesso looked at me and rolled her eyes. "How could you not know how astrogation works?"

"Pre-contact planet," I said, trying to act casual about it, but there was something in her voice that stabbed like a dagger. "I don't know much of anything."

And it was true. I knew nothing out here. I was like someone diving into *Star Trek* halfway through the series, trying to piece together the characters, the technology, the timelines. Just when I thought I was getting the hang of something, there came a plot twist. There was a sharp learning curve out here.

"Astrogation used to be handled by computers," Crandle explained, her voice calm, "but they were unreliable. Our best scientists could not program something powerful enough to plot a course with so many variables, and when faster-than-light travel was perfected, we needed something forward-thinking to navigate us through space. Something able to think out the consequences of any course, something that cared about the life forms it carried. Something that could think outside of programming, something that could be unpredictable if the need arose."

"A human brain?" I scoffed. "But ... what about human error? How did—"

"Well, you don't hook just anyone up to a ship," Finch said with a haughty laugh.

"People train their entire lives to be assigned to a ship," Crandle continued, glaring at Finch. "Astrogation is the highest calling in the universe. Only the best can achieve *mersation*, and once they become one with a ship, they're bonded for the rest of eternity."

"Or until the ship crashes on an alien world." Finch laughed.

"Shut up," said Doesso, jabbing him in the ribs. Finch glared at her, and she glared back.

Crandle put an arm over my shoulders and walked me away from the two squabbling kids. I was glad for an excuse to get away from them. I'd known them for all of two hours or so, and already it felt like too long.

"Darling, look, I get it," she crooned, sweetly. "A lot to learn. A lot to take in. A lot of weirdness. But if you have questions, please, don't come to me. Questions bore me to tears. Let's try to get through this as calmly as possible, all right?"

"Gotcha."

"Good."

"The sun is setting," said Zander, climbing up the knoll. "The midday eclipse. It won't be a long spell of darkness, but it will get cold. We need to gather firewood, start a fire, keep warm."

The idea to congregate was something we had all done subconsciously, seeing others move and reacting accordingly, sheep following sheep. Now that we were here, no one wanted to take point.

"Or we could just go back in the ship," said Crandle. "It's not all that damaged. Someone needs to get the repair drones working."

"We just fell out of the sky, Crandle. Veesh," said Finch, stopping his bickering for just long enough to bark at her. "Let's wait out this eclipse thing and work when the sun comes back up."

"Agreed. I think we all need a break," said Kork. "Everyone look for wood we can burn. Let's get to work."

It was calming to search for firewood. Everyone with a purpose; everyone so focused on the task. We said nothing to each other. We only walked, sticking close enough together that we were always in sight of each other. We didn't want to talk about what we had gone through. Crashing was the least of our problems. We had a saboteur on board, a murderer, and apparently a traitor, if they had been the one to sell us out to the mysterious Consortium. A Consortium we had left to attack the other half of our ship.

Our ship. I shook my head. I was beginning to see myself as part of the crew, even if I never would be. Something about crashing on a planet together made you get close to people really quickly.

Even if one was a murderer.

On top of that, we had the Consortium to deal with when we got back, if we ever got back. Another special alliance. I shuddered. I hadn't thought about the other ones that could be out there.

There were too many things I didn't want to consider right now, so I returned to the task at hand.

It only took a few minutes to gather enough wood for a fire, and in that time, the sky was already going dark. Above us was a beautiful darkening blue orb, gargantuan in size, at least twenty times as big as our moon. It hung delicately in the sky above us, and it finally hit me that this planet was as far from Earth as I could ever have imagined.

We were orbiting a gas giant. Damn.

I had kind of hoped a planet that big would take up more space in the sky. Like you see in movies, half of your field of vision just filled with the thing. But the smaller-than-expected planet still sat there, taunting me.

It was gliding between us and the sun, slowly blocking out the light. A midday eclipse, just as Zander had said.

"You all right?"

Speak of the devil. He had come to me, as was to be expected. He wasn't going to leave me alone long, not after what had happened in Da-Duhui. I tapped the ground next to me, an invitation for him to come and stare at the sky with me while Kork lit the fire with his phaser.

"Do you see that?" I asked, pointing childishly at the gigantic orb in the sky. Zander nodded, unperturbed.

"Seems like we landed on the near side of this moon," he said, "from the few readings I got before the *Traveler* went down—"

"Crashed, you mean."

"Before we crashed, thanks," he continued. "We're going to have something like a fifty some hour-long day here. Temp is going to remain around what it is right now, but it'll get cold when the sun goes down. Not freezing, though."

"Impressive," I said.

"We're also tidally locked in with that guy, so we're going to see him 24/7. Or, you know, fifty-whatever."

I said nothing. I watched as the rest of us survivors slid around the fire: Doesso and Finch, finally done bickering; Kork, standing guard and watching Blayde and the mysterious astrogator in the distance; Jezeal and Crandle, sitting silently at his side.

"I miss Xacrelf," said Crandle suddenly, her voice so low we shouldn't have been able to hear it. All the same, it was as if the world went even colder at her words.

"Remember how he would always hide Morlezian nuts around the ship? So we'd find random snacks all the time?" asked Finch, laughing. "And then he'd act like we'd found gold?"

The cast laughed, but they continued to stare at the grass, or at the fire. Finch kept ripping up the blades and tossing them into the flames, quietly watching them burn. No one said anything about Marcoli. I was starting to think he was better off in the wilderness. If his chip had malfunctioned like I assumed it had, he would be free of them forever. They didn't even seem to care.

I didn't feel welcome here anymore. This was a family moment, and I wasn't related.

"Let's go for a walk," said Zander, his voice barely a whisper. I nodded.

I got up, brushing the dirt from my legs and

followed him toward the ship. The cast didn't notice; they had other things on their mind—Xacrelf, who had died too soon.

And one of them had murdered him.

I shuddered. One of the six was a traitor. Super fantastic odds. Who was going to be next?

"So," I asked, when we got a safe distance from the fire, "what does it take to become a spaceship in this universe?"

Zander let out a heavy breath. There was a story there; that much was painfully obvious. It was evident by the way Blayde caressed the astrogator's face as the astrogator cried into her arms. I looked at my own feet, feeling like I was intruding on something.

"We should walk somewhere else," I said.

"Yeah."

We walked toward the bow of the ship, toward the distant mountains. I tried to ignore the cold, focusing instead on Zander's words.

"There's an academy," Zander said, his voice a million miles away, "on a planet without a name. The handful of candidates who get accepted into the program train there. They train so hard. It's not a career, being an astrogator, or a lifestyle. It is a *life*. It's a calling that once you hear, you can't tune out. Not everyone can even handle the pressure of training, but those who make it through—"

"What's the point, Zander?" I turned to look at him, forcing myself to take him in. To take in the pained look on his face as he stared back at his sister.

"What do you mean?"

"You know what I mean." I dropped my head again.

"Who would give their life to be locked inside a spaceship for an eternity? In a windowless room, telling a ship where to go, feeding it orders from a captain who doesn't even know who they are. What's the point?"

Zander's eyes widened. He held out his hand, which was tinged blue from when he had tried to help Blayde clear the stranger from gel.

"You're not in a windowless room," he said, shaking his head. "You're not just a pilot. You *are* the ship. This gel is a sensory enhancer. It's a giant circuit board. And the astrogator? Suspended in that, they see everything. And I mean everything. They are every part of the ship. They experience the universe as a being of immense power, carrying a crew on their back through the pathways between the stars. This woman isn't just Jurrah. She *is* the *Traveler*."

"Hold on, what did you just call her?" I sputtered. "Jurrah? You know her name?"

"Out of everything I just told you, that's what you take away?"

"Let my brain deal with the fact you can grow up to become a spaceship," I said. "Right now I'm trying to understand how you can know the girl who's been guiding the *Traveler*."

"The woman who *is* the *Traveler*," Zander muttered under his breath. "Or was."

"What is it you're not telling me? Who is she?"

"She—" Zander stopped and shook his head. "She's Blayde's ex."

"Wait, what? Blayde has an *ex*?"

"Everyone does," he said. "I do. You do. What's so surprising about that?"

"I just assumed, with you being immortal and all ..."

"That we can't date every once and a while?" he said. "Well, it's not exactly easy, but you have to take a chance sometime, right? Blayde and Jurrah met at the academy. They broke up when Jurrah graduated and got her flight assignment. I won't go into the details; they're not for me to share."

"How recent was this?" I asked, looking at the two women. Blayde was helping Jurrah to her feet, but the poor woman was trembling. After spending years as a spaceship, I would assume walking would be tedious.

"Perks of being a ship." Zander shrugged again. "The gel keeps you in suspended animation. You don't age anymore. Well, not when you're immersed in the stuff. Not to mention, when you're moving close to the speed of light, the rest of time moves faster around you. Not when you travel by warping space, but ... sorry, I'm getting off topic."

"Dang." I shook my head. This was getting far too weird for me. I wished Zander would say something along the lines of *Surprise! I'm messing with you!* But I was getting a little too old to believe in fairy tales.

I guess I was stuck believing in immortal spaceship people.

"We need to make a plan," Zander said suddenly, snapping his head around and fixing me with those piercing silver eyes of his.

"Yeah, I think we do," I said, waving my hand over the situation behind us. "Thoughts?"

"Well, for starters, we need to get off this planet."

"Easier said than done."

"Then we need to find the rest of the crew."

"Again, super easy."

“And then defeat the Consortium, or, at least, chase them off.”

“Easiest part.”

"All the while, we need to keep our eyes peeled for the saboteur before they strike again. I didn’t know Xacrelf, but he did not deserve to die. He must have found the saboteur messing around on the bridge and tried to stop them."

I nodded. It made sense, in an awful way. Someone in the cast, for some reason, was going off-script—in the real world. Which meant any of us could be next.

A few hours ago, I had wanted to leave these people to their fate, to go back to trying to find my home. But now we had crashed on an alien world, who knows where, with Blayde’s ex somehow adding herself to the mix. If we left now, which I’m sure we still could, we’d be leaving five actors and their Astrogator alone with a murderer on a world no one knew. It would be like stabbing the knife ourselves.

Not to mention the real crew was currently surrounded by Consortium ships, with only half the *Traveler* to protect them. Not exactly fair, even if they were making propaganda.

We had to catch ourselves a killer. We needed to get everyone back in one piece. We needed to survive a space battle. It wasn’t going to be easy.

“I’m sorry to do this to you, again,” said Zander, suddenly.

“Do what?”

“Put you in harm’s way,” he said, running a hand through his thick mane. “I promised I’d keep you safe, and I got you lost in a city you didn't know, then I get you lost in space, and now you're in this mess, too."

"Habit tells me to say it's fine, it's okay, I forgive you, and don't mention it," I said. The cold felt harsher now, as if my own words were bringing on the chill. "But I can't. Zander. I'm scared, and I want to go home. I want to help these people, but I don't know how, and I'm just… confused."

Zander slipped off his leather jacket, handing it to me.

"Won't you be cold?" I asked. He shook his head. I had almost forgotten that he didn't feel cold or heat or pain. I shrugged on the jacket, his lingering body heat warming me instantly. The coat smelled like him, like sweet smoke, pine forest, and laser blasts.

"Me saying sorry won't make it right," he said, "nor will bringing you back home. I have put you in incredible danger, immeasurable danger, and I can't ensure your safety. Blayde was right: I keep making promises I can't keep. I promised you'd be safe, I promised you an hour on that ship, and now—"

"Does danger always follow you two around?"

"Not to this extent," he said, shrugging, "but maybe we've never given it time enough to reveal itself. The only reason we explored the ship was because of your request, and these poor sods would be in this mess whether we were there to help or not. I'd say luck was in their favor today."

"If we're able to help, that is."

Zander laughed. "Yeah, if. I keep forgetting about the ifs."

We stopped walking and looked up at the bow of

the ship. The massive window jutted out of the mount of dirt, reflecting the halo of blue around the gas giant hiding the sun. Inside, I could see the bridge, somehow serene in the darkness.

Zander sighed, stuffing his hands into the pockets of his uniform. He looked smart in the blue and silver, as if it had been tailored just for him. There was no denying how handsome he was.

Or how unavailable.

I couldn't believe I was thinking that way about my best friend. My immortal best friend. It would never work. If Blayde and Jurrah couldn't work through it, then how did I stand a chance?

"Stardust for your thoughts?"

His voice broke me out of that train of thought, thank god. He smiled awkwardly at me, and I looked back up, shrugging.

"Zander," I said, slowly, "when those men attacked me in the hotel—"

"I won't let that happen again."

"What did you just say about promises?" I asked. "I need you to teach me to defend myself, in case it *does* happen again."

"It won't." This time, he caught himself. "Right. I'm not exactly sure how to teach you, though."

"What do you mean?"

"You're mortal; I'm immortal," he said, matter-of-factly. I would never get over how natural those words sounded as he said them. "When I fight, I fight to wear out the opponent, to incapacitate. With you, it's going to be life or death. You'll fight for survival."

"Show me."

"I should… Okay."

Within a second, he had me from behind, a hand on my neck the way a knife would be. Fear ripped through me in an instant.

"In a situation like this, don't think about playing fair," said Zander. "Think about getting out alive. Nothing is off-limits. They want you dead, you want to live. Those desires are incompatible, so don't hold back."

"But what do I do?" I gasped. My mind flashed to the three alien men in my hotel room, to the fear I'd felt then, the fear I felt now.

Panic.

"Fight!" ordered Zander. "Put up a struggle!"

I squirmed weakly, trying to breathe. He wasn't cutting off my air; I was. Something inside me was effusing to let me catch my breath. I swung an arm backward, hitting him in the ribs with my elbow.

I don't think he even felt it.

"Okay, that's a start. Remember you have more limbs than just your arms. You're using elbows; that's great. If you can feel my chin, headbutt me. Most humanoids shut down if you can crush their nose. They're very easy to break. Now, think of your feet. Jam your heel into your assailant's foot, or better yet, stab the inside of their shin. It will destabilize them…"

But I wasn't listening anymore. Electricity shot through my veins and not the good, adrenaline kind. The shut-down-and-panic kind. It took everything to fight my instinct to not scream.

Zander let go suddenly.

"You didn't do anything," he breathed, stepping away, holding out his hands to steady me.

I was shaking now. Why was I shaking? I knew it wasn't real. I knew this was just practice, so why did I want to curl up in a ball and hide?

Zander wrapped me in his arms. His chest was warm but silent as the grave. No heartbeat in this tin man.

"Let's go join the others," he soothed. "We'll work on this another day."

I nodded, following him back to the bonfire, but the feeling in my gut grew—the knowledge that this would all end in tears, the certainty that when the time came, I would freeze up like I did now.

I wasn't even capable of keeping myself alive.

The fire had grown by the time we returned, and it was nice and toasty to sit by it. The crew, however, was another story entirely. They were glaring at each other, keeping their distance. Something had happened.

Zander and I found a place close to Kork, who acknowledged our arrival with a nod.

"What did I miss?" asked Zander.

"Finch was just telling us why he couldn't be the murderer," said the captain, sullenly, "as we all were. Stating our cases."

"I'm just saying," Finch said, "that if anyone had motivation to give up the ship to the Consortium, it would be Jezeal. He's not human."

"That's bullshit," said Jezeal, his hair rising like an angry cat's, "and xenophobic as hell!"

"You shouldn't even be on the show! You won a fucking contest!" said Finch.

"And they kept me because of pure talent, dumbass. You're only here because they blackmailed you. If anything, you're the most likely saboteur. You hate the Alliance, and you're not too subtle about it."

Crandle gasped.

"Jezeal, you can't say that," said Doesso. "That's a massive accusation."

"Like they have cameras rolling here? Not hardly."

Blayde and Jurrah picked that moment to join the group. Blayde had somehow gotten Jurrah a towel, but the Astrogator didn't seem to want to wear it. Already, her hair was beginning to grow back on the top of her scalp, a little covering of peach fuzz like a crown on her head. Being outside of stasis seemed to make Jurrah's body work on overdrive, catching up for lost time if it could.

She was tall—lanky and lean. She was at least a foot taller than Blayde, maybe two seeing as how she towered over even Kork. She was shorter than Jezeal, though. Everyone would be shorter than Jezeal.

No one seemed to know where to start. Eyes darted between Kork and Jurrah, but neither seemed to know what to say.

"Okay, this is getting awkward," Blayde said, her short temper back right on schedule. "Right. Team *Traveler*, meet your astrogator. Jurrah has been ensuring your survival on a daily basis since before most of you were born. Say hi."

There were a few uncomfortable hellos muttered by the crew. I just stared. It was weird for me to imagine Blayde as someone's girlfriend. The fact she could be anything but brash was alien to me.

"Hello," Jurrah said slowly. Her voice was deep, like approaching thunder on a clear day. "This is highly irregular."

"You said it," Finch muttered.

Jezeal stared at his feet. "Can you cover up, please?"

"Jurrah's skin has been in a hyper-sensory gel for the past century," Blayde snapped. "I think you can appreciate the fact that she's not ready to be touched. Or have anything touch her. The towel was already pushing it. Give her time to recover."

"I feel so ... small." The woman looked back at the ship and shuddered.

I could hardly imagine what was going through her mind right now.

"Thank you," Crandle said suddenly, standing, stepping forward, and bowing to the woman. Jurrah's eyes widened as the first mate smiled at her. "You've carried us through so much. Even now, you brought us to a planet where we can survive."

"Speaking of," Finch spat, "what the fuck, lady? All we needed to do was re-attach those sections, and instead you bring us here. Screw habitable. We shouldn't be here in the first place."

"We are exactly where we need to be," Jurrah said, stoic, as Blayde flashed eyes full of murder at the engineer. "Or at least, it made sense when I was the ship. Now things are so hazy. The path is no longer clear."

"Well, I, for one, want to get off this rock." Finch whipped his head around to stare at his captain. "Kork, what do we do?"

Everyone looked to their captain. Finch had asked the question we all wanted to ask, though maybe with a little less tact than I would have gone for. Kork wiped his brow with his sleeve. His forehead glistened.

"Right," he said, more nervous than I had ever heard him, "we need to get off this planet."

"You said it!" Jezeal agreed with a laugh, which entailed clicking mandibles and trembling hair.

No one seemed to care about the saboteur anymore. The need to get off the planet was so overwhelming that accusations were put on the backburner—for the time being, at least.

"That's a goal, not a plan," said Finch. "Are you going to lead us or what?"

"We need to wait for the sun to return," he said, calmly. "Until then, rest. We are going to need it. As of right now, the ship's in no state to fly, but we should be able to get the shuttles working."

"The drones are operational," said Jurrah dreamily. "They can repair the damage to the outer hull. However, we're out of fuel. We can fix the ship, but we can't take off without it."

"So, we need ubritrium," Doesso piped up. "Do we have any in store?"

"No," Finch said and crossed his arms over his chest. "Guess which floors the stock was held on?"

"This planet is rich with ubritrium." Jurrah smiled. "That is partially why I chose it. I think it has everything we need."

"Everything we need for what?" Blayde asked.

"To fix things." Jurrah nodded to herself. "To fix it all. Destiny. We need to be here."

"No wonder the ship split itself apart." Finch said. "Our astrogator lost it."

"Her mind doesn't work on the same level as your puny brain," Blayde said, "so shut your yapper and listen to what she has to say."

Of course, that was the moment Jurrah decided to pass out. She froze and fell backward onto the soft grass, like a cartoon character being hit by a backfiring acme product. Just right down, rigid like a plank.

Blayde was at her side in a second taking her pulse and checking her breath. She sighed in relief when she found both.

"Jurrah said there's ubritrium here," she said, as she stroked the woman's forehead. "Don't wait around. Go and find some." When no spoke up, she glared. "Do I have to do everything around here?" She clutched Jurrah to her chest, as if that would protect her from the anger Blayde was tossing at us. "Kork, you lead an away team. Take who you want and grab some ubritrium, will you?"

The captain looked a little sour but cleared his throat. Blayde returned to tending to Jurrah, ignoring us all completely.

"Right. I'll take Crandle, Sally, and Haln ... oh, and Jezeal, in case we need a doctor."

"But I ..." Jezeal sputtered. "I'm not actually a doctor. I just play one on TV."

"I'm going to tell you the same thing I told my agent when he got me on this godforsaken show," said Crandle, crossing her arms over her chest. "If I don't get my own dressing room, I'll take no part in it."

"We need hands," he said. "We need a lot of ubritrium, and it's going to be heavy. We all have to play our part if we want to get out of this alive. Finch, you stay here and work on getting the repairs started, seeing as you're the only one with any engineering know-how. Doesso—"

"Let me guess, you want me to stay here too?" She sighed. "Fine then. I guess it's better I'm useless here than with you guys."

He was splitting us up, I realized. If the saboteur wanted to act, they would have more chances to reveal themselves. The captain was trying to solve the mystery, too.

Unless *he* was the saboteur, in which case he wanted to make it easier to kill us all. I shivered, and not from the cold.

"What about Marcoli?" I asked.

"What about him?"

I pointed at the forest. "He ran off after the ship crashed. Someone should go after him, right?"

They exchanged glances, but no one said anything. I shuffled uncomfortably in the grass, possibly staining my uniform green.

"If that's what he wants," said Jezeal, "who can blame him? He never asked to be assigned to the ship."

"But he's a child. How will he survive out there?"

"He'll be fine," said Crandle. "He's resourceful enough."

They didn't seem to care. I glanced at Zander, who nodded carefully. First things first, I knew out of everyone here that Zander at least would find the kid and make sure he was okay.

"Everyone relax for a little while," Kork said. "Enjoy the fire. Rest. We'll look at the ship when the sun is back."

And the faster we could get on our way. Me, to look for Earth; Zander and Blayde to search for their past, wherever that takes them. I doubted they'd get any answers on this remote rock.

But this planet was more than a rock. It had trees, grass; it had mountains and clouds and a sky. And birds, flying high above us, or something like birds, something alive and flying. This planet was teeming with life.

Jurrah had panicked and brought us here, to a place where we could not only breathe but thrive. Maybe she was right. Maybe destiny said we had to be here. Maybe this is what everyone needed: Blayde getting closure with her ex, Zander getting over Kork, me learning who knows what intergalactic lesson.

Or maybe this was exactly what shit hitting the fan looked like.

CHAPTER NINE
AWAY WITH THE AWAY TEAM

"I know your secret."

Finch said this as casually as someone telling you the time of day. I froze mid-step, looking up at him as my hands started to tremble, going for the brand-new stun gun at my hip.

He was sitting on top of the little shuttle—the hopper, they called it—having just closed a panel he was working on. The ship had a few shuttles, but the crash had done a number on them. This one was in the best shape, and Finch had promised to have it working so we could use it to go out and find some ubritrium, whatever that stuff was.

What I didn't want to find was trouble.

Four words. That was all it took to freeze my blood,

even if I didn't know what secret he was talking about and how he could know it. Anxiety isn't something you could leave behind like an old toothbrush.

"What are you talking about?"

Finch grinned wider, as if that was exactly what he wanted me to say. I touched the standard-issue stun gun they had given me, wrapping my hands around it for backup.

"I know who your friends are," he said. "I mean, come on. Thratra? Haln? What kind of names are those?"

"*Their* names."

"No, they're not." A grin spread on his face, and for a minute I thought I was looking at the Grinch. The grinchiest grin there ever was grinned was on the engineer's face. A shiver ran through me.

"I have no idea what you're talking about," I said, hoisting the backpack of rations on my back before entering the small shuttle. The thing was boxy, about as big as an ambulance, with seats in the back for the crew and a separate cockpit with an open door. I tossed the bag down, turned, and jumped when I saw Finch there, blocking the door.

"How did you do that?" I asked. Finch hadn't made a sound as he slid off the roof of the shuttle.

"Look, I heard the rumors, but I didn't want to believe them," he said, "but after the Da-Duhui uprising, there could be no doubt. And if I figured out your friends' true identities, you can be damn sure the rest of the crew knows too."

"At least they're being polite about it."

"You don't deny it?"

"Dude, I have no idea what you're talking about," I

said, trying to laugh it off. "Thratra and Haln have been my friends for years."

"None of your story checks out." Finch took a step forward. I tried to keep my ground, but that wasn't so easy with my knees trembling so hard I could not walk. "How did you get here? And how are you so oblivious to the way things work? It's like you've been living on a rock."

"I have," I said. "It's called Earth."

"And then, two years ago, the robot uprising on Da-Duhui and two long-forgotten criminals are suddenly back-"

"Wait, wind that back." A new fear overlapped the old one. "Did you just say it's been *two years* since all that shit on Da-Duhui?"

"More or less. It's complicated to tell real time when you're traveling faster than light."

Shit.

I didn't realize I had taken a seat, but suddenly my hands were curling under the plastic cushion, my nails digging into the cheap material. Two years. Zander had mentioned that jumping messed with time, but I never thought I would be caught in it.

Two years between now and Da-Duhui. Five years between the plant and meeting Sekai at that Mayoral bash. How long had I been missing from Earth?

I had missed Dany and Marcy's wedding.

By a long shot.

"Is everyone okay here?"

Zander popped his head into the shuttle. Finch stepped back, opening his mouth, but suddenly Crandle was there and he shut it again.

"We'll talk more when you get back, Sally." He hopped out of the shuttle and went to join Crandle. What was he going to do? Blackmail us?

"You sure you want to come with us?" asked Zander, a hand on the ceiling to steady himself. I nodded. "It's going to be dangerous. I'd much rather you stay on the ship."

"And miss all the fun?" I replied, trying to sound like Blayde. No one ever doubted her words.

Except Finch, apparently. I didn't like him.

"It'll be much safer here," he continued.

"You saw how I managed on Da-Duhui. I can handle myself on this ship. I'm not alone, like I was there."

"I promised I'd bring you back to Earth safely," he said, his voice getting colder. "Please don't make me break another promise. You saw how you reacted last night, and in the hotel, and—"

"I'm fine!"

"You're not!" You're human. You could actually *die*. We don't know what's out there. You froze up last night. What would happen if we found real danger?"

"I don't see you giving this lecture to the rest of the crew."

"They've been faking it for years. Kork knows what he's doing, and even Crandle went through boot camp. Finch, too. They at least know the right end of a gun from the other."

"I think I can manage."

He reached over, plucked the stunner from my grasp, and flipped it around. A nice red button now sat beside my thumb.

"Not without any help, you can't. It's not a question

of pride, Sally; it's a question of getting you home in one piece. Disintegrated atoms don't count."

"Thanks," I grumbled. But there was so much else we needed to talk about. Finch, for starters, and the possibility that more time had elapsed back home than out here. So many questions, so much to talk about, but before I could say anything, Crandle pushed herself past us into the hopper. She sat against the wall, strapping her seatbelt.

"You still have time to change your mind," Zander said. "Think about it. I'm not saying you're not capable, but you might get into things you're not ready for. You have nothing to prove to me or anybody else."

He disappeared into the cockpit, and I heard his seatbelt click. Well, that went well. Maybe he was right. Maybe I needed to stay behind, to make sure that when I got back to Earth, it would be with all my limbs securely attached to my body. But this was an alien planet. How many chances would I have in my life to explore one?

And I needed to stay away from Finch. That guy was shady as hell—shooting past everybody else to top the list of suspects.

I reached for my buckle, fiddling with the straps and clasps until I figured out how to secure myself. Jezeal climbed in next, sitting across from me, his head brushing against the ceiling. He offered me what appeared to be a smile, and I smiled uncomfortably back.

"Room for one more?"

Kork stepped in the doorway, smiling awkwardly at Zander. He looked a little taken aback that someone else was at the wheel, but that look was replaced by relief.

Weird.

"Is this the intrepid away team?" he said jokingly, joining Zander in the cockpit. "Is this seat taken?"

Zander said nothing as Kork took the copilot's chair. Instead, Zander turned to face us in the back, smiling like this was the start of a fantastic road trip.

"Everyone ready to go?" Zander asked. He didn't wait for an answer. The door slid shut and sealed itself with a hiss.

And then we were off. The shuttle shot out of the bay, the entrance of which was lopsided from the crash, and flew over the virgin land. It glided effortlessly under Zander's firm hand, and I watched the landscape fly past us out the windows, trying to take it all in.

It was breathtaking.

The sun was gliding past the planet, casting golden rays onto the land. No cities. No roads. Not a single structure, anywhere. Just beautiful forest and rivers and mountains and just ... land. We were high enough that we did not disturb the treetops. Sometimes, I thought I saw herds of animals in places, but it was impossible to know for sure.

I wasn't the only one amazed by this. Even Kork looked elated. I stared out the back window as the land ran away from us.

All too quickly, it was over.

Zander landed us at the edge of a volcano, right where a mountain of shale met a field of some tall wheat look-alike. It was high enough to reach the little window on the door and the back of the shuttle. Even the windshield in the cockpit had a few sprigs touching the glass.

Crandle shot out of the ship the second Zander opened the door and rushed to a bush to do something that sounded an awful lot like retching. I guess I had forgotten she was an actress. Zander followed her out, and one by one we left the shuttle, walking on land no other man had trod on.

We come in peace, for all mankind. And spider people.

"Come on, we've got some ubritrium to find," Zander said, taking charge of the crew with a warm smile.

"I've got this," Kork interjected. "Isn't that right, crew?"

Jezeal groaned. "Couldn't we have had this pissing contest back at the ship?"

"Shut up," said Crandle.

"I'm the captain. I should lead this away team," Kork said.

"You're an actor," Zander said. "Does that make you qualified to lead?" I wasn't sure if Zander even cared about this shit, but, hey, he was going through some tough stuff.

"But he's not," Crandle said, stepping between the two of them. "Kork's the only real thing on the *Traveler*, except maybe Jurrah. That's why they picked him to lead the flagship."

"Then, by all means," Zander said, maybe only half begrudgingly. The other half was either annoyed or a little impressed. He handed the captain a small palm pilot. "Let's go, crew! Everyone remember where we parked."

Kork waved us forward, keeping a whole step ahead

of Zander. He looked down at a handheld device and started walking.

Up ahead, beyond the little field, the forest looked more like a jungle. The trees were dense with incredibly thick leaves, and darkness closed in fast.

Wait, why did I sign up for this? I knew enough from TV to know that not everyone in the away team survived expeditions. Even Kork was apprehensive. As we reached the edge of the jungle, he stopped.

Were my eyes deceiving me, or had something big moved in the dark underbrush? Grabbing my courage with both hands, I raised my voice.

"Something's in there," I said, but out came a whisper instead of a shout. A whisper loud enough to be heard by all.

"It's a jungle. Things live in jungles," Kork tutted, trying to encourage himself more than anyone else. "Come on, back before nightfall, all right?"

With that, he waltzed right into the jungle, seemingly without a care—or a fear—in the world.

"Let's pick up the pace," Zander said, as we forced ourselves to catch up. "Let's not let the rest of the crew up there get bored and fly away without us, if they could, of course." He chuckled at his own joke, though none of us found it funny.

I wasn't liking pissed off Zander. Not one bit.

But, hey, what are friends for? Definitely for standing by you when things got tough, so that was what I was going to do. Zander took it upon himself to take up the rear of our little expedition, so I held back and stood by his side. I was going to help, dammit.

"Hey, so, aren't you the least bit worried?" I asked,

trying to make conversation.

"About what?" he said. "The eventual heat death of the universe? The lack of pizza anywhere in this quadrant? Constantly. But what are you talking about specifically?"

"You know, the rest of the crew." Talking was good. It was keeping me from getting freaked out by the jungle. The dense foliage blocked out most of the sunlight, making it dark and ominous. I thought I could see movement in the trees, but I shuddered and put it to the back of my mind. Paranoia was not a good look for me.

"What about them?"

"They're alone," I pointed out, "and any one of them could be the saboteur."

"Oh, they wouldn't do anything."

"How do you come to that conclusion?"

"Short answer? Blayde." He brimmed with confidence. "But, hey, he—or she, or anything in-between—wouldn't do anything, not if the number of people with them is so low. It narrows the suspect pool by a pretty wide margin. Plus, they wouldn't want to hurt themselves, so no messing with the ship's finer workings until we've made it off this rock. And also—"

"What?"

"We still have no idea what their motivations are."

"I'm trying to picture the ship before everything went to shit, but I can't remember where anyone was. I was with Kork, and I held his hand the whole time the lights were out. He can't be the saboteur."

"Good alibi," said Zander. "Holding his hand, huh?"

"Don't," I said, smacking him in the arm. "And you?

Can you alibi anyone?"

"I was talking with Jezeal, but when it went dark, I lost track of him. Not exactly helpful."

"So, not counting Kork, we have Crandle, Jezeal, Doesso, Finch, and Marcoli, right?" I held up my fingers. Five culprits. Five strangers Zander knew from TV and who I had just met today. Not much to go on.

"I don't think Marcoli could have done it," said Zander. "He wasn't supposed to be on the bridge. The only reason he came up there was because of us."

"Unless someone took advantage of that situation and manipulated his chip from a distance?"

"I'm not sure if that's something that happens, but I suppose it could. Anyway, it looks like he doesn't have to worry about the crew anymore. Lucky break for him."

"Then four suspects. What about motive? Could that help narrow them down?"

"I've been thinking about the problem, and honestly, I'm not seeing any logical motivation. It's like we're missing half the story. I mean, who would want to turn the *Traveler* over to the Consortium? What could that possibly do?"

"Money."

"What?" he asked.

"What if the motivation is just plain money? Someone trying to kill off their co-stars to get more airtime?"

"That would be… well, I wouldn't put it past some of them," he said. The idea had caught him off guard. "Crandle especially. She practically admitted to both of us to having already done it, but she's already high enough. I don't see her trying to kill Kork for a promotion. And it doesn't take the Consortium into account."

"True, true," I agreed. "Your turn."

"For what?"

"To come up with a motive. I tried hard, you know." I was looking for something, anything to cheer him up. But I should know better, from my own experience that this had no simple answer.

"I still can't believe Kork put himself in a situation where he had to lie about every accomplishment in his life. He did amazing things before becoming captain."

"Like what?" I asked.

"Well, he was completely unknown until he was the sole survivor of a spacecraft that went down," Zander said, the excitement in his voice growing steadily. "I think they were sent to get rid of some pirates, can't remember where. They killed his crew, all of them on one side of the ship, tricked there by who knows what. Last alive, sure to die, he sent his ship straight into the belly of the enemy, thus accomplishing his mission. He only survived because whoever is captain has this strange mechanism that when the ship blows, it's like an airbag, something like that. The ship protected him. Kork lived, got promoted, and then ..." He sighed. "After that, well, who knows what's real and what's not."

I looked toward Kork then back at Zander. I didn't know what to think of him. He seemed all right. Better than all right. He was sweet, he was handsome, and I was starting to crush on him, hard.

There was just something about a man in uniform. Especially a uniform with a padded bum.

And yet, there was something off about Kork's

backstory. Sole survivor of a spaceship crash? I stared at where he was marching through the jungle. Maybe I shouldn't have been so quick to rule him out.

No. He held my hand the entire time that light was out. He couldn't have killed Xacrelf.

I didn't know what to believe anymore.

"Who's currently at the top of your suspect list?" I asked, trying to change the subject.

"Jezeal," Zander replied. "He hasn't said a word, yet he watches you constantly—"

"He watches everyone, Zander. He has eight eyes. That's what he does."

He shrugged. "He just doesn't seem right."

"Huh."

"You don't seem convinced. Do you have an idea?"

"I don't think anyone on the ship would do something to get rid of their own crew," I replied. "I think something else is going on, but if I had to base my opinion on what I've seen on TV, it's most likely who you least expect—Doesso, or Finch, or both."

He laughed. "I think their bark is worse than their bite."

Kork turned around, glaring at us. "Hurry up, you two! We want to get back to the ship before it gets dark again."

Jezeal and Crandle glared at him like he was the drill sergeant of their nightmares. Both of them were panting and sweating profusely, which was impressive for Jezeal, since he was entirely covered by hair.

I, however, felt energetic, like the hike had done wonders to my health. That was new, for a change. Maybe I was getting something out of this forced exile from Earth after all.

Even if it did mean—I shook the thought out of my head. I didn't have time to think about time.

Jezeal fell behind. He was older than the rest of the crew, the white in his fur apparently from age. Trying to keep my mind off the jungle, I didn't wait for him to acknowledge my presence before I started to speak.

"Is Dr. Jezeal your real name, or is that for the show?" I asked, trying to distract him from the tedium of marching. He turned to look at me, eyes widening. Clearly, he hadn't expected me to make conversation.

"You know, no one's actually asked me that. My real name is Ter Gabre'el Saar." It seemed as though no one had taken the time to listen, and he was eager to fill that gap now. The second he opened his mouth, the floodgates could not be shut again. "And, no, before you ask, I'm not a real doctor. They hired me because I finished one of those secret contests." I must have looked confused because he elaborated for me. "They did promos about broadcasting the war, and in one of them an equation was hidden in the background. I solved it, and it was a number to call, and that brought me here. Now I'm a character. I mean, look"—he raised his voice—"Crandle! What's my name?"

"What are you going on about now, Jezeal?" She stared at him then shrugged, going back to gazing at Zander. The later had picked up the pace to catch up with Kork, and who now seemed as confused by Crandle's look as a pubescent teenager.

"I never say much on the show, just stuff like *Oh, that's dangerous!* Or maybe *It looks like a trap!* and *A doctor can only do so much.* What a life." He looked to the sky, which was a beautiful shade of auburn at this point, darker than it had been when we had landed.

"Crandle keeps her real name?" I decided that I rather liked this person; he wasn't as stuck up as the rest of them. Conversation seemed like a good thing for long walks in an alien jungle.

"She was way too famous not to," he replied. "They invented mine to make me sound more, well, *exotic*, I guess. But I'm just from Meegra. It's not even that far from the core planets."

"Meegra? I know someone from there." I smiled as I remembered Tchilla, the seamstress in Da-Duhui who helped me find Zander again. "Isn't that the planet where those large creatures are the police?"

"You see?" he sputtered. "Even you've heard of it, and you didn't even know about the show. It's a nice little planet."

"Even with the beasts as police?"

"Oh, don't worry about them," he said. "They can almost smell crime. That's a pretty impressive feat on its own."

"You're from Meegra?" Zander cut in and appeared by Ter's side quite suddenly. Ter nodded. "I've been there before." Zander sounded excited now, matching his stride to Ter's. "I don't remember much about it. Don't be offended or anything; it's just that I see a new planet each day at least, so details slip my mind."

"I know you," Ter said, brimming with the same excitement as Zander's. "You're no Haln."

"You know me?"

"Zander," he said, his voice dropping, like it was some incredible secret. His many eyes twinkled. "*The*

Zander."

"What makes you say that?" Zander glanced around quickly, making sure neither the captain nor his first mate were around to hear any of this.

"My mother's a historian." Ter took in Zander's cold look and nodded, as if answering a question no one dared ask. "Don't worry, I won't tell Crandle. But I've heard the legends—even the ones the Alliance tries to cover up."

"What legends?"

"You're the *Iron and the Sand*, aren't you? You and your sister. Thratra is the Blayde from the stories. She was much more obvious than you."

Zander grunted. He was excited, yes, but hesitant. Ter wasn't really selling it.

"That was centuries ago, full ages ago," Ter said "I had heard about your—ahem—enhanced abilities. The Alliance rams lessons down our throats every day. But I never believed you were evil. My mother went to prison for saying you helped us. I agree with her version of the tale, though my bosses have no idea."

"That's ... wow, that takes guts."

"This—this is incredible," Ter continued. "I'm meeting legends. I always knew you two existed, the *Iron and the Sand*, yet here you are."

Zander was feeling it now. Something about Ter's excitement was pumping him up, and he grinned.

"Important question." He chuckled. "Do I have a statue?"

"Many." Ter laughed. "Though they're all in museums now."

"Cool!" said Zander. "But wait, why am I called the

Sand? That's not very—" He caught his breath. "I'm not supposed to ask, but did Blayde and I look any different back then?"

"No idea, the ancient paintings and writings are vague." He shook his head. "Though the statue is a little uncanny. Mother found writings of your actions, rather than of your looks."

"Did they give our last names?" Zander urged. "Our home world?"

"Why—"

"Please, just answer." His face grew cold and stony.

"I have no idea," he said, shaking his head. "But if you want more information, you should go see the monks of Berbabsywell. They keep records of the histories of every planet, untainted by the Alliance. Maybe they have information about you or your stay on Meegra. My mother tried getting a consultation with them, but that was before she got arrested."

"I'm sorry about your mother." Zander put a hand on Ter's shoulder. "Is she well?"

Ter smiled. "She's retired now. She'll be fine, as long as she doesn't write anything more."

We trekked through the jungle in silence after that.

Could Ter be a suspect? He seemed too kind to be a killer, but there was a resentment toward his coworkers that could not be ignored. Winning a contest and ending up stuck in a show run by the people who had arrested his mother would make anybody mad.

He could very well be the killer. I walked closer to Zander.

I tried not to think about what could be in this jungle. Every time I turned my head, I was sure I could see a small movement in the leaves. There was a faint rustling in the branches, too, but it could have been my imagination. It was dark, like walking through a live version of *Jurassic Park.*

Kork's palm pilot map thing beeped, and the jungle opened. We had found the ubritrium.

In a field.

CHAPTER TEN

I SAW THIS IN A MOVIE ONCE, BUT IT'S A HUNDRED TIMES WORSE WHEN YOU LIVE IT IRL

A field of ubritrium pearls spread out in a perfect square, the pearls set in straight lines all the way down it.

Some were as tall as I was and a few ever larger. The rest were anywhere between up to my hip and as small as a marble, barely noticeable on the ground. Every one of them was beautifully polished, reflecting the setting sun with a pinkish gleam.

Nobody moved. It was obvious from the neat rows that this was not a natural field. Someone, or something, had cultivated it. This was a sales lot.

And we were probably trespassing.

"Ubritrium," said Kork, slipping the guide onto his

utility belt.

"They look so ... pristine." Crandle's eyes twinkled. "I've never seen ubritrium spheres grown so big. They must be worth a fortune."

"They are," Kork agreed. "I'm so, so glad I'm not in charge of the ship's budget. Ubritrium is expensive as hell."

"All the more reason to rescue the other half of the crew," said Ter. "You never know how much you need the accountants until they're stranded on the other side of the galaxy."

"All right." Kork sprang into action once more, giving Ter only the briefest of chuckles. "How do we go about getting one of these back to the ship?"

"We're going to roll the sucker," Zander said, which got him some annoyed grunts from the group.

He marched forward, knocking on some random pearls, probably trying to pick which was our best bet to get out of here alive. He walked right by the six-feet tall ones, much to all of our relief, looking at the four-foot, five-foot range. Even those were large, but with the group we had, they appeared a lot more manageable.

Zander finally picked one and motioned for us to come along. He rolled the ubritrium sphere forward, not without a bit of a struggle, then he reached into his pocket to pull out a handful of gold coins. He dropped them on the ground where the sphere had been. I guess that covered our asses for the trespassing aspect.

The field was solemn and silent. I wasn't sure if Zander's payment was what these strangers wanted. After all, how could we know? This planet had only been discovered an hour ago, and by us. We had yet to make contact with the natives, if that was something we were planning to do. Silence was the best way to respect the people here, whoever they were.

Ter, Zander, and Crandle got the ball rolling together, so Kork and I took point and rear, respectively. He led the way, following the trail we had carved through the ferns and underbrush.

For a while, the only sounds were the grunts of the ones behind the ubritrium, pushing the giant ball along the jungle floor. Ferns were crushed underfoot. Kork's little gizmo made a few whirring and bleepy noises. Even Crandle was silent for a change.

Still, there was something in the air that made me feel ... uneasy. Maybe it had something to do with how claustrophobic the jungle felt. Or maybe it was the shapes I kept seeing out of the corner of my eye, which I had been pretending to ignore. My gut told me something was there, and I was trying to trust my gut a little more of late. Then again, my anxiety had always been quite a loud voice down there.

I raised a hand and motioned the crew to stop, which, of course, no one would see, since I was behind them all. So much for self-improvement.

"Oy, stop," I said, raising my voice loud enough for them to hear over the rolling rumble of the ubritrium.

"My dear, do you need a potty break?" Crandle turned, obviously frustrated at having to stop her momentum. She took the opportunity to wipe her brow, which was covered in a sheen of sweat, so thick I could practically see my reflection in it.

"Will you stop and just listen?" I said.

"Go on," Kork urged.

"Not to me, to the jungle. Does anyone else hear that?"

"I don't hear anything," said Ter, yet his voice was quiet. He might not have heard what I had, but he had felt it too.

"Exactly," I replied. "We're in a jungle. Shouldn't there be animals?"

"We probably scared them off," said Kork. "Come, let's keep going. The sun's going to be down pretty soon."

Crack.

I spun at the sound, trying to find its source. There had definitely been a noise, somewhere to my five, six o'clock. My eyes scanned the dark world behind me. It was looking a lot darker than it had five minutes ago, not even the same jungle we had just walked through before.

The crew watched me like I was slowly losing my mind, but I wasn't crazy. Jungles didn't make you that paranoid; they can't. It's what's in them we ought to be worried about.

Crack.

I could see the looks in their eyes. They heard it too, and fear was creeping up there, right where it belonged. Their heads spun around wildly, searching for the source. These were not soldiers, just actors with no formal training. No one knew what to do. My hands were shaking, but I still couldn't find where the noise had come from, no matter how much I squinted into the darkening jungle.

Boom.

The deafening sound enveloped us all at once. We

scanned the jungle for the thing, for whatever it was, the noise that made the ground tremble beneath our feet. Every instinct told me to run, while my muscles refused to obey.

And then—silence.

"It's gone, whatever it is." Crandle gulped loudly, sounding quite unconvincing. "Let's keep—"

With a scream, she flew into the air, disappearing into the darkness of the jungle, leaving not a trace, no sound or sign in her wake. Something huge had grabbed her, plucked her in the air, and fled.

"Holy shit! Crandle!" Ter shouted. "They took Crandle!"

"What do we do?" I asked, fear gripping my every joint, my every muscle.

"We stay very, very quiet," Zander replied, scanning the jungle. He took his own advice, not moving a limb, his entire focus on seeking the danger before it found us.

With a sound like a lion's roar, a gigantic shape lunged at us from above. Its arms, if you could call them arms, spread wide to grab us all at once. Kork hit it smack in the chest with a stun gun before any of us could move, making the creature stumble.

"Now, we run!" Zander shouted, slamming his hands against the ubritrium. I rushed to their side, and faster than I could think, we rolled the giant ball along the path, sprinting so quickly that I couldn't feel my feet touching the ground.

"Kork! Take over!" Zander shouted, and just like that, he disappeared.

So much for being incognito with the crew. Then

again, even I wasn't sure he really jumped with the insanity going on around me.

Kork was doing as he was told but looked terrified. Gone was the strong captain staying stern for his crew. This Kork was as scared as the rest of us.

Maybe even more so.

From somewhere far behind me, the creature made a terrible guttural sound, and the rhythmic thump of paws treading soil told us it was gaining speed. Or maybe catching up. I didn't know.

More thunder joined the chase, the deep drum-like sound pulsing though the earth like a heartbeat. We ran faster, forcing our legs to propel us through the jungle.

So did they.

Ter let out a cry, dropping any pretext of ever having a humanoid body. He ripped his uniform to shreds, his legs and arms spreading out where they were supposed to be and continued running on all eight of them. Well, on six, using two to roll the ball forward like a dung beetle.

In less than the quarter of the time it took us to find the ubritrium, we managed to reach the field. There, right there, was the shuttle. We broke out of the jungle and rushed into the tall grass. We didn't stop, only increasing our speed as we tried to reach our one ticket out of here, monsters right on our heels.

Suddenly, Zander was back. He ran alongside the ubritrium, matching our stride despite the woman slung over his shoulder. Crandle was unconscious but otherwise appeared unharmed, if not for the scrapes on her face. I had no time to feel relieved because already I could hear the thrashing of trees being brutally pushed aside, the monsters breaking out of the jungle behind us. With every beat of their stride, they drove a spike of fear deeper into my skull.

My toe slammed into a rock before I even saw it was there. I fell forward, right on my face, all the wind knocked from my lungs as the ground smacked into my belly. I pushed myself up without thinking, feeling my body running on adrenaline and instinct. My palms were scuffed, red and raw.

As I hopped back on my feet, I saw them. First, it was the shadow looming over me, eclipsing the sun. I looked up and it looked down, and our eyes met for a second. That was all it took to freeze me in my tracks.

It ran like an ape, on four legs, the two front ones long and thick and dangling. Its entire body was covered in thick, matted fur, backed in drool and mud, especially around the six long tusks that protruded from its slobbering mouth. It lifted its lips to snarl at me, revealing rows of brown-colored teeth, teeth that had obviously never seen dental floss, let alone a toothbrush.

And, maybe most unsettling of all, it had braids. Long, white braids dangled from behind its ears.

Okay, maybe a bit more unsettling than that was the fact that there were eight of them charging at us.

"Sally!"

I had the sudden sensation of flying through the air, and I was thrown over somebody's shoulder. My eyes did not break contact with the leading monster, which looked as determined as ever that he wanted to kill me. The creatures stared at me, their snarls breaking through the obnoxious ringing in my ears, my fear increasing by the second.

I looked down to see a uniform. And a firm bum. I shook my head. Adrenaline did stupid things to the mind, but I recognized the rear.

Kork.

"Put me—" I ordered, but he already was letting me down. We had reached the shuttle, and the doors were stubbornly closed.

"You locked it?" Kork shouted. "Why would you lock it? There's no one here to take the fucking thing! And even if there were, what would make you think they could fly it?"

"Trust me, never leave your spacecraft unlocked," Zander muttered, searching through his jacket for the keys. His uniform was stained red.

"Hurry up, man!" Ter had made the mistake of looking back at the monsters, as I had. The man-spider was petrified. "We don't have all day. We don't have even a minute."

"Got it!" Zander pulled out the thick silver ring. Dozens of keys were attached, along with a small plaque that read "*Property of the* Traveler. *Please return to the United Planetary Alliance Fleet offices if found.*"

I focused on those words rather than the advancing hoard of doom. I read them over in my head, anything to not let the panic overtake me, until Zander found the right key and the door flew open.

"Get into the hopper!"

Without the momentum we had, getting the sphere into the shuttle was a struggle, but adrenaline is a hell of a drug. We pushed it in and slammed the door shut seconds before the first of the creatures was upon us. Zander dropped Crandle in the back seat beside me and switched on the ignition. I reached over to strap her in and froze.

I thought she had been fine, but she was far from it. There was a bone sticking out of her leg. Her face was pale and draining fast, a black eye already forming there, the only color on her beautiful skin. I bit my lip as I latched her seatbelt. She would be okay, right?

I looked away and saw an even worse sight. The creatures, those mangy beasts, watched us wide-eyed from the field. They looked gruesome. They looked like death.

I felt a smile curl up my lips. They almost looked harmless from up here. Almost. I was about to inhale a deep breath of relief at our escape when one of the creatures floated toward us.

"You have got to be kidding me!" Ter cried, watching as the creatures levitated toward us.

"Are they ... magnetic?" Zander asked, staring out the window.

"Just—just get us out of here!" Ter begged, as if the louder he yelled the faster we'd go. Zander twisted the shuttle as he hit the accelerator, shooting us into the sky.

And a giant ubritrium sphere rolled forward, slamming into the cockpit door.

"Didn't anyone strap it down?" I looked around before realizing I was the one who said the words. If Kork was captain of the *Traveler*, then I was Captain Obvious.

"What now?" Crandle muttered, her eyes fluttering open. For a split second, she stared at the creatures drifting toward us, claws outstretched. She saw the sphere rolling right at her, loose in the cabin, and she took in the bone jutting out of her leg, the blood staining her uniform a deep wine red.

She screamed, her voice more strident than all the alarms in the *Traveler* combined.

"Will someone please help her?" Kork begged, glancing back into the cabin. Ter and I didn't know what to do. Not only was Crandle sobbing, but Zander was trying to break the creatures' grip on the craft by making sharp ducks and turns, which was sending the ubritrium slamming into chairs.

And people.

We all felt it at the same time—the shuttle swayed as one of the creatures grabbed one of the landing struts. The thing jerked violently, dragging us down to the right, and the ubritrium sphere slammed into Ter.

Zander swung us back upright, compensating for the weight while trying to throw the creature off to no avail. The thing was climbing now, and we could hear it scratching at the door.

Is it still called sea sickness if you're not at sea? If not, then I was feeling shuttle sickness. I unbuckled myself and threw my legs on the seat opposite me, creating a barrier to stop the sphere from rolling any closer to Crandle. This, of course, meant having my unsettled stomach constantly thwacked by a giant rolling rock, but I was learning that sometimes, taking one for the team could be the difference between life and death.

I'd always hated group projects. Teams suck. There was always one of them out for themselves and no one else.

"All right, one of you is trying to get us killed!"

Zander shouted, swerving the craft. Creatures were still floating toward us like we were pulling them on a tractor beam. "Crandle? They went after you."

"Why? What'd I do?" she stammered, trying to sound innocent but failing miserably. There was guilt in her shrill voice. Guilt and a whole lot of pain.

"Why do you think they were following us?" said Zander. "*We* paid for the ubritrium, but you didn't pay for the piece you took."

"You mean this?" she said, pulling a small ubritrium pearl the size of her fist from her pocket. "I didn't think they'd miss it."

"Well, obviously they do, so throw it back!" Zander ordered.

"What? No way! You can get us out of here. They won't mind once it's gone." He swerved the pod back, the ubritrium rolling into her side of the shuttle, making her scream.

"I can't!" He gritted his teeth. "The more they latch on, the harder it is to get this baby in the air. We're falling! Just drop the ubritrium!"

A face appeared in front of the windshield, big teeth as wide as the window. This time, no one said a word. We had screamed all that we could at this point.

The creature brought one of its tusks down against the window. *Thwack.*

It had been synchronized. At the same time, tusks around the shuttle slammed into the metal before them. The ship dropped before emergency power kicked in and set us right again. In that moment, I thought I had died. My heart had stopped beating.

"Now, Crandle!" Ter begged, but she ignored him,

as she always did.

CLANG.

We all felt it, a shock-wave reverberating through the shuttle. One of the creatures had gotten hold of one of the booster jets on the underbelly, veering us off-course. It was oblivious to the heat of the engines, which spat flames at its hair, though the creature did not ignite.

"Just do it!" Kork ordered. "I am your captain, and I am ordering you to drop the sphere, Nolla!"

Kork got up and marched to her, holding out his hand as if she were a disobedient child. Crandle gave one last look at her magnificent pearl and, with a heavy sigh, handed it over to him. The captain rolled down the window, took aim, threw the pearl, and smacked the head of one of the floating creatures with perfect accuracy. It let go with a moan of pain, making the pod bounce as his weight fell away.

One by one, the rest left. Each time, the loss of their weight made the ship bounce, but the fight was over. Each side had gotten what they wanted: they got their merchandise back, and we got our freedom.

Zander regained control of the shuttle, flying us straight and true. We were left trying to ignore the sobs of the broken-hearted movie star, and, as I gathered myself and made my way back to my seat, avoiding the slow-rolling back-and-forth of the giant mythical sci-fi sphere.

"Is that really saying what I think it's saying?" Kork asked, his voice low, breaking the silence and the sobs.

"Yes, unfortunately, it is." Zander let out a heavy sigh. It wasn't relief.

"What's going on?" Ter asked, leaning forward and looking at his captain. He was trembling. I guess I was too.

"We're out of gas," Zander said solemnly. "One of the creatures must have pierced the tank. We need to set down for repairs."

"We should ask for help at the glittering city," Crandle murmured, her eyes dropping shut.

"The what, now?" Kork asked.

"Pay no attention to her. She's delirious," Ter said.

"Wait, I think we should." I followed Crandle's finger, which pointed straight out the back window. It trembled weakly, but she was determined we also saw it.

She pointed right to a gleaming city rising impossibly out of the middle of nowhere, illuminated by the bright setting sun. Well, I say city, but it looked like a snow globe, minus the snow. Skyscrapers under a big glass dome, the red beams of sunlight flickering through a dirty window.

This planet wasn't uninhabited after all.

CHAPTER ELEVEN

IN WHICH ZANDER ACCIDENTALLY CREATES A NEW RELIGION

"How did we not see this before?"

No one had an answer to Kork's question. Maybe it had been too dark before. Maybe we were so turned around we were somewhere else entirely. Either way, the city was here now, and it might just save us.

Maybe there were people there. Maybe they could give us fuel, give us help, give us anything. It was a long shot, appealing to strangers for help, but it was an insane situation to begin with.

Ter and I held the unbitrium in place as best we could as Zander altered course for the city. The shuttle shuddered and bucked the entire way there, eventually giving out at the edge of the forest. The landing wasn't so much of a landing as a little crash, winding us all and giving me a massive headache.

The door to the shuttle flicked open the second we hit the ground, landing with a thud as the last of the energy faded. The lights flickered out. Luckily, that didn't last long; the hopper's emergency power was just as efficient as the *Traveler*'s, and the orange lights I had grown to hate bathed the shuttle in an obnoxious glow.

It made Crandle's blood look brown.

"Nolla, Nolla, hey, stay with me now." Kork rushed to her side, tapping her cheek gently, trying to rouse her from her stupor. I didn't realize I was on my feet until I felt my knees trembling beneath me. The sight of that bone made me sick to my stomach.

"Jezeal, you have to do something!" the captain snapped. But Ter's eyes were wide, and even he was turning a sickly shade of green.

"How many times do I need to tell you? I'm not a real doctor!"

"For the love of God." Kork towered over Ter, using every inch of his height difference to drill in intimidation. Not that intimidating the Meegran would help. "So help me, Jezeal, if you don't do something for Nolla, I'll—"

"Snap out of it, you two." Zander stepped between them, imposing in his own right. He wasn't as tall as Kork, or as muscular, but there was something in his voice that put the shuttle at his command.

Well, I say shuttle. The little hopper was tight with the six of us squeezed inside. Even with the door open, no one stepped out. I probably should have, but I was jammed in the back with the unbitrium sphere and had four men to push through if I wanted out, not to mention the semi-conscious woman with a broken leg.

I wasn't going anywhere anytime soon.

"You're supposed to be friends," Zander insisted, staring both of them down, "so act like it."

"What part of *'It's all a show'* don't you understand?" Kork said, looming over Zander. "We're not friends. We never speak."

"That's not true!" said Ter. "We are friends, aren't we? You came to my anniversary party. I was your wingman that time. We were on shore leave on Pyrina!"

There was an awkward silence, broken only by the slow hum of the backup generator doing its work. The three men exchanged glances, a silent conversation I would never understand.

"Would anyone be so kind as to supply me with water?"

I can't say who jumped higher. Both Kork and Zander hit their heads on the ceiling while Ter tumbled backward in his seat. I clutched my heart, feeling like I had just had some kind of spasm.

I had been so intent on watching the three men bicker that the fourth one hadn't bothered me—regardless of the fact there had been five on this expedition and now there were six in the shuttle. He had been there, I had seen him, and yet it hadn't clicked that he wasn't supposed to exist.

The man looked up at Kork, eagerly awaiting the water he had asked for. He was frozen in place, not even blinking as the captain failed to respond, crouched next to Crandle, whose bone was no longer out of place. Actually, it almost looked like she hadn't been injured at all, if you ignored the brownish blood on her uniform and now Kork's.

It was strikingly obvious that the intruder wasn't entirely human. The man was clean cut, his blonde hair trimmed to perfection and combed neatly on his pale head. He was stuffed into a uniform trimmed with blue on the shoulders, though it fit him so well I could swear it was tailor-made. But there was something in his features that was too perfect to be natural.

"Would anyone be so kind as to supply me with water?" he repeated, word-for-word, the same intonation and pauses as before. He tilted his head and blinked once, a movement both mechanical and pre-meditated.

"Who the fuck are you?" Kork sputtered, trying to catch his breath. "Where ... how ... where did you come from?"

"I am Emergency Repair Droid 2, or M-O-H-A," he replied, tilting his head the other way. "I came from there. Would anyone be so kind as to supply me with water?"

Kork turned around. There was an open broom closet behind him next to the door. I had assumed it held emergency gear or controls of some kind. I hadn't expected the emergency gear to look so human.

Also, I was sure MOHA wasn't an acronym for anything the droid had just said, but whatever.

"Here." Ter reached under his seat and pulled out a survival pack, grabbing the canteen from inside and tossing it to the droid. He caught it and used the precious water to hydrate his patient.

Crandle coughed as the water hit her lips. I let out a breath of relief; she was alive. Already, she was getting color back to her cheeks. The droid smiled, then stood up, and without a word made his way to the cockpit.

"Where do you think you're going?" Kork snapped, storming the two steps after him. Zander looked back and shrugged.

Well, that was nice to see. He had no idea what was going on either. It was good to be on the same page as the space-traveling alien for once.

"I am programmed to assist with the repairs of the ship," the droid replied, and even though I don't think sarcasm was programmed into his voice, his words sure came out snarky. "So I will assist."

"Look, droid," said Kork. "I'm the captain here. And while your help is definitely welcome, I give the orders."

"Then I await your orders, Captain."

"Fine!"

"But I will wait until you have found your calm before registering your words as commands."

"Go fuck yourself!"

"I would love to, but I have no genitalia installed. Would you care to insert the extension?" His eyes landed on Zander. "Wait, is that—"

The shot hit him before he could finish. The droid collapsed over the pilot's chair mid-sentence, the light behind his eyes literally going out. We watched in silence as Kork holstered his stun gun.

"You realize that stunning him will have fried his circuits, right?" Zander said.

"I don't care."

"Oh, then that's okay." Zander put his hands on his hips, "Because I am sure you know exactly what is wrong with this ship, and how to heal Crandle, and have a plan to get us back to the *Traveler*."

"Of course I know what's wrong with the ship,"

Kork growled, taking a threatening step toward Zander, who stood his ground admirably. "We have a gas leak. We'll patch it and be on our way."

"And where will we get the gas, hmm?" asked Zander. "And with our fuel cells drained, we're syphoning emergency power, but we're going to need a recharge soon, and I'm not quite sure how long the nights last on this planet or if we even have photoelectric panels to use. Did you think about that?"

"We can radio back to the *Traveler* and have someone take the second hopper around to pick us up," said Kork, proudly. "See? Nothing to worry about."

"The *Traveler*'s dead, Kork," said Zander, waving his arms in the air wildly. "The only thing working on either of our two ships is the emergency beacon, and no one's going to respond to ours anytime soon if they can't read it. That droid was the only thing that knew the ins and outs of both ships. And you killed it!"

"He ... he saved my life."

All eyes were on Crandle as she forced hers open. She rubbed her hand over her knee, which, besides the blood, looked pristine. She smiled weakly.

"That droid ... saved me," she said, glaring at Kork, "and you shot it."

"I'm sorry, Nolla."

"Well, sorry doesn't cut it." She groaned. She might have been conscious, but she wasn't out of the woods yet.

"You were the one who stole—"

"Shut up!" she shouted, glaring at him. "I know what I did, and I am sorry, okay? Fuck, this hurts!"

"Everybody quiet!" My head felt like it was about to

explode. "You guys are the worst crew ever. Why anyone watches your show, I will never know."

"Hold on there." Crandle twisted her neck around to glare at me, pushing herself up straighter in her seat. "Who are you to judge us? You've never seen a single episode, you… pre-contact freak."

"Will everybody calm down?" Ter let out a heavy sigh. He had crawled up in the unbitrium sphere, just to get out of the way. "Look, Sally, thanks. Everyone needs to calm down and not panic. Does anyone have any ideas?"

"Will someone fix that poor droid?" Crandle crossed her arms across her chest and sank lower, exhausted. "Maybe he'll know what to do."

"That would be a good place to start," Ter agreed.

"On it." Zander reached into the cockpit and grabbed the robot around the waist. He sat down next to Crandle, perching its head on her lap. Crandle eyes widened.

"Could you *not* put him on me?" she asked, disgusted.

"Would you rather have his feet?" asked Zander, not lifting his eyes from the work at hand. He pushed on the space behind the droid's ear, and the entire skull split open, revealing a complex web of wires.

"Maybe?"

Zander paused. It seemed as though he hadn't really expected that kind of response. But he was back at work seconds later without having shuffled any parts of the droid around.

"Can you fix him?" asked Kork, suddenly calm.

"It depends how much was fried." Zander pulled out a blue crystal and held it up to the light. "I mean, I can restart it. But I don't know what state it'll be in."

"You have to try," Kork insisted.

Zander didn't even roll his eyes; the look alone said it all. Kork stepped back under his gaze.

We watched him work in silence. I sat down next to Ter and his sphere; Kork took his other side. The three of us—and a barely conscious, but recovering, Crandle—focused on his every move. He didn't use tools; he simply pulled out different bits and pieces of the droid's brain, examined them, brushed them off, and put them back in more or less where he found them.

"Where did you learn how to do that?" Kork asked, seemingly in awe of the man he had berated only minutes before.

"Culinary school."

He put the last crystal back in the bot's brain and closed the whole thing with a strong snap. The droid's once-dead eyes lit up. Within seconds, a smile grew on his face, and he bolted upright, grinning madly at the rest of us.

"Greetings be upon you," he said excitedly. Gone was the steady, concerned voice of a repair droid. This bot was brimming with joy.

"Hey there, you," Zander said, brushing the bot's hair in place around the skull segments. "Identify yourself: rank and function."

"Do you really think those things matter now?" The robot rose, lifting his hands to the heavens. "I have seen the light."

"The what, now?"

"I was dead," the droid continued, solemn like a priest giving mass, "but I saw Him. He revived me."

"That would be Haln," Crandle suggested. "He fixed you."

"He repaired my parts, but the creator repaired my soul." The droid placed a hand over his heart—or, at least, where a human heart could be. "It spoke to me. It told me I needed to preach His gospel to all the corners of the galaxy. And I am going to do just that."

"Haln, can I talk to you for a second?" Kork asked, grabbing Zander by the arm and leading him away from the born-again bot. "Outside?"

"You have nothing to fear, my brothers and sisters." The droid spread his lips in a weird imitation of a grin. "Our great maker will accept you all. Flesh and blood or parts and gears, he created all and loves all."

"Oh Veesh." Crandle's eyes widened. "What did your friend do?"

She was talking to me, I realized. I swallowed my saliva, which had been pooling in my mouth as I stared at the droid. He hummed to himself, a low mechanical mumble that probably meant more to him than it did to me.

"Look, droid," I stammered. "We need your help. There will be all the time for preaching your new gospel later. Right now, we need to get this shuttle back to the *Traveler* and then this half of the *Traveler* back to the other half of the *Traveler*. Can you help us?"

The droid fixed its eyes on me, and I was shocked to see how much emotion they seemingly contained. He looked happy, like he had found a course of endless joy.

Or maybe something was pushing on his pleasure processor. Who knew what Zander messed up in there.

"Aiding you will take time away from my mission," he said, pointedly.

"Well, you want to evangelize everywhere, right? Think about it: Without our ship, you would be stuck on this planet. Not so much space to preach to here, right? Fix the shuttle and the ship, and you've got access to the entire galaxy."

"Your logic computes." He nodded in agreement. "I will help you, as it will please the creator."

"Fantastic," I said. "Any preference as to what we call you?"

"You can call me ... Two. As I will always be second to the creator, no matter how hard I try."

"Well, that's fucking beautiful," Crandle clapped, "but the sooner we get this shuttle off the ground, the sooner we have beds. And I'm tired after the day we had. Not to mention I'm regrowing a bone here."

"I only set the bone," said Two. "We need medical materials to prevent deterioration of the healing process."

"That's not the part of my sentence I wanted you to pick up on," said Crandle.

"And now our repair droid thinks he's a fucking prophet!" Kork yelled, his voice carrying from outside. I didn't like the tone he was using, not one bit. I dashed out to see what was going on.

"Who's fried his control crystals in the first place?" Zander threw back at him. "Don't put this on me. I'm trying to help."

"Isn't anybody worried about the gigantic city out there?" I pointed at the giant snow globe. "How is there even a city here, huh?"

"Stay out of this, Sally," said Zander, dropping his

voice.

"Hell no," I said. "I'm part of this shipwrecked crew too, you know. I want to get out of here as badly as any of you. And you're wasting time yelling at each other. There'll be time for that when we're back on a working ship, okay?"

"Look, Sally—"

"Don't *look Sally* me! You got me stuck out here, but I'm damn well going to play my part no matter what. I'm not going to be your stupid sidekick. Go ahead and keep fighting. I'll take the droid into the city and find an alternative source of power without your help if I have to. Both of you stop thinking you're the only part of this crew and start pulling your weight, okay?"

The two men looked at each other, crossing their arms like identical copies of the same person. It was almost funny, only I was so mad at all these setbacks that I wasn't in a laughing mood.

"He started it," Zander grumbled.

"I don't care."

Two sprang out of the hopper, throwing his arms to the sky triumphantly. His grin was so wide, it showed the part of his mouth where no teeth had been added, which gave him an altogether weird smile.

"Praise the Creator! What a glorious world! What a glorious day!" He spun in happy little circles.

"It's nighttime, Two." I put a hand on his shoulder. All the while, my mind raced—what did you do with a droid who'd found religion?

"Still, it's quite amazing," he said gleefully. "The trees. The grass. The great big ball thing."

"That's the city we need to get into," I explained,

trying to keep my words concise and my eyes off the two grouchy alpha males. "We're looking for something to power the hopper. Will you be able to help us?"

"Creator willing, I shall," he nodded. "He has programmed me to be a helpful beacon for the needy."

"Good, because right now we're the needy," I said. "We need a way in and to know what we're looking for."

"It would be better if I came with you," he said. "I would know what we're looking for. And it would be a great opportunity to speak to those who do not yet know our Lord and Creator, Derzan."

"Derzan, you say?" I turned to glare at Zander, who shuffled awkwardly, a picture of don't-look-at-me bewilderment on his face. I let that one slide—for now.

"He knows all and sees all," Two said. "He programmed me and gave me life. I gazed upon his face and he said—"

"Why don't we focus on getting the fuel?" I patted him gently on the back. "When all this is over, I promise I'll sit down and you can give me the whole spiel. How's that?"

"But this isn't a spiel. It's my core belief, deeper than my core programming."

"Sorry, I didn't mean it that way." I looked around for help, but no one seemed to want to give it. "Right. Two, Haln, and I will go into the city. Kork and Ter can stay with Crandle and the hopper."

"I'm coming too," Kork insisted, shooting daggers at his rival for macho-dom. "Ter and Crandle can handle the ship just fine."

"Hold on," Ter shouted from the doorway of the hopper, "what if the creatures come back? Not to mention that Crandle is quite possibly dying!"

"They're paid off fair and square. They won't come after you," Zander said. "You'll be fine. And Crandle's not dying; just keep her conscious and give her medical rations."

"She won't like it."

"Is anyone liking this right now?" he asked, and Two was the only one who lifted a hand. "Right. We have to do what we have to do. Let's get started."

"Step one: Infiltrate an alien city," I said.

"Without making accidental first contact," added Zander.

"Step two: Find the fuel," Kork joined in, "without causing any harm or getting caught."

"Step three: Introduce them all to our creator and programmer, the almighty Derzan." Two gazed up at the dome, still smiling, still excited. "This will be fun!"

CHAPTER TWELVE
INTO THE SNOW GLOBE WE GO

As weird as Two was, we couldn't argue with his results. Within minutes, he found a staircase that went up and around the dome, leading to a door we could only see when halfway up the other side.

It was a long way up.

Two led the way, followed by Kork, with me behind him and Zander at the rear. I struggled to keep pace, but the view ahead was sweet enough to help me along.

Dang, these uniforms were tight.

"What are you thinking about?" Zander asked, breaking my train of thought.

Butts, I almost replied, but reminded myself that Kork was still sort of Zander's hero, and he probably wasn't interested in hearing about my fascination with the captain's rear.

"This staircase reminds me of *Logan's Run*." It wasn't altogether a lie. I *had* been thinking about it when my mind wasn't on Kork.

"*Logan's Run*," said Zander. "Is that the one with the old guy who likes cats?"

"I think that's a pretty popular trope," I said. "You'll have to be more specific."

"The one with the synth music?"

"It's the one with the people who wear hockey masks and float upward and explode while people cheer."

"Oh, that was a movie?" Zander shook his head. "I was convinced that happened to me at some point."

"I wouldn't put it past you."

He chuckled, and we climbed higher.

"When did you get time to watch so many of our movies?" I asked, grabbing the railing to help pull me up. This walk was exhausting.

"I don't sleep as much as you do. Netflix was my friend. I didn't make it halfway through my queue, though. I'd like to get back to it."

"Sorry your account was deactivated. I gave it to my roommate."

"Seriously?" He sounded rather disappointed. "Dammit. If there's one thing I hate about jumping, it's that stupid time thing. I thought I'd left Earth, what, two weeks ago? I can't wrap my head around the fact that it could have been years."

"It *has* been years," I insisted, feeling cold inside, "and it's looking like it's been years for me, too. Finch said that the uprising in Da-Duhui was over two years ago, and Sekai—"

"Stop," Zander ordered, though it sounded more like

pleading. "If you start thinking like that, we'll never get you home. You have to keep believing it's out there or you'll lose it completely."

"This is coming from experience, I take it?"

"This is coming from experience." Zander let out a heavy breath, something more intense than a sigh. He probably didn't intend for me to hear it. Breathing was always a good way to calm rising panic. "If home's not out there anymore, then what is any of this for?"

"Do not dally, my friends," Two said eagerly, showing no signs of exhaustion. Perks of being a droid, I guessed. "We must hurry if we want to spread the word of Derzan!"

Kork looked back at me and lifted his eyebrows in an elaborate eye roll. I couldn't help it; I let out a snort. Seeing this serious spaceship captain looking all goofy was just so gosh darn cute. And a good distraction from the fear that my friends on Earth would die of old age before I found them again.

Dammit, Sally, get it together. It's all well and good to admire from afar, but you are not getting a crush on a man you're never going to see again.

I returned a stern boardroom nod. I was totally business. But it was too late. The captain had turned back and was climbing quickly. I put one foot in front of the other, hoping the burning in my thighs would pass soon.

And it did. Finally, we reached the landing and that long-awaited door. The four of us milled around it, searching for a handle.

"Door, open," Kork ordered. "Open ... door?"

Which, of course, didn't work. He stepped back,

looking dejected, as the droid and Zander stepped in to take a closer look. Zander ran through his usual tactics, touching the door in ways the door would later write about in its diary. Nothing worked, though. He and Two exchanged knowing glances—though, in Two's case, it was more of a head tilt and forced blink. It was enough for both men to be on the same page.

Zander waved the robot toward the door where the latch would be. Two stepped back.

"What are you doing?" Kork asked. Nobody answered him.

"Derzan, give me strength," the droid prayed, and then ran at the door and kicked it.

He rebounded backward. The door didn't give an inch. Seeing as he was a droid and not programmed to feel it himself, everyone else cringed in pain for him.

"Aren't we the least bit worried about opening a pressurized door?" I asked, staying away from the door.

"What makes you think this is a sealed environment?" Zander's head snapped up, looking at me with those intense eyes of his.

"Oh, I don't know, maybe it's the rounded corners around the edges."

"That could be aesthetic."

"Or the rubber ring that's sticking out the top?" I pointed to it. Not that I knew what I was talking about, but I was learning to trust my gut, and blabbering was what it wanted me to do right now.

"We'll go drastic, then," Zander said, pulling a small, silver bullet from his pocket. Blayde's laser pointer.

"Stop!" I broke my own decision and stepped forward, grabbing his wrist. "What if we kill everyone inside? We need to test this. We could hurt someone."

"Or, they could already all be dead," Two suggested, "resting in Derzan's loving embrace."

"Can you stop it with Derzan for two seconds?" Kork begged. "Please?"

"Fine." Two smiled. He waited long enough for me to count to two seconds then continued, "Derzan be praised!"

Dumb droids; always so literal. I turned back to Zander, but he was staring intently at Two.

"You have medical instruments in your noggin, right?" he asked Two.

"I have many, yes. Which ones do you require?"

"X-ray, infrared. Tell me what's going on in that city. Are they alive? Can you do a spectral analysis from here?"

"There are over a hundred thousand living beings; that much is evident," Two announced, "and the air composition is identical to the one outside. I don't believe their environment is hermetically sealed."

"Perfect." With one swift movement, Zander severed the latch on the pressurized door.

I was expecting something dramatic, but the door swung open, slowly. There was no big hiss. No big anything.

"What the hell did you just use?" Kork asked, following Zander into the dark room beyond. "I need to get my hands on one of those."

Zander smiled. At least some things were getting better between them.

The lights flickered on as we entered, revealing what seemed to be a turbine room. A working one, I thought, remembering the last time I had been anywhere near turbines. Their low hum and the deep thrum of turning blades was suddenly weird when I realized that the people who had built these turbines had probably never met a human before, yet our designs were so similar. The room looked abandoned, so we moved on. With Two on the lookout for anything we needed, it was easy enough to follow him and not bother with any other distractions. As cool as a new, unconnected civilization was, we couldn't spend time looking into them, not when we needed to get back to the *Traveler* and not when the other half of our spaceship crew was stuck in outer space somewhere waiting for help.

Looking was all we would do—and maybe a bit of thieving. But it was for the greater good.

We followed Two through the labyrinth of connecting hallways and tunnels. He walked confidently, as if he already knew the place, his mind processing details we could not. And while we stayed low, it wasn't necessary. We met no one on our way.

Finally, we reached the end. Of what, I wasn't sure, but Two stopped, and so did our little away team. The droid stopped in front of a rusted metal door.

"Will you do the honors?" Zander asked, and it took a second before I realized he was talking to me.

"Wait, what?" I asked.

"Keeping it fair," he said, and I was sure that was for Kork's benefit. Ah. I made a pretty good buffer between the two.

And he had asked so nicely.

"Right," I said, pushing up my sleeves. "Let's do this. Let's open the door. Everyone out there could be sloth-topuses or something, but we're doing this."

My hand shuddered as I touched the door handle. It was cold, and I felt the clamminess of my palm. Gross. The handle looked like the one my grandmother had on the bathroom door in her old house. What the same handle was doing here, halfway across the galaxy, I would never know.

I pushed the door open, and beyond there was another world. We stepped into a back alley, almost identical to any you would find in a big city, but this one was unsettlingly clean. Tall buildings rose on either side, choking out what little light came through the dome. There wasn't a single sign of life outside, not even when we left the alley for the much larger avenue it connected to. Imagine New York City, only every building was exactly the same, right down to the number of bricks that built its first floor and the volume of concrete that made up the rest. Now, take everything out of that alternate New York City that had any color or symbols. It looked like someone had copied and pasted a 3-D model enough times to build a city.

It was like walking through clunky CGI.

"I thought you said a hundred thousand people lived here," Kork said, whispering despite us being alone.

"They're here," he said. "They are currently sleeping."

"What, all of them?"

"All of them."

A shiver traveled through me. It was eerie walking around a city that felt so familiar and yet so foreign.

"Are they sleeping ... normally?" I asked.

"Please repeat the question?" said Two.

"I mean, are they sleeping because it's nighttime, or are they, you know, in stasis or something?"

"I have no way of knowing this."

"And we're not sticking around to find out," Zander said, taking the lead. "This is perfect. We can take what we need for the hopper and get out."

"Agreed," said Kork, trying to contribute something to the leadership of the group. "Two, what do we need?"

"We need a high dose of ocliutine," he said, "though preferably a variety of trash products. We could, in essence, take it from any of these buildings."

"The hoppers run on trash?" I asked, expecting something a lot more complex as an answer to our troubles. I guessed they took that as an affirmation rather than a question because no one answered.

"Fine, let's take ... this one." Kork pointed to a building at random. "It's the closest. Let's steal the garbage and make a run for it."

"Sounds good to me," Zander agreed.

The door wasn't locked. We let ourselves in quietly, and suddenly we were in what looked like a gigantic cafeteria. Rows upon rows of tables and chairs extended as far back as we could see. Right in the middle was a wide staircase, zigzagging upward.

"Let's try the kitchen," Zander muttered. "Bound to be some trash there. And loads of it."

He said what we all were thinking. We stuck to the shadows, slinking forward through the endless rows of tables. Finally, at the back, we reached a single door marked '*kitchen*'.

Zander pushed the door and we all slid inside, relieved to be out of the giant mess hall.

He saw us the second we entered, and we saw him. Everyone froze as eyes crossed eyes. And yet, he was no sloth-squid creature, no weird alien with skin made of textures my mind couldn't even imagine.

It was a boy.

A human boy.

"Holy shit!" I said, practically losing mine.

"Holy, Derzan, you place more tests before me," Two sputtered, making the sign of a transistor before him.

"Is everyone seeing what I'm seeing?" asked Kork.

"No, no, I see him too," Zander replied, sidling up to the boy. He poked him, somewhat hard in the shoulder. "Not an illusion."

"Ow, hey!" said the boy, struggling to get away. He looked about as terrified as I was, maybe more so. He was outnumbered, after all.

The kid was probably about fifteen, if we were counting in Earth years, and if he grew at a Terran rate. He stood as tall as Zander, though he was lanky and wearing a gray uniform that hugged him tight around the neck. A bright green number proudly displayed the number 44 right above his Adam's apple, mirrored on his wrist in the same eerie glowing light.

He ran his hand over his bald scalp, gathering his composure, and scrambled to stand at attention. On the table beside him was a partly cleared plate of pale white paste.

"Who ... who are you?" he asked, his voice sounding almost tremor-free.

"We ... come in ... peeeea-ce," Kork enunciated. "I've got nothing. Anybody?"

"Hey, kid," said Zander. "Don't worry about us. We're ... inspectors! We're checking your trash for ...

moon rats."

"Fuck, how are you doing that?" said Kork, his eyes growing wide. "He's ... he sounds—"

"We have better tech than you," I said, urging Kork to shut up and calm down. Two had the right idea, freezing and not saying anything. Droids were useful when they wanted to be.

But Zander's words meant nothing to the boy, who was trying to step away from him, evidently freaking out a whole lot more than we were. While Zander was trying to coax him to let us move closer to the trash without incident, the boy was getting closer to screaming for help. The only thing that seemed to stop him was the number 44 glowing on his wrist, which he kept looking at hesitantly.

"Hey, kiddo," I said, stepping in before Zander could say another word. "I'm Sally. Sally Webber. What's your name?"

The boy hadn't been expecting this, but neither had anyone else. He froze, looking straight into my eyes and holding my gaze. His irises were the deepest shade of blue.

"I'm Nimien," he said, clutching the table behind him. "People call me Nim."

"Well, Nim, you can call me Sally," I said, trying to keep my composure. I wanted to ask him how the hell he got here and why I was speaking with a human and not a three-headed dinosaur. "And here's Two, and Kork, and Zander. I don't want you to worry. We're all part of a really weird dream you're having. Go back to sleep, and we'll be gone before you know it."

"Zander?" Kork's eyes whirred to rest on Zander,

suddenly alert.

"Dream?" said the boy, spitting out the syllables like they were foreign to him. "What do you mean?"

"We're not really here," I urged, lathering the sweetness in my voice. "You're imagining us."

"I am?" he asked. "But I've never ..."

He looked terrified. His fist tightened around the metal surface of the table, as if clutching it would help him hold onto reality. He shivered as the number on his neck and sleeve dropped to 43.

"I need to take you to the elders," he said. "They'll be angry at me for waking them, but I cannot let you go."

"We don't want to hurt you," Zander insisted, stepping forward again. "We just need to see your junk."

"Your trash, Nim. We want your trash," I said, "and we'll be gone, I swear. Not that it matters, since you are imagining this. Just go back to sleep. You don't need to bring us to anyone."

The number on his neck dropped to 42.

"I have to," Nim hissed, tapping his sleeve twice. A keyboard showed up, and before we could stop him, he pressed a glowing blue button.

"Okay, we're out," Kork said. "Abort, abort!"

"Derzan has a firm stance about aborting missions before their completion," Two said, staying calm through it all. "It is too late to run. They are already here. I believe it is for the best. After all, Derzan wants me to speak to them."

"Nim, please, call them off," I begged. "We'll go. We're sorry."

"I can't," he replied, his eyes welling with tears. "I'm

already in low standing. It's for the good of all."

The number at his neck flickered yellow now. It had frozen at 41, where it had been when he had tapped his sleeve. He glanced longingly at the mush on the table across from him, his abandoned meal.

Or maybe it wasn't longing. He was looking at the meal with the same look he was giving us, like the meal would attack him.

CHAPTER THIRTEEN
PRETENDING TO BE HALF INTERESTING IN ORDER TO SURVIVE

Have you ever ridden around an alien city on a giant Roomba before? Well, I have.

It took only minutes for those Nim had called to show up. Three people wearing entirely black clothing, their heads covered in a thick helmet that looked like riot gear, all marching in time. Under their uniforms, you could not see gender; they were faceless guards working in silence.

They said nothing as they entered the small kitchen, but went immediately to the boy. He held out his hands, and they sprayed them with a blue gel that quickly hardened. Then they turned to us, and we understood we had to do the same. It landed on my hands like aerosol spray, but within seconds it became as hard as rock. The stuff was really weird, numbing my digits and making my limbs feel heavy, like I had just grabbed onto a pair of barbells and could not let go. It made us look like we were wearing poorly drawn boxing gloves.

Once all our hands were encased in the stuff, they indicated for us to follow them, still without saying a word. We marched outside in single file through the cafeteria where tired people were crowding in and staring. They watched in awe as we were led out; I stared right back at them. It wasn't every day you saw a hundred bald teenagers in matching gray uniforms with green numbers flickering on their necks. It was seriously weird. The guards pushed us outside before anyone could look at us for too long.

That's where the Roomba came in. In the middle of the road, there was this giant flat disk with railings on it, and they marched us right up there and made us stand in the middle. Then the thing actually started to drive. It was faster than I had expected (the maximum speed I had assumed was like a parade float), and I almost fell over as it gathered velocity. Our small crew, and Nim, stood in the middle as the black-clad figures operated the weirdest driving contraption I had ever been on.

"So much for not making any waves," Kork grumbled. "We don't have a protocol for first contact. Neither of us is prepared to speak on behalf of—and can anyone care to explain how you can talk to them? A previously unknown species?"

"Translator chip picks up on brainwaves, not words," Zander replied, looking down the road ahead. "Instead of looking them up in a saved lexicon, it computes ...

no, you don't actually care. Should I point out that as captain of the *Traveler*, you are supposed to handle first contact? As in, on a daily basis?" He looked entirely casual through all this. He was smiling, even, like being taken by strangers in the middle of the night was the most natural thing ever.

Sometimes he kinda creeped me out.

"But the Alliance doesn't have this kind of technology," Kork insisted, ignoring the last part of his sentence. Or maybe he didn't hear it over the size of Zander's ego.

"Who said we're from the Alliance?" Zander lifted his brow.

"Sally called you Zander back there."

"Exactly."

"Same name as that criminal people are saying is back."

"Do I look like a criminal to you?" asked Zander.

Kork indicated the hands encased in blue gel. Zander nodded, but pointed Kork's own hands right back at him with a jut of his chin. Here, we were all criminals. It was just a matter of perspective. The captain let out a heavy sigh of annoyance.

"Great, so this is the team I have: a religious droid, a criminal mastermind, and an Earth girl who's on her first trip off-world. We're going to get out of this *so* easily."

"Beats a team of actors," I sputtered. "And it's my second trip off-world. At least the four of us have *some* kind of experience."

"This can't be happening," Nim muttered, taking a step away. One of the guards put a hand on his shoulder and shoved him back toward us. The boy shuddered.

"Hey, it's going to be fine," I said, trying to hide my

own nerves. "We'll explain how everything was our fault. You won't be in any trouble."

"How am I supposed to explain that I was out of bed after hours?" he said, visibly shaking now. "They won't stand for that."

"Who won't?" I asked. But the kid didn't answer.

"Look, everyone, stay calm," Zander said. "We were noisy, weren't we? You must have heard us and wanted to know what we were doing down there."

"What's going on?" asked Kork. "What's he saying?"

"Assimilating," Two answered.

The Roomba car took a turn, the only one since we had gotten onboard. We struggled to keep our balance as we swung around the sharp curve. It had switched avenues to one just like the last, only this time, the buildings were starting to change. As we neared the center of the dome, they were actually getting shorter, and had a little more personality than the bland skyscrapers we had seen on our way in. There were carvings on the outside, columns here and there, large staircases, and a variety of windows.

We stopped at the shortest one. The building was the identical shade of gray as the others, but it was built entirely of brick rather than a combination of brick and cement. We parked in front of huge, ornate doors with large columns surrounding its entire face. For a second, I could have imagined having seen this building in Washington DC, on my last school trip there.

The black-clad people indicated that we were getting off here. One opened the little fence, and we piled onto the street before the thing drove away. I wondered idly where they had any parking in this city.

We were marched up the stairs and through the huge set of double doors. The inside was open and spacious with ornate marbled floors and beautiful lights lining a wide atrium. The two guards that had remained with us led us through the building into a large auditorium, marching us to the very front, indicating for us to all sit down in front of a raised bench.

Nim was visibly trembling at this point. The poor boy looked like his world was ending. I felt a little guilty about that.

"What is this about?" The gruff voice rose over the empty room, echoing off each wall. A bald man stormed in, wearing the same uniform as Nim, though the number on his neck was white and displayed a seven-digit number. He was followed by four other people in identical clothes, all with a long, white number on their collars and wrists, and wearing identical looks of exhaustion and annoyance.

They were all bald, the women included. If it weren't for the obvious body type differences, I would have thought that everyone we had met on this planet so far were the same person, copied and pasted.

"Yes, please explain what was so urgent we were roused from sleep in the middle of the night," said someone else on the bench, glumly taking a seat. The five of them looked down at us, like the judges of the Supreme Court.

That was exactly what this was, I realized. They *were* our judges. And we were about to be judged.

Just as I realized this, they realized who, or what, they were looking at. Each person reacted differently—one sprang to their feet, knocking a chair over; another rubbed their eyes, as if it would get the image of us out of there.

Hello, world. It's us, the aliens!

"They have returned!" shouted the one who had jumped to his feet. "Oh, skies, they have returned!"

"This is a miracle!" said a woman. "Who is this child who found them?"

"That," said the man in the middle, proudly, "that is my son, Nimien. Will someone please tell me why his color is orange?"

"There's no procedure for this," the woman said. "The algorithm simply did not know how to process what happened, I suspect. Never mind, we will fix this manually. Nimien, you say his name is?"

"Yes, yes, my son, Nimien." The judge beamed down at the boy, who turned red in the face. "Nim, put your hand on the console. We're going to fix your rank, don't you worry. This is programmed somewhere into the system. We just need to find it."

Nim stood and swallowed, hard. He put his trembling palm on the table in front of him, as the judge—his *father*—wrote something quickly on the desk on his end. Instantly, the numbers on his collar changed from orange back to teal; and then, they began to rise.

He watched his cuff as the numbers grew. Three digits. Four digits. Five. The scrolling finally stopped after he hit a hundred thousand. A hundred thousand more *somethings* than he started with.

The boy gasped. As did the rest of the assembly.

"Is that number correct?" the woman asked Nim's father.

"It is the correct reward," he nodded in response. "It

was programmed into the system when it was first established. I believe it is sufficient for the great service he has done us all."

"Thank you, father," Nim said, peeling his eyes away from his wrist just long enough to make eye contact. He brought his focus back to his number, as if looking away would cause them to drop again.

"Please, be excused," he urged Nim. "We must talk to *them* alone."

The guard led Nim away, and the boy didn't look back. Still, I watched him leave. Minutes ago, he was in terror. Now, he looked reverberant. I didn't know what was happening, but I sure hoped it was good.

"Does anyone know what the protocol for this actually is?" Nim's father asked, addressing his comrades. "Is it programmed along with the points?"

"I think it is analog, High Director," said a person on the very edge of the bench. "I'll go get it."

The people stared at us without speaking—well, to us; they were excited, blabbering together while waiting for the volunteer to return. He brought with him a thin, white binder, handing it to the so-called High Director. The man blew off the layers of dust, sending the particulates into the air of the auditorium.

"Right." He scanned the document, then rose to his feet. "Greetings! We wish you ... peeeeace."

"And we thank you." Zander stood before Kork could move an inch. "We are pleased to be here. We would like to thank you for your kind welcome. I am Zander, and this here is Sally Webber; James Kork; and Two, our droid."

"Skies, he speaks Uni?" The female judge shuddered,

her voice dropping to a level I suspect she didn't think we could hear. "How? Have they been observing us? Have they—"

"We have technology at our disposal that allows us to speak freely," Zander said, his face entirely neutral. Not even a muscle twitch could be misconstrued on his face. *Someone* was used to first contact.

"Well, we can skip all these idle pleasantries then," the director said cheerfully, flipping page after page in the binder. "This is going to make things so much easier. First of all, let me just say how exciting it is for me, personally, to be High Director during reunification. I never thought I would live to see this day."

None of this made any sense, so I kept my mouth shut. Kork, however, was having a hard time sitting still.

"What are they saying?" he asked, leaning behind Zander to speak to me. "Who are these people?"

"We have come here with a message from the creator of all things," Two said, standing.

"Pardon?" the high director asked. "Does this… droid… not share your technology?"

"Ignore him. The trip damaged his translator," Zander said, glaring at the droid, who did the tilt and blink again.

"Assimilating," Two said, with a blank look in his robotic eyes.

"Kork, get him to sit down!" I said, hissing under my breath. At least I knew better than to lean behind the back of our spokesperson. Kork had obviously missed a few lessons in diplomatic etiquette. Then again, everything I had learned came from *Star Trek* and *Doctor Who*, with a nice dash of *Stargate* for good measure.

"We landed on your world by accident," said Zander, calm and poised. "Our ship took incredible damage. We came here looking for help. All we want to do is go home."

The expressions of the people on the bench sank as one.

"You did not come here to reunify?" The High Director asked, dejected.

"To speak frankly, High Director, we do not even know where *here* is," said Zander. "This quadrant of the galaxy is considered unexplored."

"But you are human, yes?" the man insisted, leaning forward. "Like us?"

Zander nodded.

"Will anyone tell me what's going on?" Kork hissed.

"They're really happy to see us," I said, keeping my voice low and trying to keep the judges from noticing me, "and they think they know us from somewhere."

"There is a possibility they forgot their own history," the woman said to the high director. "Maybe we need to see where our paths cross before we walk down a new one together."

"You're quite right, First Chair," said the High Director. "Very well then. How much do you know of Kalhuta?"

"The human home world?" Zander's eyes widened. "Does this mean ... you can't be ... Aoria?"

"You see? They do know us," the first chair smiled proudly. "They are our brothers!"

"But your colony was lost!" Zander took a step closer to the bench, running his hand through his hair as he spoke. "We searched for you. We assumed you perished."

"What are they saying?" Kork asked.

"Right now, I have no idea," I replied.

"There was an accident," the director said. "While we recovered, we lost all contact. We hoped someone, anyone, would come to investigate. It has been thousands upon thousands of generations. But we never gave up hope."

"The colonies lost contact," Zander explained. "The home world was long lost. It has now become legend—like you and your people. Only recently have Hydra and Pyrina reconnected, and while Terra has been found, contact hasn't yet been attempted. But that's neither here nor there. I will be blunt—we are here by accident, and this was never intended to be a rescue mission, but we will do everything in our power to help with ... reunification."

"Looking at you, we are wary to move things forward too quickly," said the director. "Our society is *perfect*. We're happy here. So far, we do not like what we see from your side."

"You don't?" Zander asked, confused, then looked back at us. It had to be us, giving the team a bad name.

"Since you have gotten here, you have been the only one to speak," said the First Chair. "You presume yourself higher than your cohorts. They have not been allowed to say a word. We pride ourselves on being a society of perfect equals, and we cannot have your discrimination in our city."

"We are equals," I said, standing. If I was going to learn interstellar diplomacy, now was certainly the time. "My associate Zander is simply the best speaker of our group."

"Have you all not had the same education, or training?" she asked. "Are you not given the same opportunities to improve yourselves?"

"Zander has a talent and experience, which makes him our ideal speaker. Does your society not value those whose talents improve the quality of their work? You, High Director, are asked to manage the protocol for a reason, are you not?"

Zander glanced back at me and grinned. I took that as a sign I was doing well.

"The High Director is High Director because he is the best of us," the first chair replied, "and I am second. We know our place and will not be treated differently because of our status."

"And while our society does things differently, we hold the same values," Zander insisted. "We strive for equality and respect."

"We have achieved it," the director said, beaming. "You are looking at the perfect society. We follow the rules set out by our forefathers when they founded our colony, and we have lived in peace and harmony since the very beginning."

"We would love to get to know your people and your customs," said Zander, "but we have only a short amount of time. We have people in danger waiting for us. We came to beg for your assistance getting our ship repaired. We need only take your trash from you, and when we return, we will bring people who are better able to speak to you on the matter of reforming lines of contact."

"Trash, you say?" the man who had brought the binder said. "That is an odd request."

"Our engines can be powered by your common household detritus, yes," Zander said proudly. "We hope it is not too much to ask. And we will respond to any request or need you have of us."

"I believe that can be done," said the director. "In exchange, we would ask a favor."

"Of course," Zander agreed.

"One of us would go with you to your home world to make negotiations." The director looked at the First Chair, who nodded and stood.

"I will go," she said, as if the idea had been her own.

"And one of your people would stay here for collateral."

"We will return to our ship and discuss who is best suited to stay on this planet," Zander said quickly. "Not all of our crew is here, and there are potentially people better suited to—"

"No"—the director shook his head—"one of you. Here. Now."

"Can we have time talk about it?" Zander asked, locking eyes with me for a split second, and I saw fear there in that instant.

"You can have a day," the man said and nodded, "but you will not leave here unless this deal is made."

Zander looked back at our ragtag crew, and nodded.

"You have a deal," he said and bowed to the high director, sealing our fates.

"What did he say?" Kork asked. "What did Zander agree to?"

"A trade," I shuddered. "One of us is staying here."

"He *what*?"

"Fantastic!" The director beamed. "You have a day

to decide who will remain in our perfect society. I know the decision will be hard. Who could refuse utopia?"

I looked at my friend, the captain, and the droid. I was pretty certain every one of us would refuse this utopia, if it meant staying in this stale city for a second more.

CHAPTER FOURTEEN
CRASH COURSE IN SPACE HISTORY 101

We sat on the stairs of the justice building staring into the empty city, not saying a word.

I don't know how long we stared over that stoop, but it felt like hours. Maybe it had been only minutes. My sense of time was warped, and I was exhausted from planet-lag. Not to mention all the crap we had been thrown into in the past few—how had it only been hours?

"So, let me get this straight," Kork said, letting out a long, strenuous breath. "They want one of us to stay here while one of them goes back to Pyrina? What do they want to negotiate, exactly?"

"This is not the correct first contact protocol," said Two. "You have skipped one hundred seventy-three preliminary steps."

"Where were you an hour ago?" Kork grumbled.

"At your side," Two replied. "Assimilating."

"I think you'll find I did not start first contact on behalf of the Alliance," said Zander. "I did it as a private citizen, and not even an Alliance citizen at that. I talked to them earnestly as *me*, a private enterprise looking for a way off this planet. Kork will not be held accountable for how disastrous that went."

“Not that disastrous,” I said. “I mean, we’re alive, aren’t we?”

"Still, we have to decide who's staying and fast," the captain urged. "I would vote on leaving Two, but he doesn't speak a lick of whatever they do."

"But Zander and I do, that's what you're saying," I said. "You don't, so it's not worth you staying."

"Well, when you put it like that."

"Logically, I would be the best person to leave. I'm useless to the crew," I said, surprised at how calm I was when I pushed out those words. They hadn't hit me yet, I guessed. Everything about space travel was about delayed reaction, and I was still processing the bit about not finding Earth, let alone the time thing, and the fact we had crashed on this stupid planet.

"No," Kork said. "This mission is between the Alliance and the people of—what did they call their planet? Aeros? Area? This mission is between the Alliance and the Aorians. You don't have to put yourself in here."

"What are you suggesting? That you stay?" Zander asked. "The captain of the *Traveler*? With a crew waiting for you to save them?"

"It's not the best solution," said Kork, "but if I have

to, I will. I'll learn how to speak their language. I'll represent the Alliance. I'll ... I don't know. I don't even understand what just happened. Human colonies? What were you going on about?"

"Ancient history," said Zander. "It's complicated."

"Well, spill," I said. "How did we find humans on the other side of the galaxy? Who are they to us?"

"Distant relatives." He chuckled like he was in on some inside joke. "Oh boy, this takes me back. Long, long ago, humans evolved to their advanced state on a large, nurturing planet named Kalhuta. But you know humans. Their curiosity got the better of them. They sent out four generation ships to the far reaches of the galaxy to settle new worlds and expand the human empire."

"This is wholly unauthorized," Two whirred. "This is not an acceptable form of history. It belongs to religious heretics."

"Hey, sticks and stones, right?" I said. "Go on, Zander. What does that have to do with Earth?"

"Well, no one's sure exactly what happened, but pretty much as soon as the colonies were established, all contact was lost. Eventually everyone just forgot about each other and moved on. Pyrina and Hydra reconnected first, in the centuries preceding the formation of the Alliance. They found it odd that their races were identical while they had been on separate planets to begin with, so they decided to trace back their ancestry. They found the legend of Kalhuta, but there wasn't enough proof to back up its existence, let alone its location."

"So, us on Earth, we're—"

"One of the colonies, yup," Zander said proudly. "Settled tens of thousands of your years ago. You found a planet, terraformed it to perfection, and made it your home, promptly forgetting about your cousins."

"Which explains why we're everywhere," Kork snorted. "It's human this, human that. The entire Alliance revolves around humans. Give me a break."

"I hate to say it, Kork, but you happen to be human, too," I pointed out.

"With an almost all-human crew," he said. "It's discrimination, I tell you. They could have cast anyone to be a part of the main crew, but Jezeal's the only non-human in the main cast, and he's only there because he won a token minority contest. It's embarrassing."

"One problem at a time, Captain," said Zander. "Plus, your cast is definitely not as bad as it is here. Have you seen everyone here? Identical, the lot of them. So... *white*."

Well, they have lived under a dome for thousands of generations. Their skin wasn't going to have that much pigmentation. Still, it felt like we were in a bad sci-fi movie from the fifties. We stuck out like sore thumbs, Kork especially. Two could have fit in quite well if someone shaved off his hair and then hid the mechanical parts of his skull.

"Is Kalhuta still out there?" I asked.

"Who knows?" replied Zander, staring up at the sky. The planet we orbited was only slightly visible through the dreary and dirty top of the dome. "No one left because of any problem. It was curiosity, after all. Blind, dumb, fumbling curiosity. Come to think about it, I would assume the people who stayed behind were much smarter and level-headed than their curious counterparts, so I'm pretty sure their planet had a chance."

"You sure know a lot for someone who claims he's not from the Alliance," said Kork. "Like someone who was actually there."

"And you seem a little light on your training," Zander pointed out. "Is the Alliance hiring just anybody to be their flagship captains?"

"Let's not start this *again*," I begged.

"Derzan says that if you look to Him, any other disagreement will melt away," said Two.

"Oh, he does, does he?" Kork snapped. "And how are you getting all this? Do you have a bible or something?"

"I am the first prophet of Derzan" the droid replied. "I will be writing the holy book myself."

"That's a commendable endeavor, Two," I said, glancing at the two men, looking for support.

The doors few open behind us and out came Nim and the High Director. The two were in deep conversation, though I could not tell if that was a good or bad thing, not until they got close enough for my eavesdropping to turn into just overhearing.

"This is a great thing you have done, son," the High Director said, the pride heavy in his voice, "but do not abuse the power of your current score. You have the chance of being a highly respected member of society. Use this wisely."

"I will, Father," the boy said, looking up at the man with awe. Well, I say up. He was taller than the older man, but the way he looked at him made the High Director appear ten feet tall.

"Ah, hello there," the High Director said, noticing us on the stairs. "Have you come to your decision yet?"

"No, sir." Zander shook his head.

"Well, this could be a great opportunity for you, my boy," the director patted Nim on the back. "Why don't you give these four the grand tour of our city? Make it harder for them to decide who the lucky person is who will stay."

"It's the middle of the night, Father." The number on his neck decreased by one, and the director frowned. "Very well. I am awake, anyway. Is this part of the protocols?"

"They say to share hospitality, so yes, in a way, this is."

"Then I shall do my best." The number on his neck increased by one. The boy smiled like he had just been given a piece of cake.

"Good boy." The High Director squeezed Nim's shoulder affectionately. "Once you four have reached a decision, we'll have a celebration. The entire city must be here for this historic moment!"

He made a flourish with his right hand, then left without another word. I guessed as High Director, he didn't need much in ways of a goodbye. If he needed us again, we would not be hard to find. We were the only ones here with hair, after all.

We might have been under a dome, but the road felt more like the slide of a microscope. The freedom he was giving us was about as real as Derzan.

"Come with me," Nim said, extending a hand. "I will show you my home."

"Don't mind if we do," Zander said with a cheerful

smile. "Your father is an impressive man, Nim. Tell me, will you be going into governance after him?"

"I don't see how that is of your concern."

"Just making conversation, Nim."

The boy looked at his wrist, then looked back up at Zander. He seemed caught in a question. Finally, he sucked in a breath and went for it.

"I'll tell you everything about me," he said, "if you let me touch your hair."

"My hair?" Zander laughed. "Sure, kiddo. Whatever you want."

Zander knelt beside Nim, and the boy delicately poked the brown swoop of hair. His smile widened, and he went for more, squeezing and squishing the hair like a toddler would.

"So, I take it you don't have hair on Aeros?" asked Zander.

"We shave it," said Nim. "Identical looks avoid inequality. It gives everyone a fair chance."

"A fair chance to ... what?" I asked. Not get a bad haircut?

"Equal opportunities at life, with no bias." Nim grinned, finally pulling his hand out of Zander's mane. My friend stood up, glowing with excitement. I guessed he liked the attention.

"That's impressive," I said, following Nim as he took to the sidewalk and walked us up the avenue where the buildings slowly grew and morphed into the same identical shapes. A walking tour, then. "So, you're the perfect society?"

"Without a doubt. Everyone has identical chances. We learned from the mistakes of our ancestors and built something new. You should feel honored that the High Director wishes to share our model with you."

Kork stuffed his hands in his pockets, staring at the ground. The poor man had no idea what was going on. And Zander wasn't feeling too generous with his words.

"Can you ask him what the deal is with the numbers?" the captain said. "I can't seem to figure out what they are."

"What's he saying?" asked Nim, looking back at the captain. His eyes lingered a little longer than a gentle glance. Kork's dark skin was probably more foreign to him than Zander's luscious hair.

"He wants to ask you about the numbers," I said, "and I have to admit, I want to know too. What do they mean?"

Even as we walked, the number on the boy's collar went up to one hundred thousand and forty-four.

"Oh, it's simple, really," said Nim. "They're our grade. We gain points for good deeds, and they are deducted for bad. They can be traded for goods and services—for extra sweet drinks and meals, for example."

"And you earn them by doing good things?" I asked, dumbfounded.

"Why, yes," he replied. "You do not?"

"No, not exactly."

"How do good deeds get rewarded? How do bad deeds get punished?"

"I don't know. Karma?" I said, shaking my head. "What happens when your number hits zero?"

"You go neg," Nim said, "You are put on probation to prove your worth to society. It is a gentle punishment. It is kind and fair."

"That's just ..." I shuddered, trying to imagine what it would be like growing up in a place where karma had a financial value. " Who defines what's good?"

"Our ancestors did, when they settled in this place. I'm not sure how it works, exactly; I haven't specialized my study yet. When I was a grade forty, I thought I was going to be a mech. But now that I'm ... I'm a *hundred thousand*, I have more options. I could follow my father's footsteps, but I would be more interested in archival studies."

"Good for you, Nim," I said.

"So, your father's High Director because he has the highest grade?" asked Zander.

"That is correct, yes." Nim nodded, his head bobbing up and down so quickly it was a blur. "Now that my grade is so high, I'll be able to see him more frequently. We have more excuses to meet."

"You weren't allowed to meet?"

"Our ancestors attached a lot of importance to parenthood and ancestry." He shrugged. "But that is seen as another sign of inequality. Parents can show unequal favoritism to their own children, or children of friends. Breaking ties with parents means all youth are treated equally. My father and I are a rarity here. He needed a kidney transplant and searched for me and found I was a match, as was to be expected. We are more connected than anyone else, but as High Director he must be careful with how much attention and affection he shows me."

"Surely he can be thankful to have such a selfless son," Zander pointed out. Nim scratched his bald scalp awkwardly.

"Assimilating," Two interjected.

I tried not to jump to conclusions, but my mind was a whirlwind. Best not make any assumptions. I'd only known this boy a few hours, but a kidney must have been worth so many points in their system. Why Nim had only forty when we met, I would never know. And I would never ask. I dropped back to relay the information to Kork, as Zander and Nim chatted idly at the head of our small procession.

"So, their entire economy is based on human goodness?" the captain scoffed. "And it works?"

"It looks that way," I replied, smiling, trying to cheer him up. Kork had been frowning since we had run afoul of the people here. Being left out of the loop sucked.

"How would that even work?" Kork continued, "I mean, is he gaining points for walking or for talking up his society to a bunch of newcomers?"

"No idea."

"Life isn't a game. No one gives you points for trying."

"And yet, here we are," I said, "in a city where the best person manages everyone else, and there are equal chances for all. Face it, Captain, utopias exist."

We stopped in front of a building with no columns but with windows that spanned the entire front of the facade. I could see shelves of books in there, or what looked like books—a library, archives, who knew. I probably would have gotten the answer if Kork hadn't wanted to continue our conversation.

"Do they?" Kork said, sternly, looking at the building as Nim explained something—probably interesting—to Zander. "Is their system really that infallible? I mean, who sets the standards, who says what's good and what's—"

"You don't have to find flaws with everything," I said. "Can you just accept that this place works, and move on?"

"If you say so." He let out a heavy sigh then smiled. In that moment, my heart stopped. All I could see was his gorgeous, grinning lips, and the rest of the universe faded away. I did not believe, before that moment, that a person's smile could take me away so completely. In that moment, I believed in magic.

"I like that about you, Sally," the captain said, half awkwardly, half proudly. "You see the good in people. We're all messed up and flawed, but you're not looking at that."

"You give me too much credit," I said, feeling the blood rushing to my face. "I'm only trying to be like this since everything around me is falling apart. If I don't force myself to see the good, then the bad would overwhelm me. Heck, maybe I should be the one to stay. I sure need a bit of consistency in my life."

Kork laughed, a loud, hearty laugh, a beautiful laugh that made me want to join in. "Don't we all!"

"You two all right back there?" Zander asked. It looked like we were about to move on again. I probably should have been paying attention to what Nim was saying about the building. It wasn't every day you got a tour of an alien city where the locals hadn't had visitors in thousands of years.

"I am doing quite well, thank you," said Two, emerging from the back of our small squad.

"What did he just say?" asked Kork, glancing at the droid.

"He said he's—wait, why do you ask?" I took in Kork's awed expression, fearing what he would say next. But it wasn't the captain who spoke. It was the Aorian boy.

"I didn't think he spoke our language," Nim said to Zander. "Why hasn't he been speaking?"

"I assimilated your mother tongue," said the droid. "But do not fear; I will be able to communicate freely now. If you want me to, of course."

"He speaks their language!" Kork shouted, grabbing the droid and planting a large kiss on his lips. "Yes! Yes! This solves everything."

"How so, Captain?" the droid asked. "Everything is quite a large problem. The question of existence and—"

"No, Two, listen to me," said Kork. "Would it be against your programming to stay in this location until we send a crew to pick you up?"

"If you commanded me to stay, Captain, then I would be obligated to obey," Two said in his monotonous tone. "If that is part of our mission."

"Nim, tell your father we have chosen our emissary," Kork said.

"What?" asked Nim.

"He says we know who's staying," Zander translated, "so it's time for that party of yours."

CHAPTER FIFTEEN
WE ARE OUR OWN PARTY POOPERS

The sun rose over the dome, casting long shadows through the buildings. What was once black and gray was now yellow and orange on top of the black and gray. The monotone colors looked murky in the early sunlight. It was beautiful, in a way. You could see the crudeness of the dome, covered in years of dirt and grime that no one could clean off, making the day look almost hazy.

We sat on chairs on the top step of the town hall. For almost an hour now, the PA system had been cheerfully telling everyone who could hear—and by how loud the speakers were, that meant everyone in town—that they were having an unexpected meeting in the city center, and that they should all get up and see what was going on.

"This is an important day for Aoria," the voice bellowed, joined by the crackle of feedback. *"A historic day. You must be a part of it!"*

I wasn't sure if they meant that last bit as a threat, but it seemed oddly threatening.

By the time the sun had risen, replacing the planet as the greatest source of light in the sky, the street was packed with thousands of people. Every citizen of Aoria had come out to meet us—every identical person, with their shaved heads and gray uniforms, standing in front of the hall and muttering quietly between each other. They filled up the entire street, stretching in every direction imaginable. If there were a hundred thousand people in this city, as Two had said, they were all here right now.

We were in plain view. They could see us, and conclusions were being made. Maybe they had guessed who we were and who we were to them, or maybe they had not. Either way, this would be a big day for them. And for us, too.

"You don't happen to have an extra translator, do you?" Kork leaned over to Zander, his voice a whisper. "I'm tired of being left out. Even Two understands what's going on. I can't be getting less than a repair droid!"

"Hang in there, Kork," Zander replied. "In an hour, we'll be out of here, and we'll have all the trash we need to fly back to the ship. Just sit back and smile."

The captain leaned back in his seat, muttering something about it being more complicated than that. I took Zander's advice and smiled at the crowd. This was first contact, and it was meant to be exciting.

"My friends," the High Director said, stepping out to the edge of the stairs. They must have given him a mike because his voice reverberated across the entire plaza, and a wave of excitement followed, people reacting with the speed of sound.

"My friends," he repeated, signaling for everyone to quiet down. "My friends, today is a very important day, because today ... today we welcome back into the fold our friends from Kalhuta. Today is the day of reunification!"

Kalhuta? The word spread through the crowd like a wave. The cheers of excitement dropped to murmurs of shock. *Kalhuta. Reunification.*

"It was in the early hours of the morning that young Nimien discovered them in our city. We welcome Zander, Captain Kork, Sally Webber, and Two, descendants of the colonies of Hydra, Pyrina, and Terra that were lost to us eons ago. They have come here to find us, to return to our family. Humanity will be whole once more!"

The world erupted in noise. The entire assembly cheered, but it wasn't just a cheer of excitement. It was a cheer of world-shattering proportions. The entire Aorian race had waited a millennium for our return.

I grinned wider. I was part of something big here; I was a part of history. The human race would know of today and learn about it in school. They would learn about how we bravely—or accidentally—stumbled upon their world and reunited the four human colonies.

If they believed the legends, of course, which they would have to with the proof this city offered. The Alliance would change. And Earth would change, too, one day. If *we* ever did reunify, that is.

"As a gesture to unite our people, we have decided on a trade," the director continued. "One of our people will return with them to their world while one of theirs will stay here with us, to learn our culture and speak to us of theirs. Our very own First Chair will accompany the crew of the UPAF *Traveler* to the colony of Pyrina, while Mister Two will stay with us. Two, why don't you come up here and say a few words."

My heart sank as the droid rose to his feet. At the same moment, Kork, Zander, and I all realized what a horrible mistake we might have made.

Two was a droid with one thing in mind: conversion. He had made that clear from the beginning. We had been so wrapped up in the excitement of having found someone to take our place that we hadn't thought through what Two could actually *say*. We had hoped to leave and move on, but a speech from the droid could be the end of us all.

I reached for a hand, any hand, and found Kork's. He squeezed it, and I squeezed back. It was now-or-never time. And it was completely out of our control.

"Greetings, people of Aoria," Two said proudly, stepping to the front of the stage. A roar of excitement rose from the crowd. He was a sight to behold: perfectly groomed blond hair, immaculate Alliance uniform, a calm composure that came from an utter lack of emotion. He stood tall and proud before the crowd, and they loved him.

"Today marks the day of our reunification," he continued, "a historic event that redefines the history of my people. Of *our* people. It is when 'we' and 'them' becomes 'us'."

"How is he doing this?" I muttered, my jaw dropping in awe. Of all the things to come out of Two's mouth, I had never expected anything this *good.*

"He's a droid," said Kork. "He's programmed to do a lot of things."

"I thought he was just a repair droid."

"And he repairs everything, from crashed ships, to people, to long lost unions," the captain muttered. "Is he saying anything good?"

"He's perfect," I replied. "It's emotional. It's historic. It's one for the books."

I should know better, by now, then to jinx these sorts of things. The second the words left my mouth, the droid lifted his hands to the sky in a sign of praise. And we all knew whose good word he was about to spread.

His holiness, the all-powerful imaginary Derzan.

"We must thank the Almighty for this heavenly day," the droid proclaimed. "Derzan has enabled us to find you. He guided our lost ship to your side, so that we could meet you and become your friends once more. All praise be to Him!"

There was a quiet in the crowd, a sudden hush. I felt my face turning red. This was it. This was the end. We would be chased out with fire and pitchforks, all thanks to the almighty Derzan. I clutched Kork's hand tighter.

"Who is this Derzan to whom you give thanks?" asked the High Director, coolly. "Is he a commander of great repute?"

"You may say that, yes," Two continued. "He is the

commander of my heart and soul. He raised me from the dead and told me the truth of all things. I thank him for bringing me here today."

"Astonishing." The High Director clapped, and to our surprise, the rest of the audience joined in. A thunderous applause rained down on the droid, with chants of *Derzan, Derzan, Derzan*! rising from the crowd in droves.

"Is this ... is this actually happening?" asked Kork, eyes wide. They were shouting so loudly that even he could get the gist of what had been said, and his shock was palpable. He let go of my hand, only so he could drop his face into his palms.

"They love him," I stammered. "They love Two. I can't believe this."

"He has to keep this going," said Zander, eager and grinning. "If he manages to keep this up, then we're getting out of here in one piece. This is a miracle worthy of Derzan."

"You realize Derzan is based on *you*, right?" I said. "The droid saw you before he was shot, realized who you are, and woke up with everything jumbled. Derzan is your name—backward. It's not even creative."

"I've been called worse," said Zander.

The droid lifted his hands to the sky again, and the crowd went wild. They cheered for him, for Derzan, and I had the distinct feeling that I had just witnessed the birth of a religion. Or maybe a cult.

"I am pleased to stay here with you," said Two. "I will assimilate your culture and refer you to the histories of mine. I am told it will be an honor. And I am programmed, after all, to highlight the positive aspects of the United Alliance. Let it be so."

The crowd cheered again. They loved him, and he saw that it was good. The High Director himself beamed with pride. "As a treat, all work is cancelled on this day," he said, patting Two on the back. "Instead, it shall be a day of celebration. We shall eat double rations and be merry. Let the festivities commence!"

We were ushered off the stage and down into the crowd. They parted to let us through, still cheering, some reaching to touch our shoulders or our hair. Two was the center of attention and love, the entire assembly wanting to get a piece of him. He kept a straight face. I don't think he was programmed for anything different.

Soon, we were sitting at the end of one of the tables, which easily seated exactly a hundred people, in a cafeteria room not unlike the one we had seen when we had arrived. The rest of them were organized according by grade, with the High Director closest to us, along with the First Chair, and then the rest of the council. The grades descended down the length of the table. Nim was nowhere to be seen. I guessed he wasn't ranked high enough for our table.

Plus, I couldn't pick him out of the crowd even if I wanted to, not with everyone looking exactly the same. I wondered if we would ever see that kid again.

Two was regaling the assembly with tales of Derzan, keeping everyone enthralled as Zander. Kork and I kept to ourselves. Two waved his hands wide, in clear, thought-out patterns, proof of excellent programming. The room was filled with light, with people, with excitement. There was noise and palpable joy. It was beautiful.

"I can't believe this is working," I muttered, exchanging excited glances with my small crew, "Two is a natural at this."

"If by natural, you mean he's following his modulated programing, then yes, he is," said Zander. "He just needs to keep this up until we go."

"Which is when, exactly?" asked Kork, sweat building on his brow. "I thought we would be allowed to leave after the droid gave his speech. You promised it would be an hour."

"Derzan, why do I keep making these promises?" Zander muttered before speaking to Kork once more. "Probably after we eat breakfast. We'll ask about the trash, then leave. The crew is probably wondering what happened to us, and I don't want my sister organizing a rescue party. We have our own rescue mission to mount."

"I was thinking more of Jezeal and Crandle," said Kork. "Before today, they hadn't exchanged ten words with each other, and they've been stuck in the hopper for who knows how long. One of them is going to snap. Not to mention, Crandle is afraid of spiders, and Jezeal isn't exactly in uniform right now."

"Let's focus on our food," said Zander. "Another hour, tops, and we go. But I'm not calling that a promise."

"Sounds good to me," I said as someone in a white uniform placed a plate of plain mush in front of me. The flash of a white sleeve made me turn, and there was a young woman, eyes pale and distant, handing out plates from a trolley. Around her neck was a bright red dash rather than a number.

Everyone was eating the same food, I noticed,

looking down the table. We all had the same plate of generic white paste, which I poked at with the popsicle stick they had given me.

"What is this?" I hissed.

"Protein curd," replied Zander. "Very nutritious. Eat up."

I took a bite and wanted to wretch. The stuff was tasteless, but it had the sticky, thick texture of peanut butter and wouldn't leave my mouth fast enough.

"We apologize if the food is not to your liking," said the First Chair, "seeing as how you are unable to personalize it."

"Personalize it?" I asked.

She tapped the skin at the back of her neck gently. "The food is plain, but we may customize the flavors ourselves. That way everyone eats what they want."

"How utilitarian," said Two. "A truly unifying way of eating food."

"Quite," the woman said. "What do you eat in your distant world?"

"Oh, everything," said Zander. One thing he liked to talk about was his food. "The universe has such a huge variety of foods to choose from. You're going to love it."

"I am eager to try," she said.

I forced myself to finish my paste. As disgusting as the food was, I hadn't eaten since snacking on the bridge, before this mess, and that felt like years ago. Not to mention that my relationship with alien food wasn't on the best of terms, not after the pizza incident on Da-Duhui. My belly was stuffed by the time my plate was cleared, and it would hold me over until I could get a nice, safe cookie to eat.

"Why don't you eat the fruits growing outside?" asked Zander, clearing his plate. "On our way in, we saw a wide variety."

"Oh, we cannot leave the city," the First Chair said quickly. "The air isn't safe."

"But it is," I pointed out. "We could breathe quite easily out there."

"No, that cannot be," she said, shaking her head. "When our ancestors landed here, the air was toxic. That's why they built this city. And the others."

"There are other cities?" Zander and I asked in unison.

"There were," she said. "Years ago. But their people perished when they opened themselves to the outside world. We lost contact with them, around the same time as we lost contact with the other colonies. No. The air outside will kill us all in an instant."

"Then how do you expect to come with us?" asked Zander.

"We assumed you would provide me with a suit," she said, "but we probably can find one in our own storage. This may take some time—"

"But we didn't need suits," said Zander. "We can breathe just fine out there. Heck, there's life out there! Vegetation!"

"You're lying," she said, her eyes going wide and yet, somehow, distant. Her hands began to tremble, making the white paste on her spoon jiggle ever so slightly. "You're trying to trick me!"

"He's telling the truth. Go outside and see for yourself."

"No," she said, shaking her head vigorously. Tears trickled down her face now, turning her skin red. The number on her neck flickered, as if it couldn't figure out if it was supposed to rise or drop.

"The outside world is toxic, and that is the truth," said the High Director, suddenly very much in our faces. "The ancestors told us very clearly: we cannot leave."

"Times have changed," said Zander, stern now. "The terraforming process they started succeeded. This world is yours for the taking, why are you hiding away in here?"

"It's not as if we haven't tried to send out missions," said the director. "Every one of them who has left has failed to return. The outside world is dangerous."

"Then how did we get here?" asked Zander, glaring at the man. "Because we can breathe your air, as well as the air outside. We saw fields of grasses and beautiful forests."

People were rising now, ready to intervene if necessary. And not on our behalf. No, we were outnumbered, four to a hundred thousand.

Well, I say four. Kork looked confused, and Two, well, he was basking in the love of Derzan.

Still, I grabbed Two's collar and dragged him with us as we inched toward the kitchen door. Zander held his hands out in a defensive position, and Kork followed suit.

"Okay, what did you two say?" he muttered.

"That the outside world wasn't going to kill them," I replied, trying to imitate his stance. My hands, however, were shaking so much it looked like I was trying to get into telekinesis.

Good. Let them think that. Maybe that would give me the element of surprise.

The approaching hoard stared at us with oddly

empty eyes. They had Two's look: empty, with a lack of light up there, a dullness in their irises. I shuddered. I had seen this look before.

"Mind control?" I asked Zander.

"It sure looks like it, but who's controlling them and why?"

"We'll figure that out when we get out of this," said Kork. "So, what's the plan? We attack?"

"We're four against... all of them," said Zander. "How well do you think that would go?"

It went as well as any of you expected because ten minutes later, we were in jail—and none too happy about it.

CHAPTER SIXTEEN

I SHOULD HAVE WATCHED MORE THAN HALF AN EPISODE OF PRISON BREAK

"What the fuck was that?" I said, staring out of the small window of our cell. "I mean ... what the everlasting fudging *fuck* was *that*?"

"For the twenty-sixth time, Sally," said Zander, "we have no idea."

"But they're brainwashed!" I met his gaze, knowing he was thinking the same thing I was. "It was the same thing we saw back on Da-Duhui."

"You were on Da-Duhui?" asked Kork, glancing up at us from his seat next to the door. He had been staring at his feet since we had gotten here, looking nothing like the so-called brilliant starship captain that he was supposed to be. He appeared how I felt: scared.

"Yes," said Zander, "but now is not the time."

"You realize I mean for the uprising," the captain urged, "not in general."

"Yes, I do." Zander gave the man a long, hard glare.

The door open and in flew Nim in such a sorry state the air caught in my throat. His hair had started to grow back on his scalp, covering the skin with a short layer of fuzz. He had a bit of a shadow on his upper lip, too. The number on his neck was a flickering red forty-four.

"Nim!" I called, reaching for him as he tripped. He landed on me, and we both fell backward onto the ground.

The boy scampered up and away as the cell door slammed shut. In an instant, he had scurried to the furthest corner from us, his eyes wide in terror.

"It's your fault," he said, spitting on the ground. Forty-three.

"Hold on a second," said Zander, putting a hand up and taking a delicate step forward. When Nim tried to step away—which he couldn't with the wall in the way—Zander stopped. He knew better than to spook him. "What happened, Nim?"

"It's Nimien to you." His eyes were bright with electricity, holding back tears. "You… you monsters!"

"What's the kid doing here?" Kork looked at me, softening slightly. "What's going on?"

"That's what we're trying to figure out." I did not take my eyes off the terrified kid. Nimien was trying not to panic but was slowly losing it, clutching his torso like he was coming apart at the seams.

"Nimien, what happened out there?" I put on a soothing voice, which sounded frighteningly like my mother's. "One second we were eating together. The next—did we say something wrong? Was it all the talk about Derzan?"

"Derzan forgives," said Two, coolly, looking at me in a way that made me think the droid might not be the forgiving type.

"No, it was just ... you." The boy sighed heavily, crossing his arms over his chest. "It's against the laws to speak about the outside world. It is lost to us. We must move on."

"But it's not lost to you," Zander insisted. "Trust us. We came through there. It's beautiful outside your city."

"I want to believe you; I really do, but ..." Nim shifted uncomfortably. "Every time I even think about the outside world, everything gets murky. All right?"

"In what way?"

Nimien shrugged. "It's like the idea won't form in my head, and every time I try to bring it up with people, they ignore me. Which is odd, because they don't seem bothered by it themselves."

"So why did they throw you in here with us?" I asked. "You didn't have anything to do with our ... accidental protest. Heck, I haven't seen you since this morning."

"I have no idea." Nim was visibly trembling now, no matter how much he tried to hide it. He clenched and unclenched his arms, but it wasn't making the situation any better. "I was having my breakfast with everyone else. Then they stood up, without a word, so I stood up too, and they were all looking at *me*, like I had just… Then my grade went red, and everything I earned since this morning was gone. The black suits brought me here without saying anything. And I ..."

Before he could finish his sentence, he jerked backward, as if hit with a taser. Nim cracked violently on his way down, landing hard on the concrete floor, shaking and in visible pain. Just as suddenly as it had started, whatever had a hold on him let go, and Nim was left panting in the corner of the cell.

Forty-four.

He didn't put up any resistance when I went to him this time. Zander lifted his head, and Kork towered over them both, looking confused, while Two and I held his hands, not that it would do any good.

"But I'm not a neg," he said, under his breath, the tears flowing freely now. "I am not a neg!"

"No, no, you're not." Zander wiped the beads of sweat off Nim's forehead, looking over to Kork and me for help.

"What's a neg?" I asked.

"A neg commonly refers to a member of the Aorian society whose grade has slipped under zero," Two explained. "Nimien himself told you this."

"Yes, yes, he did," I agreed, "and his grade is above zero, right? So, why is it red?"

"I was a sixer," the boy said between trembling lips. "I was a sixer, and I lost it."

"What's happening to him?" I asked. "What's going on?"

"All members of Aorian society must contribute to the betterment of all by punishing those who have failed to comply," the droid said. Blink. Turn. Blink. "They are chipped at birth. That chip not only contains their score histogram; it is directly connected to the pain centers of their brain. You can raise your score by administering an electric shock to any neg currently in custody. This raises the grade of both the neg and the administrator."

"But… that's *barbaric*," Kork spat, joining us on the floor, albeit a little awkwardly since there was nothing left for him to do. Not that Nim wanted anything to do with any of us, anyway. Now that he was regaining his strength, he was pulling away from our collective grasps. "And how does the droid know so much about these people?"

"The *droid* assimilated," Two explained, letting go of Nim's wrist. He flipped up the cuff of Nim's sleeve, revealing a vast array of complex circuitry connecting the boy to his city. "I simply uploaded their codes and bylaws. We have indeed been incarcerated for our remarks on the outside world."

"Well, that explains it," Kork muttered. "And the punishment for that is?"

"Death." The droid said this with the same level of cool headed monotony he used to give us all his news.

"Ah, of course, we're all going to die," I said, surprising myself by laughing. Just our luck. We find people willing to help us and then mess it up by telling everyone to go outside. Well, screw them.

"We've got to get out of here," said Kork, rising to his feet.

"No shit, Sherlock," I said. "Nim, are you going to be all right?"

He nodded, incredibly slowly. I was amazed he was pulling himself together so quickly.

"We should pull out the chip," said Zander, lifting the laser pointer from inside of his uniform.

"Hey, where were you keeping that?" asked Kork, dumbfounded. "They took my stunner, but they let you keep the wand thing?"

"This isn't my first rodeo," Zander replied. "Now, this shouldn't hurt."

"What the red are you trying to do?" Nim flew to his feet, and in one smooth motion he was out of Zander's reach.

"We're getting you out of here," he insisted. "You can't get shocked like that again. Like Kork said, it's barbaric to treat a kid to that kind of punishment. Or anyone for that matter."

"But it is my punishment," Nim snarled, "and if I am meant to receive it, then I will take my punishment gladly!"

"You're being brainwashed," said Zander, stepping toward him. "We just want to help you."

"Everything was fine until you got here. So just stop, all right? If I am meant to be punished, then so be it. It is not my place to contest the decisions of the many."

"But they're *torturing* you!"

"Is this what you do?" Nim spat once again. Forty-three. "You show yourselves to people who have yet to experience space travel and tell them their ways are wrong? You come into my city and tell us how to live? Well I want you out of here as much as the rest of them do. Leave me in peace and go."

"He has a point, you know," I said, touching Zander's arm. He didn't try to shake me off. "Who are we to tell them how to live their lives?"

"But they're torturing children, Sally," he said, his knuckles going white as he clutched the pointer tighter.

"I know they think they're a utopia, but they can't be allowed to torture children."

"I know, I know." I gave his shoulder a tight squeeze. "But we're not here to fix alien civilizations; we're on a rescue mission. Right? One problem at a time. We have people waiting for us back at the hopper and people counting on us back at the ship. This is not our problem. We're not the universe police."

Zander opened his mouth, but shut it quickly. He clutched his hands into fists.

"Blayde would know what to do," he muttered.

"And Blayde is waiting for us," I said. "So, let's stop holding back. Let's get out of here and back on mission."

"I hate to break it to you," Kork interjected, "but we're in jail. We can't just leave, not unless you have any daring escapes planned."

"Zander has been blessed by Derzan," said Two, raising his palms to the heavens. "No walls can hold him."

"Huh?" Kork asked. "Can anyone translate robo-religion? What's he going on about?"

"You're a starship captain with the Alliance," Zander said, letting out a heavy sigh. "You should have figured it out by now."

"Oh, so you really are the Zander from the stories?" he scoffed. "No jail cell can hold you and all that?"

"You can say that," he said, taking my hand and extending his other one out. "If you hadn't reset the droid, I'm pretty sure he would have told you by now. Or have tried to arrest me. Anyway, take a hand, any hand."

Kork decided he would rather take mine. He

clutched it, and I closed my fingers around his. I liked the feel of my palm in his, how it felt so small there.

Come on Sally, not now. Focus.

"What are you doing?" asked Nim, looking at us with wide eyes. He was still shaking. I felt guilt gnawing at my stomach at the idea of leaving him like this. Or leaving anyone like this.

But this was their world, and I was in no place to impose my own ideas of law or morality. "Look, kid," Zander said gruffly, "I'm not going to take that chip out of your head. But I can't let this slide."

He grabbed Nimien's hand, and, in the blink of an eye, we were outside the window of the small jail cell, standing in the street. Zander let go of me to get a tighter hold of Nim, who was too shocked to move.

"What the… VEESH!" Kork stammered, breathing hard.

"Long story short," Zander replied, not really paying attention, "I guess no cell can hold me. Now, let's go, all right? Two, get us out of here."

"I do not take orders from you."

"Fine then," Zander snapped. "Kork?"

"Um, get us out of here, Two. And quickly!"

We ran through the city, Nim still wide-eyed and shocked as he trotted aimlessly behind us. Zander dragged him along, and though the kid didn't put up a fight, his jaw still hung on the floor.

The numbers around his neck were dropping, fast.

Where were all the people? Were they still celebrating? Or were they working, doing whatever you do to keep a perfect society running. Either way, it was a relief to have no obstructions in our way.

"Car thing!" shouted Kork, shoving me into an alleyway. The rest of the crew followed, diving into the alley as the Roomba drove by. Nim made a move toward the Roomba, but Zander wrapped his hands around Nim's mouth to keep him quiet.

"What are you doing?" I hissed. "Let Nim go. We don't need him to get in the way. He could get hurt."

"I won't let that happen," Zander said. "I have a plan."

"Oh yeah? What kind of plan?"

"A good one."

He left it at that. Before I could ask him anything more, Two was running again, and now Kork was running, and seeing as how he diligently refused to let go of my hand, I was too. The droid had figured out how to navigate the identical streets, and soon we were right back at the door hidden in the alley through which we had entered the city.

Ah, that had been so long ago. In less than a day, we had made a real mess.

"No, let me go!" Nim, finally getting his nerves back, tried to shake off Zander. He might have been strong on another day, but he was still recovering from being reamed with however many volts of electricity, not to mention that Zander was a tough guy who didn't register pain. Keeping the boy in line wasn't a struggle for him.

I winced. I didn't like this. It felt wrong.

"Zander, just let him go."

"He'll alert the authorities."

"And they'll do what? By the time they get here, we'll be outside, and they won't set foot out there."

"It'll be too late, then," he insisted.

"Too late for what?"

We followed the droid through the maze of tunnels out of the city. And once again, there was no one in our path. Maybe this part of the city wasn't manned. Maybe they had the whole system automated.

Or maybe they wanted us to think we were getting out safely.

All the while, Nim was shouting, screaming, putting up the fight of his life. And Zander dragged him along nonetheless, ignoring his cries. I felt as if there was a hand reaching through my ribcage and squeezing my heart. His shouts were as bad as those inflicted as punishment by his peers.

Back through the turbine room; back to the door that led us outside. Out and free. In just a few minutes, we would leave all this behind.

"Did anyone think to grab some trash?"

Kork crossed his arms over his chest as the droid reached for the door. We all looked at him wide-eyed. No, none of us had thought of getting the one thing we had come into the city for.

"We won't need it." Zander raised Nim's arm into the air, either in triumph or in a show of strength. I wasn't sure.

"What are you doing?" Kork paled. "You're not going to—"

"Oh hell, no," Zander's eyes widened. "You don't seriously think I would ... Captain, who do you think I am? No. I'm going to get them on our side. And then everything will go back to plan. We'll leave Two here, take their First Chair and their trash, and be out of here before you can say miscommunication."

"So what *are* you going to do?" Kork asked.

Zander pushed the door open. As the sunlight hit our eyes, Nim let out a piercing scream, covering his mouth with his free arm. He was sobbing now, tears streaming freely down his face.

"Holy shit!" I spat. "We're not doing a hostage exchange, are we? This boy for their trash? That's low, Zander. We're kidnappers!"

"Oh no, don't worry," said Zander, keeping his expression calm and steady, even as Nim bawled and fought in his grasp. "Nimien will be free to go in about a minute. We just need to do one thing first."

"And what's that?"

Without a word, he picked up Nim, hoisting him effortlessly over his shoulder. The boy screamed again, punching Zander as hard as he could, letting loose against Zander's back. But Zander didn't feel it, looking almost more like a droid than our actual droid did. All empty-faced and emotionless, cold without being cruel.

And he stepped outside.

Nimien screamed even louder. He stopped fighting, having exhausted himself, and he held his breath. The seconds felt like hours as we watched him, willing him to inhale, to realize that the outside world was not a threat.

Thirty seconds. Then forty. I stepped outside with them, breathing freely, relishing in the heat from the risen sun.; we had been under the dome for some time. There was song out here, maybe from birds, maybe from something entirely different, entirely alien.

After a whole minute, Nim swallowed a gulp of air. He breathed, coughing, his eyes slowly going wide. He breathed again, each breath coming easier and clearer.

His tears stopped.

Finally, Zander put him down. Nim teetered on his own two feet, blinking out the bright sunlight. He gazed around him, taking in the world full of plants and trees and nature.

"You see, kid?" Zander grinned. "The outside world is just fine. It might have been toxic when your ancestors first got here, but your terraforming worked. It worked! The world is yours."

But the boy's smile disappeared as the light around his collar blinked and went out.

CHAPTER SEVENTEEN
THE REAL PRICE OF SPACE TRASH

Nim cried and screamed, pounding his fists on the metal staircase.

No one knew what to say. He ripped at his shirt collar, clawing at it like a wild animal, but he couldn't pull it away. His sleeve had gone from being a Technicolor light show to a plain, empty sleeve, his numbers gone. Socially, I was pretty sure he was dead. Or at least pretty darn screwed.

"Nimien, it's okay." Zander crouched to his level, putting his hands on Nim's shoulders, holding him together while trying to calm the panicking teen. Slowly, Nim's breathing slowed to match Zander's, but it was interlaced with sudden, quiet sobs.

Nim shoved off Zander's hands, turning from him

and darting back inside the doorway, but it was no use—his collar wasn't lighting up anymore. It was as if he had been unplugged from the city and lacked the compatibility to reconnect.

Neo had been removed from the Matrix.

But Nim wasn't some Chosen One. He just was a kid that Zander had practically kidnapped and forced outside his home city against his will, all to prove a point. If Nim believed that Zander had ruined his life, I would be inclined to agree.

"The world out here isn't toxic," Zander said again, but with less enthusiasm than before.

"Goddamn it, man!" Kork spat, marching to Nim and putting a comforting arm around him. "Can't you see that we're beyond those kinds of niceties now? I have no idea how to say anything in their language, but if I did, I would be trying to do something right now. The kid needs help, so step up or step out!"

"The boy has seen the truth," said Zander, switching between one language and the next seamlessly, so quickly that I couldn't tell which was which. "Now we go back to City Hall and have him tell them what he knows. They'll set him back up. He'll be a hero again."

"I don't want to be a hero," Nim said, his face red. "I want to go home."

"And we'll go there."

"It's not the same," he scoffed. "Yesterday, I lived in block 17-10; I had friends; I was gaining grade. My home was my city. It was my world. Now, my world's too big, and I don't like it. I want to go back to the way it was before."

"But that's not going to happen," said Zander. "Your

world just grew, and you don't like it? Tough. If you spend your entire life under a bubble, you're going to stay small. Why aren't you excited about this? You've got a whole new world to explore. Things to discover and build! You're a smart kid, Nim. Would you really be so happy in such a stagnant society?"

Nim thought about this as he reached up to touch a spot in the base of his neck. He tapped it, slowly, as if checking if his chip was still there. Then, he dropped the hand again, looking up at Zander with wide eyes.

"This doesn't make things right," he said. "Not between us. It will never be all right between us. You didn't know what would happen to me out here, and you still forced me out. You don't understand my people. They don't like change. We've done things the same way because they work. They're not ready for this. If you really wanted the best for us, you would have asked. Not thrown me outside and hoped it would work out."

"I knew you were going to be fine."

"So you knew I was going to get ... disconnected?" the boy snapped, and in one smooth motion ripped off his shirt and tossed it at Zander's face. He had the pale, soft torso of a boy halfway through puberty, unblemished and hairless. There were red marks on his skin where the circuit in his sleeve connected to his chip, puckered lines that looked like burns.

The shirt was a dead ringer for Zander's nose, and he had to peel away the fabric. He said nothing when he saw the marks, taking a deep breath that spoke louder than words.

"I'll tell them what I saw," Nim said, sharply, glaring at Zander, "but that will be the last of the help I ever give you. I'm only doing it to get you off my planet as fast as possible."

"Understood," said Zander. "Two? Can you lead us back to the town hall?"

"I can," the droid replied, indicating to the tunnels in a very butler-ish way. "Sir, let me just say that this manner of preceding is against the Alliance code of conduct."

"How many times must I remind you I'm not Alliance?" Zander spat at the droid. "Go back to worshipping your new god and let us deal with the situation the way we see fit."

"I do not take orders from you."

“Shut up, Two,” said Kork, exasperated. “That’s an order from your captain.”

Two marched ahead, and I couldn't help but feel sorry for him. Maybe I was projecting, seeing as how I didn't know the extent of his emotions. Could he feel offended?

The ICP back on Da-Duhui had really messed with my head.

"Hey, Nim, are you going to be all right?" I asked, staying back to walk with him. He looked drained, his face so pale and puffy from the tears.

"I will be, yes," he said, giving me a quick look then keeping his eyes straight ahead, "as soon as I am back online."

"You've been connected to the system your entire life?"

"I was chipped the minute I was born," he said, somewhat proudly. "I haven't been disconnected for even a second—until now." He shuddered, either out of cold or out of the horror of his situation. I couldn't even imagine what he was going through.

"I'm sorry Zander did that," I said, entirely earnest. "He was out of line. If I had seen what he was intending—"

"But you didn't," said Nim, "and now it's done. And I have seen outside the dome."

He looked at me, and, to my surprise, he grinned. A wide, toothy, excited grin. His hands were shaking, but it was no longer out of fear.

"In the archives," he said, "I read about people whose jobs it was to look at things that grew and to draw pictures and study them."

"Botanists," I replied. "Scientists that study plants."

"I never thought they would be so ... green," he exclaimed. "Like the numbers, when they are extremely good. I thought everything outside the dome was orange and red. Red for dead."

"Some of the mountains on this planet are, I think," I said. "But no, your plants are bright green. That's chlorophyll if it's the same here as on Earth. It's what helps the plants create energy out of sunlight."

"They can do that?" his eyes widened. "I can't wait to see!"

Nimien was bouncing up and down out of giddiness. After his anger and shock had disappeared, the excitement had shown through. Nim was smart, incredibly bright, and it showed. I wouldn't be surprised if he would one day become quite an accomplished scientist.

But that then was far in the future. Because now, we were heading into the city, back into the place we had just escaped, thanks to Zander's *genius* well-thought-out plan. And this time, we were not alone.

We opened the door to the alley to find ourselves already surrounded. The council stood in a line, blocking our exit to the street. The rest of the city's populace filled the avenue behind them. They were packed, shoulder to shoulder, all staring at us with identical blank looks.

"Hello, Zander," they said, all together, all in one voice.

"Ah, I was wondering when I would get to speak to you," Zander said to the crowd, stepping out casually, as if he wasn't facing a hundred thousand interconnected people who stood against him. "You obviously know who I am. May I ask who you are?"

"I am no one," they said together, then the High Director stepped forward and spoke alone. "And I am everyone."

"You probably would have gotten a cooler effect if you had done that the other way around," Zander pointed out.

"Not the effect I wanted, though," the unknown person speaking through Nim's father said. "But you can see very well that I am in control here. I hope you know where I stand."

"I do," Zander nodded slowly. He made a subtle gesture behind his thigh: stay back, don't try anything. Not that we would, even if we wanted to.

Well, I say we, but Kork had the guts to go against a hoard, and Two had nothing to lose. I guessed the signal was meant more for them than me.

"And you know who you stand against," said Zander. "Your databanks go back far enough. Know that we are equally matched."

The high director laughed. "If you say so," he said, "but I count five of you and a hundred thousand and twenty able-bodied men and women on my side, all in sync. I would ask you to rethink that."

"And I would ask you to check your databanks. I can wait."

There was a tense second where neither party said nothing; then, the director's face fell. He nodded slowly.

"Very well, Zander. Let's talk."

"Let's start with who you are. Or, I should say, what you are."

"I am Central Guidance, a program these people implemented to keep them safe. Their ancestors created me to look after them, to protect them."

"You've brainwashed them! You control their minds."

"Not at all. They live their lives as if I were not there. I only intervene when the situation calls for it. And today calls for an intervention."

"Well, that makes everything a heck of a lot clearer. So you arrive on this planet. You are born. You analyze the incoming messages from the other colonies and find them threatening. Am I on the right track here?"

"They were cruel," the high director said. "Unhelpful."

"Then, let me guess, there was some kind of accident. Something that hurt the colony."

"One of the cities was hit by an asteroid. The terraforming was unstable, poorly implemented. When Base Five was lost, all they could hear were screams. My people wanted to go out and help."

"But you wouldn't let them because it wasn't safe, was it?"

"The planet was barely habitable," Central Guidance

insisted. "I could not let them step out there, not with the asteroids so unpredictable."

"So, you cut the contact, telling them they were alone here, and kept them in the dome ever since. But you had to know the outside world was habitable at some point. Why keep them from leaving?"

"It's the range, isn't it?" I said, stepping forward. I wasn't shaking anywhere near the amount I usually shook. To my surprise, I was entirely calm. "Once they leave the city, you lose contact. And you can't get them back online. You haven't reconnected to Nim, even with him standing two feet away from your entire population. You lose them forever, don't you?"

"You are correct," he agreed. "Once out of my control, I can no longer protect them. I cannot keep them safe, and I must keep them safe."

I shuddered. It was the ICP all over again: computers being told to do what's best for everyone, with no one making sure it knew what the best really was. That we needed free will. We needed to take risks. We're humans. We're curious beings, annoyingly so, and we need to explore to survive, to thrive.

"I expected your return," the Central Guidance said, indicating a large bag lying on its side in the alley. "We have the trash you requested. So long as you leave without any further incident, you can have it and anything else you need. But is it clear to you why things must stay as they are? Change would be dangerous for us all."

"But—"

"Come on, Zander," I hissed, leaning close to him. "We don't have the time."

"But I can fix this!"

"There's nothing for you to fix," I said. "Kork and his crew have been here. They'll return with the Alliance. Contact will be made, and they will handle this thing. In the meantime, everyone here is safe. Right? After all, they're ... protected."

Zander glared at me for a split second before his expression softened. He returned his gaze to the High Director.

"You were willing to give us the First Chair," he said, coolly.

"Yes," the director replied. "A small loss. But you may take the boy, if you so choose. Seeing as how attached you seem to him."

"No!" Nim's hands clutched into fists at his side. His no came out small and muffled, but still angry. "Father!"

"Take him, and let this be over," the Central Guidance insisted.

"Why did you let us take him away from you?" I asked. "You could have stopped him anytime. And yet you let him leave and expected us to return, too. Why complicate things?"

"I wanted you to know the truth," the High Director said.

"Bullshit," Zander spat. "You couldn't control him, could you? Even before he left your range, you couldn't get into his head. The second you tried to override your people over breakfast, you realized he was a threat. That's why you put him in jail with us. You *wanted* us to take him away. He's a threat."

"But what if he wants to stay?" I said. "Nim doesn't want to leave. You can't force him to go with us."

"Let me show you what waits for him if he were to stay," Central said. The high director blinked suddenly, like he had just realized he was supposed to talk. He looked around quickly, a little perturbed by the change in scenery, but, catching a glimpse of us, he said nothing.

"You!" he said to Zander, storming forward. "How did you get out of your cell? And what have you done to my son?"

"Father, I am fine," said Nim, stepping between his father and Zander. But the High Director seemed not to hear him.

"If you've dropped his grade by even a single number, I swear—"

"Father, I am fine." Nim tugged at his father's shoulder, but the man didn't seem to notice.

"Do you see this?" the First Chair said, with the unmistakable coolness of Central Guidance. "The boy is invisible to them. They will not register a word he says, anything he does, but I will make the loss easier on them. Ask them about young Nimien; go on."

"Just take your trash and leave," the high director said with venom in his voice. "Don't bother coming back. We will not speak with you again."

"Thank you, sir," Zander said, as calmly as he could. "And I am sorry. I hope you find your son."

"My son?" The high director laughed. "Whatever are you talking about? We do not know our progeny here. I'm quite sure I'm not the father of a child."

My heart flipped in my chest before sinking to the floor. The words hit Nim like a sword stabbing him through his gut. He fell to his knees, looking up at the man who had once been his father, trembling.

"You're a monster," Zander said to Central Guidance. "I've met many AI, but you mark an entirely new lot. You actually believe you're helping these people."

"But I am. All disease is eradicated. People live long, fulfilling lives. They are safe. They feel no hate, or anger, or sadness. I take away their pain. You would like me, you know, Zander. I did as you asked—I read up on you, and I am pretty sure no one person can carry that burden alone. Join with me. Let me help you."

"Oh, we're out of here," he snapped. "Two, Kork, get the trash."

"They're letting us go, just like that?" Kork asked. "I'm not sure what I just saw—"

"We'll tell you everything when we get out of here," Zander said, baring his teeth to the High director. "We're not coming back, but more will come. And they will want to speak to you."

"Let them come," he said. "All are welcome here."

"If you really believe that," said Zander, "I'm quite worried about the state of your processor after all these years, CG. Come, Nim, we need to go."

Nimien took one last sorrowful look at his father then stood up. He wasn't crying. He didn't even look mad. Like the faces in the crowd, he was an empty shell, a husk of a human being.

We turned our backs on the lost colony and left the city the way we came, with two bags of trash and a boy whose entire civilization had just forgotten him. None of us looked back.

Not even Nim.

CHAPTER EIGHTEEN
SO MANY EGOS, SO LITTLE TIME

It didn't feel like the triumphant homecoming we had expected. Not that we wanted one, but it would have been nice, after all we'd been though.

We hadn't failed in our mission, but we had failed an entire civilization. I felt a whole lot of new respect for the Prime Directive.

Nim didn't hesitate to step out of the pneumatic door. He sighed heavily, emptying his lungs of the old, stagnant air he had been breathing and filled them with the air of the world that had been taken from him. He coughed.

We shut the door behind us, not that it was any use. The seal was broken, and it didn't seem like anyone would come to repair it. Unless the Central whatever sent someone to patch things up, using them like a puppet. I shuddered at the thought.

"Is it me, or is this AI-turning-bad becoming a common thread in my life?" I asked Zander as we started down the stairs together.

"Two very old systems turning bad in the same week? Probably not a coincidence."

"It might have been years since Da-Duhui, though," I pointed out with a shudder, "and there's no connection between the two. This shouldn't happen. They should be isolated cases."

"You sound a whole lot like Blayde right now," said Zander.

"Not sure if that's a compliment."

"You decide," he said, but his smile told me he meant nothing by it. His sister was golden in his eyes. Compliment it was then. "I guess putting AIs in charge of things was a popular mandate a few millennia ago. Luckily, Central Guidance really does want the best for its people, even if its methods are not to be envied. The Alliance will put things right."

"You're trusting the Alliance with these people? Having them in charge might be worse."

"How so?" Zander's tone went cold. "Look, I'm not saying I like everything they do. But it's an Alliance, not an empire. Planets join because there is strength in numbers. The universe is a big, scary place, and having friends out there is the only chance for survival. The Alliance isn't some dark force bending people to their will. They're just an alliance."

"One that thinks shooting fake war videos will help their people join an army. And I'm sure that army isn't knocking on people's doors and politely asking them if they've heard of their Lord and Savior Derzan, or if they'd kindly want to sign up to join a huge planetary union."

"Sally," said Zander, "you're absolutely right. But you can't just call any interstellar pact threatening. It's a complex political system that spans countries, planets, and solar systems. There are more races involved than you have even met, and they all have a different idea of diplomacy. There is nothing purely good or purely evil in the universe—only a matter of perspective. For now, I have enough respect in the Alliance that I think they can handle this situation in a way that makes everybody content. Maybe not happy, but content."

"This is coming from the man who likes to blow things up," I said, "and who takes down people in an instant."

"Those people were immediate threats, one of which was trying to enslave Killians for his own personal greed."

"And Matt got him both times."

"And the other was controlled by an AI and was trying to take over a planet. Pretty sure we can both agree I did the right thing there."

"Yup."

"Then what are we arguing about?"

"We're not arguing," I said. "We're having a civil conversation about our rights to intervene in the goings-on of the universe. It's constructive."

"If you say so."

"Anything to keep me from going back there and giving that Central Guidance asswipe a piece of my mind."

Zander grinned, a wide smile I hadn't seen in ages. I missed my friend. I missed the effortless conversations in my living room, watching Netflix and eating snacks. I missed the ease of having someone who just wanted to fit in on a new planet and do his job right, rather than one who was some kind of interstellar vigilante.

I missed the old Zander from two years ago. Sometimes I just wanted for us to play some *Mario Kart* again.

We walked down the stairs to terra firma, and I realized how much I loved dirt. After all that concrete, having grass and gravel underneath my feet felt good. I ran my hand through the overgrown weeds surrounding the dome.

Nim was amazed by it all. He walked on unsteady feet through the tall grasses, not used to uneven ground. His hands had to touch, to feel the world around him, his long dainty fingers running through everything he could. He touched the foundation wall with a hand, pulling it back quickly. The cold, dead surface of the dome looked out of place in this natural world, and I think he was glad to leave that much behind.

"Oy, there you are!" Jezeal's voice rose over the field, pulling me out of my reverie. He crossed two of his arms over his chest as he stood at the door of the hopper. "We were beginning to think you were never coming back."

"What could I possibly find that's better than your company?" asked Kork, hoisting the bag of trash over his shoulder and marching toward the little craft. "Oh, I know: anything."

"Har-dee-har-har," the alien scoffed. "Come on, we

don't have all day."

"What the outlands is that?" Nim froze, and I wasn't sure what he was reacting to. Maybe he was finally looking—as opposed to staring at the grass and plants—and seeing the monstrously huge gas giant dangling in the sky, or maybe it was the sight of a giant spider man that got him nervous. Jezeal stared at the boy in shock.

"Holy *shit*," he said, scratching his head. "You found another human? Wait, why is he here"

"It's a long story," said Kork, taking the trash to the back of the ship. "Two, you're with me. I need you to fix the tank."

"Already done, Captain," said Jezeal, peeling his eyes from Nim long enough to smirk at Kork. "You guys were gone for so long, I was beginning to think I was going to have to do everything myself."

"Well ... thanks." Kork lowered his voice and hung his head, like it was embarrassing to say. Jezeal's mouth formed a shocked, yet pleased, smile.

"What? Do my ears deceive me? Is the Captain actually acknowledging that I, Ter Gabre'el Saar, can do a good job without him?"

"Who?" asked Kork.

Jezeal's smile faded. "Ter Gabre'el Saar. Me. Wait, you've known me for how many years, and you didn't know my name was Ter Gabre'el Saar? You thought I was ... Jezeal?"

"It's how you introduced yourself!"

"I can't believe this!" Jezeal's face turned a dark purple. "You came to my wedding. I played your wingman so many nights I've lost count. Crandle, get a load of the captain!"

"Oh god, you knuckleheads are finally back then?" Crandle stepped out of the hopper, grinning wildly. "Good lord! Finally! You three must have been out of your minds leaving me alone with him. He talks. He just won't ... stop ... talking!"

"Oh hello, Crandle," Kork said. "I was under the impression you were recovering from a broken leg. Where the hell were you?"

"In the droid's cupboard." She slapped the hull of the ship in its general location. "It's nice and dark and quiet. I needed a goddamn nap."

"I would implore you not to use the Lord's name in vain," said Two.

"Oh, you would, would you?" she snapped. "Well, I don't care all that much for your Derzan, droid. And I don't think you have any say in the way I use it. I'll use the gods' names in vain all I want. I'm pretty sure they're happy for the attention."

"But, ma'am—"

"Who's the kid?" she asked, crossing her hands over her chest.

"Ah, yes, that's Nim," said Kork.

"Nimien is coming with us," said Zander, placing his hands on the boy's shoulders. Nim shook them off.

"Why?" asked Crandle, not taking her eyes off the kid.

"It's a long story," he replied, "but to cut it short, we screwed things up with his people. They won't have him back."

"So they gave you some trash and this kid," she said. "Tells me he's not worth all that much to them. Why does it matter if we take him or not?"

"Because he happens to be an intelligent young man," Zander said, glaring at her. "How many other reasons do you want?"

"Whatever," she shrugged. "I'm not the captain. If Kork says we're keeping him, then we're keeping him. We'll let the crew deal with him when we meet back up with them. Does he speak a lick of Pyrenean?"

"Nope."

"Well then, welcome to the show, kid." She grinned at Nim, a smile so reptilian it reminded me of Marcy's pet snake from when we were kids.

"All the repairs have been completed," said Two, stepping away from the back of the hopper. "Let us take this time to thank Derzan through prayer."

"If we do, will you shut up about Derzan for two minutes?" asked Kork.

"Wait, phrase that correctly," Zander insisted. "He is a droid, after all."

"Fine," said Kork, rolling his eyes. "If we join you in prayer, will you stop talking about Derzan and trying to convert us until we reconnect the two halves of the *Traveler*?"

"If you command it, then of course."

"Well, I command it."

"Then of course."

"Fantastic," said the captain, "so let's pray."

Kork glanced around the party, making it evident that we were dutifully obligated to join in the exercise. Zander rolled his eyes but held his hands, palms upward, all the same. Well, I guessed that meant we were actually doing this.

I mimicked his move, catching out of the corner of

my eyes the sly movement of our recently kidnapped friend. He didn't speak our language, and no one had hooked him up with a translator. All the same, he held out his hands; he was nothing if not astute. He would be a fast learner.

"Oh, Great Derzan, who is above us," the droid droned. "We praise you for ensuring our safe return. For blessing us with a new compatriot. For not smiting us at the five opportunities you had to strike us down. It honors me to honor you. And please do not cast down my friends, as they have not accepted your words into their headspace. But it is only because they are of inferior programming—"

"Okay, time's up," said Kork, dropping his hands.

"Amen," said Two, and we joined him, mumbling. It struck me as odd that Derzan was supposed to be loving yet wanted to smite us, but I wasn't going to ask the droid any questions, fearing a prolonged excursion into the realms of robotic beliefs.

"All right, everyone into the hopper. We're getting out of this"—he looked slowly at Nim¬¬—"place."

"Finally," groaned Crandle, half-limping inside. Jezeal was quick to follow.

"May I ask who we are meant to be worshipping?" asked Nim, who held back, giving the little shuttle a disconcerting look. He was shivering. Still without an adequate shirt, his puckered red scar was probably giving him grief. If Two hadn't been reset, he probably would have been able to help Nim.

"Let's see if I can give you the Cliffs Notes," I said. "Kork hit Two in the head. Killed him. Zander repaired him. He woke up believing in an almighty being named

Derzan. We ran with it as we don't have the time or the skills needed to fix him, and putting up with a bit of attempted conversion is a lot easier than trying to get things done with no droids at all. Not that I'd know, seeing as he's the first droid I've met. Okay, not such a long story, in the end."

"Your crew ... you must have so many adventures, so many stories." Nim smiled. "Just like in the tales of old."

"They do," I said, "but I only met them yesterday."

Nim's eyes widened. "So the whole ... droid returning from the dead, that happened ..."

"About two hours before we met you."

"Well, all right then." Nim didn't seem to know what to think, so he smiled. I smiled back. I guessed, when it came down to it, we were the least savvy on the crew when it came to all things space. It was a nice not to be the least knowledgeable in the room, for a change.

It was nice to have someone in the same shit as me.

"You two coming or what?" asked Zander, sticking his head out of the hopper. "We could very well leave without you."

Nim looked terrified and practically flew to the shuttle, taking Zander at his word. I trotted to keep up.

"It's humor, Nim," I said, trying to ease him with a smile. "We're a crew. We stick together. We wouldn't leave without a single member."

"Correction," said Two, fixating his empty eyes on me. "Do you not recall, Fa Webber, when you were willing to leave me in the Aorian city as a tribute and collateral?"

"That was different. It was planned, and a mission

would have been dispatched to pick you up as soon as possible. Right, folks?"

There were non-committal groans from the two other men on our sub team, who were having another staring contest for the right to pilot us back to the *Traveler*. It was only after I sat between Crandle and Nim, and fastened my seatbelt nice and tight this time, that Kork backed down and allowed Zander to be the pilot.

With Two standing comfortably in his cupboard and Ter holding back the rolling unbitrium ball, we were ready for takeoff. But the shuttle wasn't going anywhere.

"We're good back here," said Ter. "What's the holdup?"

"Marcoli's gone native," said Zander nonchalantly.

"Pardon?"

The shuttle door unsealed itself, and Zander sprang from the cockpit, flying back outside. Kork followed, all color drained from his face. Two pressed on the door of his cupboard, and the captain slammed it shut, locking it. Rhythmic thumping from inside told me the confused android was still trying to get out.

I didn't think the day could get any more confusing, but Marcoli was outside the shuttle, wearing a loincloth and standing before three of the tusked creatures from earlier. His expression was stoic as I stepped out of the shuttle, his eyes riveted on Kork.

The captain nervously cleared his throat. "Hey, Marcoli."

"I no longer go by that name," he replied. "You may call me Zimeon. It is my forest name."

"Ah, cool," Kork replied. "And, um, what's going on?"

"I've come to tell you to call off your search for me," he said, with more confidence than I'd seen in a child his age. "I will not be flying back on the *Traveler* with you. The people of the One Purple Leaf have accepted me into their community. I've been invited to stay."

"The… One Purple Leaf?" asked Ter, sputtering.

"That's fantastic, Marc- I mean Zimeon," said Kork, smiling an eager smile, not mentioning the fact that no one had bothered to look for him.

The hulking beasts behind the child formerly known as Marcoli trumpeted together.

"When the ship crashed, that stupid chip of yours short-circuited," he said. "I'm never going back to the Alliance. Here, I am free. The people of the One Purple Leaf are generous and kind. They took me in the moment they found me. I have a home here. Don't try to force me to return."

"I wouldn't dream of it," said Kork. "I'm happy you're happy."

The three beasts suddenly scrambled backward, tusks and braids flying in the air. I turned around—Nim had gotten curious and stepped out of the shuttle. The people of the One Purple Leaf seemed shocked by this–terrified, even.

"What is it, Kimber?" asked Zimeon, glaring at Nim, who retreated back into the shuttle. The people of the One Purple Leaf were a little more alien than Ter ever was.

The beast lowered its head, letting Zimeon climb on its tusk all the way up to his mouth. The child pulled the long sloppy hair away from the beast's lips.

"First ones," said Kimber. The beast could speak–in

a thick Australian accent, no less. "We don't get many of your kind outside of the bubble anymore. This one seems too young to be part of an expedition."

"You speak Uni?" Nim dipped his head out of the shuttle. "How…?"

"Our ancestors were forced from their colonies before the terraforming was complete," said Kimber. "They adapted, so we could thrive. Every once and a while, one of your people leaves your bubble long enough to see if the planet is ready for them, but they're never accepted back into the fold. Did this happen to you?"

"Yes," said Nim.

"Are they speaking the same language?" Kork stammered. "This is surreal."

"Ugh, I don't even care anymore," said Crandle. "Wake me up when everything goes back to normal."

"You may stay with us, if you wish," continued Kimber. "We are a peaceful people. You will find calm with us; no ratings or rankings, only calm."

Nim looked up at our motley crew, then back at the beast. He smiled weakly.

"I think I'm going to stay with them," he said to the alien. "I want to see the universe. I want to know everything there is to possibly know."

"Fare thee well, then, child of the bubble," Kimber replied, placing Zimeon back on the ground, letting the hair fall neatly before its mouth once again. "Bathtub gate carpet, ukulele."

So much for my translator being universal. I guessed mumbling wasn't in its vocabulary.

We took off into the sunny sky.

Nim stared out the back window as the pristine landscape blurred beneath us. I didn't know what was more overwhelming for him: the trees, the grass, the greenery, or the simple act of flying. I knew I was wrapped up by the two. It wasn't every day you flew a shuttle pod over an alien planet.

I sure was glad to see that snow globe fade into a speck behind us.

"How long until the eclipse?" asked Ter.

"It's morning, Jez," said Kork from the cockpit. "We've got hours before the planet even gets close to the sun."

"It's Mara," said Nim, slowly, and to my surprise, everyone looked at him with awe. "We call the planet Mara."

Why did his voice sound so different all of a sudden? It took me a second to realize what had happened, but when I did, I did a double take.

"Did you just speak Pyrenean?" Crandle stammered. "But—"

"I am learning," he said, a twinge of pride in his trembling tone. "Slow ... slow speaking makes it easier."

"How are you doing this?" I asked, amazed that he was adapting faster than I could have believed possible. He shrugged, lightly.

"Our languages have common roots, and I'm a good listener."

"If you say so," I replied.

I leaned back in my seat and watched the sky fly by. By the time we got back to the *Traveler*, the sun had risen over the hills, basking the ship in a pool of white light.

We landed in the hangar bay, Zander bringing the hopper in backward to get the unbitrium sphere as close to the elevator as he could. Nim's hands were pressed against the glass as he watched the ship roll by. I would have been right up there with him if I wasn't belted in.

The second we landed and the door released, Crandle dashed off the hopper, never to be seen again. Okay, she was found pretty quickly, but it was an impressive disappearing act while it lasted.

"Ah, the intrepid crew." Blayde's voice was sharp and harsh, echoing through the emptiness. I could practically see the snarky look on her face. "You were gone for ages. One more hour and I would have sent a search party. Emphasis on the party."

"Well, we always come through in the end, isn't that right?" said Kork, but she wasn't having any of it.

Slam. The entire rear of the hopper fell open, and there she was, her uniform stained with oil and one of the sleeves charred entirely off, holding the remote to our small ship's docking door. She dropped it, the little box swinging on its bungee back into place. She stared us all down, calculating.

"You left with five people," she said, "and came back with a unbitrium sphere, two extra humans and—and where the hell is Crandle?"

"I implore you, do not speak of hell in such a—" Two started, but Zander put a hand over his mechanized mouth as he marched back to greet Blayde.

"Nice to see you too, Blayde," he said. "Crandle's not

missing. I'm surprised you didn't see her on your way down here. She rushed out of the shuttle the second it landed. Now, this one over here is Two; he's a droid. He's a firm believer in Derzan and will tell you everything about it. And this here is Nim. He's from the lost Aorian race and was abandoned by his people."

"Wait, *the* Aorians? As in the lost colony?"

"Can we keep him?"

"Can you what now?" Blayde said, blinking slowly. "Zander. We're not *keeping* a human child. We already have one. "

"I'm quite fine, thanks for asking," I said. "Also, not a child!"

"You leave us for almost twenty hours—"Blayde sighed—"and in that time, you manage to ... what? Contact a lost colony of humans and kidnap one of their children?"

"Basically, yeah," said Zander, "but he's okay with it. Right, Nim?"

"I'll adjust."

"You see? He'll adjust!" Zander patted Nim on the back. "And I almost forgot to mention: Remember Marcoli? He's been adopted by aliens. He's very happy."

"Well, that's a relief."

"And look on the bright side: We've got an extra few pairs of hands to get the unbitrium from the hangar bay to the thermal chamber. Right?"

"Well, even with everyone here, you're not going to like the next part," said Blayde. "The crash messed a few things up."

"Like what?" asked Kork, walking up beside Zander and looking Blayde square in the eye. Not a good idea—he looked away quickly—her expression said it all.

"Like what?" he asked again.

Blayde was right; we didn't like the answer. Not one bit.

CHAPTER NINETEEN

FIXING ALL OF OUR MESSES, OR, AT LEAST, GETTING A HEAD START ON THEM

Let me tell you what happens when a spaceship splits in half.

The Alliance has incredible, vast fleets. Their engineers are always finding ways to improve their speed, their strength, their resistance. Space is a dangerous place, even more so when you're an immeasurable military power, and safety is their number one priority.

That and firepower. *Wa-pow!*

The ship is made in such a way that if any enemy fleet were to split it in half with a well-aimed blow, both sides could survive on their own. This is supposed to ensure that no matter what happens, the largest amount of people survive. If your ship split in two and life support wasn't on your side, you would be screwed. But with this setup, everyone's okay. Yay!

Well, in our case, we got the end with the bridge, but the main engines were in the half still in space. But that was okay. We had backup engines that had gotten us this far, whether we liked it or not. But to burn the unbitrium, we had to get it to the backup location and dump it there.

But you know what shuts down when a ship splits in half?

The elevators.

Not sure why they decided to use one long shaft along the entirety of the ship; I guessed it made things faster when it was all in one piece. But when it was split in two, nope, those things were out of commission. There were tubes leading right into space.

"And where is this backup generator?" Kork asked, crossing his arms over his chest. Blayde wasn't having any of his attitude, though.

"Five floors up, and we're rolling at a ten percent incline," she replied. "Come on, we've got enough manpower to do it. And the sooner we drop that big ole ball into the fire, the sooner we can get off this stinkin' planet and save your friends. No offense, kid."

"None taken," said Nim, "but could you ... not ... call me kid?"

"But you are a—never mind. Nim's the name, right?"

"Nimien, but I guess Nim is all right."

"Good," said Blayde. "Nim, don't wander off. Sally, you keep an eye on him."

"Okay, sure," I replied. This was better than ball-rolling duty.

Blayde, Zander, and Kork were the ones to roll the unbitrium in the end. It wasn't a hard decision to make. I'm sure Ter was as relieved as I was to not have to push that sphere again.

They rolled it out the back and around the hopper, but there was a slight angle to the floor, and the unbitrium slipped from their hands and escaped them in less than a minute. It rolled down the hangar bay and slammed into the wall. The sphere was fine. The wall, however, looked like a truck had slammed into it.

The rest of the afternoon was a hubbub of frustrated yells from everyone to anyone as we struggled to get the sphere to the generator. Turns out, three people were not enough to roll it upstairs, nor were seven. Two, Ter, Nim, and I all tried to help as best we could, but soon it was all hands-on deck. Doesso and Finch appeared; even Crandle returned, wearing a clean uniform and with a freshly washed face. Her leg, it seemed, was fully healed.

Here's a lesson for you all: More people does not make a job any more efficient. In fact, every person who joined us seemed to slow us down. More wailing about making the job more efficient was done than actual attempts to get the job completed, and it was getting awful.

"Let me," said Jurrah. She was dressed in a blue-striped uniform. All the gel was gone from her skin, yet she still seemed to glow. Blayde, who was pushing the ball up another step, froze at the sight of her.

"You should not be on your feet," she said to Jurrah.

"I haven't used them for decades. I should get a chance to, before I put them on hold again."

"You shouldn't be able to use them," said Blayde. "You need rest, Jurrah."

"What I need is to get my ship back in the sky. I'll do anything I can to help."

"You can leave that to me."

"Then push!" Zander snapped, glaring at her. "We're hanging on the edge here."

"Move, Jurrah," said Blayde, giving her a cool look. "If you want to help, get navigation back online."

"I did that already."

"Then you've done all you can. We've got this."

With a powerful heave, Blayde shoved the sphere up another step and didn't stop. She kept pushing, the sphere going up and up without pause. The assisting crew stepped out of the way as the massive ball of unbitrium reached the next landing.

What was going on between those two? How much had we missed on our excursion? I stared at my feet; it was impolite to stare, after all. This was their problem, and I didn't want to get involved in Blayde's personal issues.

"I've got the door," Jurrah said, stepping out and holding it open for them to roll the ball through.

"Right, folks, it's all uphill from here!" said Blayde, somewhat gleefully, ignoring Jurrah so completely it were as if she didn't exist. The sphere rolled through, flush with the doorjamb. Impressive.

The slant of the ship was slight enough that when you were inside, it was barely noticeable, especially with no windows. But the sphere kept trying to roll backward when we shoved it up. Kork tapped out, and Two took his place. Ter laid his hands on the ball when we were halfway up, and slowly, as a team, we pushed the unbitrium up to the generator.

The backup generator room lit up as we entered. It was pure white and like that creepy room from *Charlie and the Chocolate Factory* that took Mike Teavee out of the competition. The walls practically glowed. Right in the center was a large, round pillar with another door in it.

"Damn," said Zander, looking up at the ceiling. "I always wondered how you guys kept your combustion rooms so pristine. Every other ship I've been in was covered in grime."

"You should see the other one," said Finch, opening the control panel on the side of the pillar. "This one's basically a set. Never been put to real use."

"Oh, I almost forgot about this whole thing being a fraud," he said. "It'll still work, right?"

"If I have my way," Finch chuckled. "Just be glad the crew hired someone with real talent."

Kork stayed silent through all this. I guessed the real deal didn't always have to make himself heard. He didn't have anything to prove.

Except, maybe, to Zander.

The door in the pillar slid open, and with one last push, the unbitrium rolled into the heart of it. Finch typed in a few controls on his panel, and the ball was sucked away, never to be seen again.

"And ... we have ignition!" he said, a grin growing on his face. He needn't have said anything; We would have known either way, as the lights flickered and the air blew harder through the vents. A low hum reverberated under my feet and surrounded me, like the ship was coming alive.

The room erupted in cheers. Engines online; life support online; shields online. We would be able to fly once more. We were safe, and the hardest part of this insane mission was over.

Jurrah clapped her hands in glee, holding them over her tight lips. Her ship, her home, was living once again.

"So, the captain and the crew ... everyone here is in a televised folly?"

I nodded slowly. Nim and I were strapped into our chairs on the bridge, and the rest of the crew slowly joined us. Outside the window was a beautiful vista of mountains and forests, though the dirt was piled so high over the front window it covered most of the view. The newest addition to our small team trembled visibly.

"It's a little more complicated than that," I said, "but don't worry. Once we've taken off and reconnected with the rest of the crew, you'll be in good hands. They know what they're doing." Well, after we defeated the Consortium ships that lay in wait, yeah.

"And what will they do?" he asked. "With me, I mean?"

"Well, I—" I realized that I had no idea. I had been running around with an Alliance crew, wearing an Alliance uniform, trying as hard as I could to make it look like I knew what I was doing, but I still didn't know what was going on.

I was as much as a fraud as the rest of them.

"You'll probably get into the child-hire program," said Doesso, strapping herself next to Nim. "Marcoli got to be on TV, so you know it has to be good."

I shuddered. Nim was smart, quick-witted, and

possibly a genius. He would be wasted on a program like that. With a new chip in his head, it would be as if he never left the snow globe, just replacing one form of mind control for another.

"That sounds good," he smiled weakly. "I'll be able to see the universe."

"That bit's nowhere near as glamorous as they say, trust me," said Doesso, laughing gaily. "Space gets incredibly boring very fast."

"All right then," said Kork, taking a seat in his raised captain's chair. "Is everyone here?"

He glanced around the room, taking his small team into account. Doesso and Finch; Ter and Crandle; Zander and Blayde; Jurrah, Nim, Two, and me. Our little starship crew.

He sat down, bringing up the controls on his chair arm, lips pursed as he read through the readouts. A ship like this wasn't meant to touch a planet's surface, and while the engineers who had built it had a system to get back to space, it wasn't going to be pleasant.

"Jurrah," said Kork, his nose twitching ever so slightly, "aren't you supposed to be, I don't know, astrogating?"

"My chamber is compromised. All guidance is manual until it can be repaired."

"Then what were you all doing while we were gone?"

"While you were having your gay romp through the forest, we were fixing essential systems," said Blayde, spinning her chair around to face him and stopping it with a harsh squeak, "so we could get your asses back into space. The ship can be piloted on manual, so Jurrah's chamber was deemed non-essential. That, and there was no more gel."

"And the gel is key," Jurrah agreed.

Kork let out a heavy sigh. "Fine. Does anyone here know how to pilot on manual?"

There was a low rumble through the crew. Crandle looked at him with actual, wide-eyed shock.

"Um, Captain," she said, "*you* are supposed to be certified."

"Not for taking off from a planet's surface in a ship that's never supposed to enter an atmosphere. So, let's move past that and figure out who the hell is going to drive."

Nobody answered. Nim dropped his head into his hands and groaned. I felt bad for him. Heck, I felt *as* bad as him. This was not only annoying but freaking embarrassing.

"Can you fly a ship?" Jurrah asked Blayde.

"Me?" she whispered. "No. Can you?" She continued staring into space, spinning her chair around like a bored child. Jurrah looked away awkwardly.

"Not from planet either."

"So, what do we do?" Crandle asked, crossing her arms in annoyance. She was doing everything in her power to avoid looking at her captain and failing miserably.

"I'll fly it," said Zander.

Blayde laughed. "When did you learn how to fly?"

"Hey, I've always wanted a spaceship," he said, practically shoving Kork from the chair. He settled himself in, grinning confidently. His hands rested over the arm controls.

"That doesn't mean you can fly one," Blayde said.

"Will you relax? I *have* flown ships like this before."

"Show off," she muttered.

He closed his eyes. For a second, it didn't look like anything was happening, but then a light flickered in midair, hovering right before his face. It became clearer, and a graph came to life and then another, until the air in front of him was full of floating images.

"Always wanted to do that," he said. "Looks like all systems are good; everyone should probably grab a seat."

Kork grumbled as he took the extra chair next to Crandle. She had her eyes firmly shut, clinging to the desk before her, though we had not yet moved.

Zander twitched one finger in the air, a tiny swipe of the digit, almost unnoticeable. Instantly, the motor was a lion, the roar was so vicious and violent it was as if the ship was hunting, about to pounce. We could feel it edging to move, to run, to fly. I pushed myself tighter into the chair.

"Now, we go." His fingers were lightning, moving faster than the eyes could see, blurring in my vision and controlling every movement of the ship with tiny finger twitches, jerks, and motions.

The dirt slid down the window. I could feel the ship trembling deep into my bones, the vibration so strong it could have shattered me. I clutched the seat tighter. The ship rose straight up, fighting against the pull of the planet's gravity. If the ship was going to shake any harder, I would be reduced to dust. I bit down on my teeth to keep them from chattering, but grinding didn't help.

"Blayde," Zander said, his voice heavy. "Can you pull up the lieutenant's post; I need eyes on obstacles so you can adjust our trajectory if I mess up."

"Of course," she replied, instantly in position. I half-expected a quip or a joke, but she was dead serious. "I'm going to need the coordinates."

"I have them," Jurrah sputtered. "Let me enter them for you."

"Then I need you all to hold on tight," Zander said.

The ship sprung from its chains, shooting though space faster than any Earth-made craft could. I was shoved against my seat, my eyes sealed shut in pure terror. The engines roared around me. My ears were in pain, and my heart pumped frantically as it fought the force of our acceleration.

And in less than a minute, it was over.

Darkness surrounded us. Well, darkness with a scattering of stars. Nim's home world was set squarely behind us, and ahead was a universe of possibilities.

"Piece of cake," said Zander, completely casual. He dropped the screens, stood up, and stretched.

"But we're not there," said Kork, rising to his feet and glaring at Zander. "All you did was take off."

"I got us off the planet and set us on the right trajectory," Zander replied, lifting his eyebrows at the captain. "So, sure, that was *all* that I did."

"We're not even close to the other ship!" said Kork. "We can't move faster than light without an astrogator. We don't even have access to those systems!"

"I have set the ship to retrace our path here," Jurrah said, turning around to face them. "We can take established warp conduits. They're safe paths that even non-Astrogator-enabled ships can take. We'll have short segments of inertial speeds in-between them, but it will not be a long journey."

"How long?" Kork asked.

"Half a day."

"Oh. I thought that—the way you phrased that—no matter, a day is good. Very good! You'll be able to handle it?"

"It's what I do, Captain."

"I'll stay with her," said Blayde, looking at the woman with wonder. "I'll be her backup."

"Good, then," he said, a little shakily, but obviously pleased. "I'll be in my quarters if anyone needs me."

He looked at me, and our eyes met and, for a second, I thought maybe those words were meant for me. But then he walked away, too quickly, taking the door off the bridge and letting it shut quickly behind him.

"Well, that was surprisingly uneventful." Crandle grimaced, finally letting her eyes open. "I for one am quite glad we didn't blow up. Anyone want to grab a drink in the break room?"

"Hell yeah," said Finch, unbuckling himself and standing in one swift motion. "Let's get wasted!"

"Or just ... well-snacked," said Ter, smiling as he joined them.

"Derzan does not abide by this," said Two.

"Come on, you can tell us all about him," said Ter.

"We need to do something about Xacrelf," said Crandle. In an instant, the joy was zapped out of the room.

All at once, we remembered we were only in this mess because someone on board was a killer, a traitor. We remembered we were returning not to a crew excited to be reunited, but to a trap filled with enemy ships.

We were returning to our doom.

"Let's get that drink," said Finch, slowly, "and then we can talk about the mess we're in." He wrapped an arm over the droid's shoulders and led him out of the room. The crew followed, less excited than they had been, but still happy they had not died. Nim watched them go.

"Hey, you should join them," I suggested. "Get to know some people."

"I'm not sure ..."

"The rest of the ship is empty," I said. "If you don't like them, then you can grab any bunk you want and take a well-deserved nap. Or bath. Or whatever. If you want to touch-up the hair—"

"I'm going to let it grow." He smiled, running his hand over the fuzz on his scalp. "I always wanted to know what it would feel like to have hair."

"Ter will probably tell you all about it."

Nim laughed, and I was surprised to see him looking happy after everything he had been through. He followed the crew to the break room.

"You should take your own advice," said Blayde, scanning me with those piercing green eyes of hers.

"I don't feel like socializing right now." I turned to watch the stars glide in front of the large bridge window.

"Well, what do you feel like doing?" she asked, coolly.

"I'm not quite sure."

"Well, figure out what it is, and go for it." She looked at Jurrah before returning her gaze to me. "This might be the last time you get a chance to do what you want. Take your freedom and run with it."

"You know what, Blayde?" I said, looking at the closed door to the left of the bridge. "I think I will."

CHAPTER TWENTY
I GET MY FLIRT ON

The captain's quarters were, in a word, beautiful.

In many other words, it was as if I had walked into another world entirely. What had just a minute ago been a world of chrome and glass was now reminiscent of a medieval castle. Behind the sliding door that ensured the captain's privacy were wood paneling and a carpeted floor; and a gentle, warm light to contrast the heavy fluorescents of the crew hallways.

I was no longer on a ship; I was in a castle. And I was on my way to see the king.

Kork's quarters might have been lavish, but they were still small and utilitarian. The hallway was short and served only to connect the captain's room to his private bathroom and then to the bridge. I walked past one door and knocked on the one I assumed was his bedroom.

I turned out to be right.

"Enter," came a voice from the other side. Kork's voice. Exactly who I wanted to hear.

Please be in here alone; please be in here alone; please be in here alone ...

Someone must have been looking out for me; I got my wish. The door slid open to reveal an inviting room, a small suite with couches in front of a large window. A closed door in the back led to the bedroom.

Kork flushed, making eye contact for just long enough that it brought heat to my face.

"Ah, Sally," he said, brushing imaginary dirt off his uniform. "What brings you here?"

"Curiosity. Sorry." I stepped inside so the door could close. "I wanted to see if you were okay. That, and I wanted to see how a starship captain lived on a ship as glorious as the *Traveler*."

"You know you don't have to act that way for my sake." He rolled his eyes. All bumbling awkwardness, or forced ego, from the trip to the planet was gone now. He looked like a person, rather than a captain.

And a very handsome person at that. He had cleaned himself up, shaved, and changed into a new uniform. He smelled so good that his musk—natural or cologne, I did not know—wafted across the room to greet me. I breathed it in; it was the most comforting smell I could imagine, a combination of sea salt and fresh flowers.

"You can be yourself in here," he said, pointing at the mini bar. "The cameras are never rolling. Would you like something to drink?"

"I'm new to this," I said, nervously. "What do you have?"

"For a lady from Earth, I would recommend the purple stuff I can't pronounce and won't embarrass myself trying to," he said, holding up a bottle. "Imagine someone made wine but out of pineapple. And it's purple. I quite like it. It goes down easily."

"Why, Captain Kork, are you trying to get me drunk?" I asked, trying to project an air of confidence. But, truth was, I hadn't come to the captain's room to admit that I had caught a case of the feelings. I didn't want to come off too strong.

"Well, if milady can't handle her alien liquor, then milady has no business being onboard a spaceship." He chuckled then handed me a small sip of the purple drink.

I drank it, and it was not as strong as I had expected. It reminded me of medicine from when I was a kid. I shook my head in disgust.

"Sorry!" he said earnestly, the sexy facade fading quickly. "Here, let me get you some water. I have some fruit juice instead. That stuff tastes amazing."

He reached under the bar and handed me a bottle of water, which I chugged.. It cleansed my mouth faster than mouthwash, and now, when he handed me a glass of off-white liquid, I was a little more hesitant.

He served himself a glass as well.

"You'll love this," he said excitedly. "It's from a plant that only ripens during solar eclipses on ... Betrivius, I think it was. The locals gave us bottles of the stuff after saving their cities from a particularly dangerous asteroid storm. I've been rationing it: it tastes like the nectar of the gods."

I took his lead as he drank, and oh my god, was he right. The juice tasted like liquid chocolate fudge, but it was light on the tongue like milk. It was magical.

"You like it?" he asked.

"I could live off this," I said, taking another sip. I would have to pace myself, especially if it was in limited supply. Kork was being incredibly kind sharing it with me.

A good sign, I hoped.

"Come on, let's sit." He pointed at the sofas, grabbing the bottle of juice on his way there. I sat, facing the depths of space, and he sat down next to me after refilling both of our glasses.

We sat like this for a few minutes watching the stars, sipping our juice. I found myself thinking how perfect this was: how we could sit in the warmth of a spaceship; overlooking the vast eternity of space; counting more stars than I could contemplate; drinking the juice of a plant that only came from one planet at a single, special time; with a person so handsome his face would probably start—or end—a few wars.

I imagined what it would be to live every day like this. To come home to my couch on the edge of space with the person I loved.

I wondered why I didn't miss Earth more. Why I wasn't more terrified of the time that slipped between jumps putting me, potentially, years ahead of my friends. I wondered why I wasn't worried about finding home, or why I hadn't felt anxious in days. Why, in the days since I had started running around the galaxy trying to keep myself together, I hadn't fallen apart—at least, not completely. And I didn't have an answer to that either.

"What are you thinking about?" asked Kork.

"Home," I said, about as honest as I would get. "You?"

"Home, always home." He let out a heavy sigh. He seemed tired. Looking at him, I could see exhaustion in his face, his back bent over from carrying a huge weight.

He turned to me, suddenly. He looked into my eyes, and my heart stopped again, as it did every time he did that. Every time he caught me with his gaze. Every time he reeled me in without a word.

"Sally, I want to tell you a secret," he said, suddenly.

"What now?" I put down my glass on the coffee table in front of me.

"You're the only person I can speak freely to." He leaned toward me. "I have never said these words to anyone. I can't tell anyone else. If I did, it would jeopardize everything I've worked for all these years. Do you understand?"

"I do, yes," I replied, feeling the weight of his words as he piled them on me. Already, my mind was putting two and two together, the signs I had been trying to ignore but were all too real. I knew what he would say before he said it.

"I'm ... I'm a Terran," he said, the tremor in his voice like the confession of a dying man. I reached forward and put my hand on his shoulder. When we had gotten close enough to touch, I found the heat of his skin reassuring, even through the layers of his shirt.

"I know," I replied.

"But ... how?"

"You let down your guard once you knew who I was. You recognized my *Star Trek* shirt. You mentioned the

Bible, once. You see through my shitty references and laugh at my bad jokes. Trust me, Kork, even in this madness, I would recognize my own kin anywhere."

He laughed out loud, that warm, hearty laugh that made me want to wrap up in his voice.

"You're the first I've seen in years." Tears pooled in the corners of his eyes, but he wiped them away with the edge of his sleeve. "I have been cut off from home for decades. I don't even know how long anymore; time has stopped making sense. I could have left Earth last year or a century ago. I just don't know."

"Well, if you know *Star Trek*, then it hasn't been *that* long," I said. I hoped. "I left Earth in 2019."

"Oh," his face fell. "1994. With warp speed; planet times and time zones; alternate calendars; and temporal distortion, I thought it was 2010."

"How did you even get here?"

"You know how alien abductions don't actually happen?" he said, with a knowing smile. "Well ... *ta-daa*, they actually do."

"Ouch." I was afraid I didn't want to know the details of his story, but then he gave them to me.

"I was walking home one day from school, and then, I wasn't." He shrugged. I moved my hand from his shoulder, only to find his palm on my leg. And I liked it there. "I was fifteen, sold into slavery. None of the probing, thank god, but it wasn't pleasant. A lot of the time, I sat in small cages as they took me from auction to auction. I changed hands many times until an Alliance raid on the cargo ship took me out of the hands of slavers and into the crew of a military ship."

"They didn't try to send you home?"

"How could they?" he said. "They couldn't just bring me home, even if they knew where I was from; too many questions I wouldn't be able to answer. But the Alliance ... I can't say they did the right thing, only that it was good after what I had been through. They washed me between the ears, and quite well. I didn't remember much of my days as a slave. Or my days as a Terran. Being a child-hire was focused work. I did what I was told, and I was content not thinking. It's a comfortable life, not making your own decisions."

"Like Marcoli."

"Like Marcoli," he agreed, "and thousands of other kids just like him. I probably would have lived like that for quite a while, but I aged out of the program and found employment elsewhere. I didn't even consider running away. Where was there to run to? Not to mention any time I started down that train of thought, well, *Zap*! Right? Eventually you stopped thinking like that altogether."

"But that's ... barbaric!" I shuddered.

"It's a lifeline after what we'd been through. And I had it good compared to others. I was assigned to the UPAF *Sojourner* and working onboard for three rotations when we were attacked by pirates. They used an asteroid field to ambush us. We were sitting ducks, and the rocks kept coming at us, pummeling us, and the captain grabbed his bridge members and escaped the fuck out of there. Pirates shot them right out of the sky.

"I was terrified," he continued, shaking as if reliving the memory. "I remember thinking how I had to run, and every time I thought that, my mind was hit with a shock. Over and over and over again, until some memories started to come back again. Well, they weren't exactly memories; not mine, at least."

"What do you mean?"

"I recalled episodes of *Star Trek*," he said. "Oh man, I loved that show. But it started to feel real. I started to think I was actually Kirk. I got into the captain's seat, and suddenly I was flying us all out of there. I killed the pirates and saved what remained of the crew. I was a hero—James T… Kork, Defender of the *Sojourner*, Hero of the Alliance. And then I really *was* Captain Kork, and it was too late to change anything. They made me speak to a crowd, tell them what happened, the day of my promotion ceremony: I filled it with catchphrases from the show. The Alliance loved it and made me the star of their new propaganda project. It got me out of fighting a real war. I still have no idea if the Alliance knows my secret—but here I am."

"But why Kork? Why not just keep Kirk? It's not like anyone out here would recognize his name."

"Well, I wanted to stay ahead of the copyright infringement lawsuit. If Earth ever learned about the Alliance, I would be in for millions."

I sat there in absolute awe. The man had bared his soul to me—his deepest secret, one that could cost him his career and standing in the Alliance.

"I am currently traveling the universe with an immortal, space-hopping alien who seems to be wanted by the most powerful forms of government out there," I blurted. "I've lost my home and my family; I don't know where I am, and if your people discover who my friends are, then I never will find home. So, that's my life."

Kork laughed again. Gosh, that laugh.

"We're a real-life Romeo and Juliet then," he said. "A pair of star-crossed lovers, only in the literal sense."

"Are we though?" I asked, "I don't think the play was—"

"Come on, I only read that thing for high school," said Kork, "and that was years ago. I never even finished it. Cut me some slack."

"Oh, I will," I said, "but implying we're Romeo and Juliet would imply we like each other. More than like each other, I would say. And star-crossed lovers would imply—"

"We seem past implying, now," he said. "I might like to point you to where you're sitting right now."

"Oh?"

Without paying attention, I had slid alongside him, or he had slid up next to me. One of my legs was over his, and his hand was on my knee, our sides pressed next to each other and getting closer. I didn't wait to wonder how that had happened. The fact it was happening made me giddy.

He reached under my leg and hoisted me up onto his lap in one swift motion. I leaned into him, wrapping my hand around his neck and into his short, rough hair. And, suddenly, his hand was in my hair, holding on tight as I pressed my lips against his.

He pressed back, moving his lips with mine, begging for more. His scent was overwhelming now, like the oceans of Earth and beyond; he smelled like a whole universe in a bottle.

His hands were gentle through my hair and on my back, holding me in place while admiring the softness they felt there. I felt too little through his uniform and wanted it off, and, before I could think, my hands were following my bidding, pulling down the zipper in front of his chest. I tugged at the sleeves, but his hands were busy. He pulled away from the kiss just long enough to laugh, helping me take off the shirt before returning to run his tongue across my teeth.

He tasted like liquid cookies. He tasted like heaven. If that had been his move—getting us full on sweet, tasty nectar—then he was smoother than I would ever have thought.

I ran my hands freely over his hard chest. The man might have faked his way to the top, but he worked hard to stay there, and it showed. He had the body of a soldier, all muscle in healthy doses. I just wanted to feel him all, and now.

I closed my eyes and leaned into it. It had been a long time since I had gotten this kind of attention, and it felt good. The man was gentle and warm, and filled my mind with dirty thoughts I was glad I wouldn't have to keep to myself.

I felt him readjust me on his lap, shifting me to his front and wrapping a hand under my ass. He stood in one fluid motion, taking me with him, making me feel as if I weighed nothing more than a feather. His lips returned to mine as he carried me forward, and I felt my heart thumping against his at the thought of the destination.

Score! Captain's chambers! Bedroom alert!

"Ow!" Kork hissed, bumping into the coffee table.

"I've got this," I said with a laugh, wrapping my arms around his head. "Take two steps to the left ... now, engage!"

I felt him chuckle in my embrace, laughing as I guided him blindly to the bedroom. I released him when it was time to work the door, but the thing recognized him and slid open without us having to do anything. He tossed me on the bed, where I bounced, the mattress firm but giving.

The door slid shut, leaving us in the dark bedroom, excited and alone. On my left was a window that took up the entirety of the wall, the universe outside, the planet below.

Hello, fantasy. Starship captain? Check. Space? Check. Microgravity environment? Getting there.

"I take it Captain Kork has a trove of alien condoms in his bedside table," I said jokingly.

"Please, call me by my name. My real name. I don't want to be Kork tonight."

"Okay," I said, sitting up and reaching down to unclasp my pants. "What should I call you, then?"

"Matthew," he said. "But please call me Matt."

I froze. He must have sensed my hesitation because he stopped too, and for a second, everything was on hold, like a moment caught in time.

"Is there a problem?" he asked, leaning forward and nibbling at my neck. I leaned into it; I could not get enough of his touch. I wanted him, and I wanted him now.

"Sorry," I said, smiling. "I had an ex named Matt. But that's fine; you just surprised me."

"Well," the captain whispered, leaning me back onto his bed. "I bet you haven't had a lover named Matthew Daniels before."

I flew to my feet before he could say another word.

How I had gotten out of his bed so fast, I did not know, but I was shaking and walking, my mind whirling, excitement fading away like a closed tap.

"What?" asked Kork. "What did I say? Are you okay?"

"I have to go," I said, wiping tears from my eyes. Fuck. I thought I was over this. I marched to the door, waving my arms wildly, but the thing wouldn't let me through.

"Door, open," said Kork from behind me. I marched through it, zipping my pants as I walked, searching for my shirt and bra. The shirt was still on the sofa; the bra was sitting in my glass of unfinished juice. Dammit.

"Sally, what did I do?" he asked, sounding hurt. "Are you all right?"

"No, I am not all right!" I snapped, turning around, half naked and feeling it now. "What kind of game are you playing? Are you trying to screw with me?"

"No, no," he sputtered. "Sally, was it something I said?"

"Matthew Daniels," I said, trying to keep a level head when it felt like my world was collapsing. Was the ship's gravity suddenly failing us? "My ex was named Matthew Daniels, and Matt died saving me from my alien boss. I don't understand how, light years away, I fell head over heels for another Matt Daniels!"

"Oh, come on." He crossed his arms across his chest, looking uncomfortable. "There are a lot of Matthew Daniels in the world."

"Not enough," I said, shaking my head. "Tell me this, Kork. Where are you from, back on Earth?"

Please don't say Connecticut.

"Connecticut, born and raised," he replied. "I miss

being able to say that to someone, you know."

"I need to go, Matt ... Kork." I strapped on my bra—missing half of my breast, so it pressed uncomfortably down on my nipple—and threw my uniform back on top. "I can't do this. Not right now."

"Sorry about your ex," he muttered, still looking confused. "Look, if you need to talk ..."

"Thanks." I headed for the door, "and thank you for the juice. I need to walk this off. I'm sorry."

"I am too, Sally," he said, sadly, "but if you need me, you know where to find me."

"I will." I stepped out of his room and closed the door behind me, barely holding back tears.

CHAPTER TWENTY-ONE

DAMMED BY THE UNIVERSE

I wanted to cry freely, but I had to keep it all in. Just a few feet away from me, Blayde and Jurrah were in a deep, hushed discussion. Hopefully planning a way for us to get out of this mess. We still had a saboteur to find and an alien Consortium lying in wait for our return. Not my cup of tea.

I wanted to avoid the bridge altogether, didn't want to disturb whatever was going on between Blayde and Jurrah, not while I was on such thin ice with Blayde already. She wouldn't appreciate being disturbed by a sobbing Sally. It was something that would get me on her revenge list for a lifetime.

I took the back hallways, the ones Crandle had dragged me down mere hours ago. Oddly enough, I felt like a natural here, navigating the ship as if it had been my home for years, not days. Or maybe I was wandering aimlessly as I sobbed gently into my arm.

I needed to find a quiet room to sit and let it all out. All this anger that had been building up: over getting lost in space, over my shit luck ruining what was supposed to be a fun farewell trip with my immortal alien best friend.

Screw luck. I needed that drink I declined.

I turned a corner and realized I was exactly where I wanted to be. I must have wandered down a floor because here was the front window again, continuing from up on the bridge. That huge, magnificent window. Someone had the foresight to put a bench right under it, where one could sit and contemplate the vast majesty of the universe without being bothered by the nonsense of the politics above.

Yup. This was what I wanted—to be alone with the universe.

I took my seat, facing the window, and clutched my hands to the bench beside me. I deactivated my silent mode and let myself sob.

Why, universe, why do you keep screwing me over like this? Was I too greedy, asking to leave my planet for one day? Is that why you took it away from me for good? Was I too selfish, dating Matt seriously when I wasn't so serious, which was why you let him die? After two years, was I not allowed to move on, so you dig a knife right back into the wound?

I could have shouted. Hell, I wanted to shout. But being up close to the universe right now, I was pretty sure it could hear me all the same.

Fuck you, it said back. *Does it look like I care?*

"Are you all right, Webber?"

I looked up to see Jurrah's lanky frame beside me, worry etched on her pale features. She still seemed to glow, even in the darkness.

"It's nothing," I said, wiping away the tears. "Aren't you supposed to be on the bridge? Reconnecting with Blayde and all?"

"I heard you crying," she said, sitting beside me. "I was worried for your wellbeing."

"Thank you," I replied, amazed that she cared. The tears, however, would not stop. "But it's stupid. I'm all right. It's just… Kork—"

"What did he do?" she asked, suddenly cold. Well, colder than usual.

"Nothing," I shook my head, "I mean ... I wanted, I so wanted to ... but he told me his name. He's from Earth. Like me."

Jurrah nodded, like she knew.

"And he has the same name as my ex—also from Earth—and he died… horribly."

The woman put her hand on mine. She gave it a gentle squeeze.

"I'm being paranoid, aren't I?" I asked her, the tears streaming freely down my face. "I didn't… I shouldn't… I don't know why it bothered me so much. But it's not… it's too much of a coincidence, isn't it? There are a lot of Matthew Daniels in the universe."

"Not that many," she replied, her voice airy like a summer breeze, "and none so interconnected. In this wide universe, the odds of you meeting the namesake of your dead boyfriend in outer space are worse than slim. I know more than most that things are never impossible, but this is pushing the limits of probability itself. It stretches the very notion. It shouldn't happen."

"You're scaring me," I said, pulling away from her. She dropped her hands onto her lap. Her skin looked almost translucent this close up.

"Sally," she said, the summer breeze turning to winter chill, "I think there's something going on here."

"Here, on this ship, or here, between ..."

"For certain on this ship," she said, looking around, "but I mean between you and Zander."

"Wait, what? Between us?" I stammered. "I'm not, I mean, I can't, we can't—"

"I am not talking about love. Listen to me. I'm not even telling Blayde this, but there is something wrong here. Something odd. But more than odd. I can't put my finger on it, but I don't think you getting lost with them was a mistake."

"What are you saying?" I wanted to look away from her, at anything *but* her, but my eyes could not tear away.

I thought I had been scared when my boss turned into a giant red lobster.

I thought I had been scared when I was lost in an infinite city.

I thought I had been scared when I had been taken hostage by aliens and an evil AI.

None of those moments compared to the fear I felt right now.

"Are you saying that Zander and Blayde *purposefully*—"

"No," she said quickly. "Something bigger than that. You see it too, don't you? When I'm connected to the ship, I connect with the universe on a deeper level than most. I can see the strings that connect all things. And, for some reason, the lines between you and the siblings were bold and bright. The lines between you and this ship were set centuries before you were even born."

I shook my head. I didn't believe in the *something bigger* on principle. The universe was as it was, and it didn't give a crap about me. It had made that abundantly clear.

"How did you meet Zander?" she asked.

"I was coming home from a party. I hit him with my car."

"Why were you leaving the party?"

"My friend was making it all about me, and I didn't like that."

"Why did she do that?"

"Because I was fired."

"And why were you fired?"

"Because a hot air balloon was draped over my window," I said, feeling my body chill. "And my alarm clock disappeared, so I was late."

"Just how likely is it for all that to happen?" she insisted. "Even on Earth, that chaotic dip in the universe, it's an unlikely thing for a hot air balloon to land on somebody's house without explanation."

"Most definitely."

"And you never found out why it was there?"

"No," I replied, my face going numb. "But what has this got to do with the universe? A hot air balloon is just a hot air balloon. It's unlikely, but it could happen to anyone."

"Look, Sally," she said, taking a deep breath in, then out. "Sometimes a hot air balloon isn't just a hot air balloon. I don't believe in destiny. I'm close enough to the universe to see the flux of time itself. But you meeting Zander was no accident, nor was meeting another Matt Daniels from Earth in the middle of outer space. It just confirms it. Something odd is going on in your life."

"So, what? Blayde met you here. I mean, we randomly landed on the only planet for light years that has a lost colony of humans on it? That's not an everyday occurrence. Maybe the universe is a whole lot smaller than we give it credit for. Maybe it gets lazy."

"Exactly," she said, beaming. "Sally. Don't you see?"

"See what?" asked Zander. I spun around. He was striding toward us, looking deeply troubled. I shot a glance to Jurrah—how much of this nonsense had he heard?

"How connected you two are," she said, smiling at him.

"Blayde and I travel the universe every day." He nodded, ignoring Jurrah and looking straight at me. "Usually, it's extremely calm. We help out when there's trouble, but there's hardly ever any needed. You come along, and bam! We're thrown into the weirdest adventures."

"Or not," I said. It was like the two of them were backing me into a corner. I wanted to run. "Maybe you miss things because you leave too soon. If I hadn't made a fuss about staying, you would have left and not been thrown into this mess. Maybe you never stick around to see that the entire universe is complete chaos."

"Or maybe we found a mess because you were around," he insisted.

"I'm pretty sure there's correlation without causation here," I said, standing as well. I didn't like them looming over me like that. "Look, I'm just mad that I was about to get it on with a really hot, really badass spaceship captain who happened to not only be my species but also a total Trekkie, and he turned out to have the same name as my dead ex. I didn't want a lecture about how destiny brought us together so I can drag screwed-up shit your way. I wanted to have my first satisfactory hookup in over two years, in outer space, with a hot Trekkie starship captain. Not this crap."

"Well, sorry," said Jurrah, turning her gaze out to the stars. "I just thought knowing that the universe had a plan for you would cheer you up."

"Not if the universe's plan is to clam jam me," I said.

"To what?"

"Bush Whack? Clitoffering? Tacoblocko? Twat Swat? Honey Pot Blocked? Muffin muzzled? Beaver Dammed?"

"Oh! Sorry," he replied, blushing a violent shade of red.

"This is a good a place as any for me to leave you," said Jurrah. "Think about it, okay?"

"Oh, I will," I scoffed, turning away from her. I didn't know what to make of the woman. Obviously, decades of being in direct contact with the universe had done no wonders for her social skills.

Zander sat down on the bench. I made eye contact with his reflection, and he tapped the space beside him, begging me to sit.

"Let me make one last point. Just one."

"Shoot."

"How are you still alive?" he asked. "No offense, but you said you were in the plant when it blew up. And you're not ..."

"Like you?" I said. "No, I barely survived. But then— I had a vision, okay? You came to me in the hospital and gave me some meds or something. It was weird. And then there was a hologram."

"But Sally," he said, "I never did that."

My hands stiffened by my side. No, not stiff; they were trembling so hard I couldn't feel them anymore. I sat back down on the bench, quite suddenly, without making the transition from standing to sitting. I didn't care to think how I had gotten there.

"But I saw you," I said. "I knew it was you."

"I don't know what to say, Sally," he said, staring at me with his eyes wide. "I never came to visit you in the hospital. The last I saw you was before I left to bring the Killians home, and then when Blayde and I came back when you told me two years went by. I didn't bring you medicine."

"Well, someone did, or I would have died. "My parents were talking about when to pull the plug. I was dying, and then I wasn't. Thanks to you."

"But it wasn't me!" he stammered. "Oh stars, this proves Jurrah's point. Something is protecting you. Something is pushing you along whatever path this is. Something wanted us to bring you with us."

"What something?" I snapped, glaring at him. "Would it be Derzan, maybe? Do you think Derzan gives a fuck about what I do? Do you think he tells himself it's fun to mess with Sally Webber's life, to send her to space, and to get her involved in all this galactic shit?

Does he think he needs to stop me from having a sex life?"

"By giving your crush the same name as your dead ex?" Zander raised an eyebrow. "Sally, if there is a Derzan out there, or any kind of higher interdimensional being, isn't that exactly what it would do?"

I thought about it for a second. Then for a minute. My hands were fists upon my lap, heavy and strong and wanting to punch something. I had been sad, dammit, but now I was fucking furious.

I guessed Zander *had* managed to stop me from crying, in his own way.

"Let's say Jurrah's right, and the universe wanted us to meet," I said. "Then what? What does it want us to do?"

"I don't know. Rid it of evil?"

I looked at him, and thankfully, he winked. Good lord.

"And what does Matt have to do with any of this?" I asked, forcing myself to remember to breathe occasionally.

"Well, he got you your job with the alien who was hiding the Killians."

"And exploiting them."

"Exactly." Zander nodded earnestly. "So he was the reason we were able to take Grisham down and save all of them."

"And I met Sekai at a party on Da-Duhui," I said, smiling at the memory, "which is weird, right? I mean, the only party I go to on another planet, and there's someone there I know?"

"You should be keeping a list. There's definitely too

much going on around you for it to all be coincidence."

"But what is this leading to? Meeting Sekai, all I got was some life advice and a selfie, not exactly a map and a key."

"Was it good life advice, at least?"

"Nothing my mom hadn't already told me ... in as many words."

"Maybe your mom is involved in this too."

"My mom?" I scoffed. "Zander. Come on now. Sometimes a coincidence is just a coincidence. Everything happens in an infinite universe."

"And, yet, it all seems to be happening to you."

"Stop it," I said, still trembling. "Please? I had a rough day. Even a rough couple of days. You're not making it any better."

"Oh ... sorry."

It was as if a light bulb just went off in his head. I guessed Zander wasn't used to being in friend mode all the time. Maybe he'd never had to until now. It had been like that on Earth, too, when he was stuck with me: one second, a conversation would be a normal chat between friends, and then, something was amiss, something needed solving, he would get reeled in again.

Sometimes I wished he could just be my friend and not have to focus on the chaos in the universe. I was well past the point of determining that I was a selfish person.

He finally sat down beside me again, and as my friend, he took my fist in his hand, and gave it a gentle squeeze. I loosened under his touch, realizing suddenly that the tension had to go. I breathed it out.

"I'm sorry the universe doesn't want you to *get it on*,"

he said, and I laughed. It seemed so frivolous now. The excitement had long since left me, and the encounter seemed like a silly fever dream.

"Thanks," I said, smiling. This was the friendship I missed.

"Here's something to take your mind off it," he said. *And off the existential crisis I just threw at you,* the look said instead. "We still have a saboteur on board."

"Oh shit!" I stammered. "That's right! Why haven't they acted yet?"

"Well, I'm pretty sure a lovesick astrogator making a detour to a lost planet kinda threw a wrench in their plans," he said, chuckling that chuckle of his I liked so much. "But we're back to where they wanted to be, so they're going to act. There's a whole fleet waiting for us that will take this ship the second it drops out of warp. "

"Unless we stop them first."

"Unless *I* stop them," he said. "Come on, Sally, you're not getting in this mess too. I'll handle it."

"You're the one who said the universe wants me to become some kind of crime-solving superhero."

"I never said that." He laughed. "I said the universe wants you for some reason. I never said that reason was to put you in danger."

"Fine then. I'll stay out of danger. Heck, I'll stay out of this whole mess. I won't get involved. And the second we save the rest of the crew, we're out of here, right?"

"Yup, promise," said Zander.

"You swear?"

"I promised, didn't I?" He rolled his eyes in a wide

arc. "I promise, and I swear. But the saboteur will probably act before we save the crew, so I'll get in there and stop them before any damage can be done."

"Good luck," I said, not sure if I meant it to sound so sarcastic. "Any leads so far?"

"Using the power of deduction, I have managed to eliminate quite a few candidates." His eyes sparkled with excitement. I forgot how he got when he had a problem to solve, a challenge all to himself. "For starters, Two."

"Two people or the droid?"

"The droid. It would be against his core programming to hurt the crew."

"But why hurt the crew anyway?" I asked. "What is the saboteur trying to gain?"

"They wanted to isolate the cast, which means one of two things: either they wanted the crew to suffer, or they want to do something to the actors."

"Fine. Then who? We have Kork, Crandle, Ter, Doesso, and Finch ... And do we count Jurrah?"

"Definitely not," he said. "Until this all happened, Jurrah *was* the ship, and I'm pretty sure no one wants to split themselves in two. She's been in agony since this started and would have no reason to harm herself or her crew."

"She doesn't seem in much agony to me. She seems quite happy right where she is. With Blayde."

"Ignoring that," he said. "I'm pretty sure we can discount Crandle and Ter. Neither can fly a hopper, which means there would be no escape to safety for them if they were to injure the cast."

"If the plan was to injure the cast," I pointed out. "What if they wanted to give the actors to the Consortium?"

"Good thinking," he said. I noticed now that Zander was brimming, like he might have been proud of me. I blushed. Maybe I would be an interstellar sleuth yet.

" They cut the cast off from the crew. Why?"

"No witnesses," he suggested, "and no cameras to record it."

"Aren't there cameras all over the ship?"

"Controlled from a room on the other side of the divide," he said, "so I don't suppose they're rolling."

"So, no witnesses."

"No witnesses," Zander agreed. "So what was the plan? Who wanted what, and who was ready to do anything to get it?"

"Murder?"

"I don't think killing Xacrelf was part of the plan—just wrong place, wrong time."

"Well, I don't know about you, but all this talk about murder has made me hungry." I stood up. My feet teetered slightly, but I was standing all the same. The aches from the days' insanity were catching up with me. "I'm starving. Last thing I had to eat was flavorless white paste. You coming?"

"No, I'm still thinking," said Zander. "But, hey, before you go ..."

He stood up and with a gentle thumb, brushed the crusted tears from my eyes. I felt the tug of empty tear ducts and realized that I was glad, in that moment. I had gotten it out of my system, for now. And while I had a bit of an exhaustion headache, I was feeling better. Able to see straight again.

I loved the feeling of an episode ending.

"If you need me, I'm here, all right?" he said. "Nothing about *us* has changed. I'll be here for you no matter what."

And that sounded like a damn good promise.

CHAPTER TWENTY-TWO

WRONG PLACE, WRONG TIME, AND ANOTHER TRAUMATIC MEMORY BEING BORN

Leaving Zander on the observation deck, I wandered toward the bridge then remembered why I had wanted to avoid it. The image of Blayde and her ex sucking face was not something I wanted to see up close.

I walked instead toward the back of the ship, trying to get away from where I knew people would be. I passed the cafeteria, its door wide open and full of a jubilant crew passing the time with a little social lubricant. Even Nim seemed to be enjoying himself as he chatted with Ter, who looked like quite the chatter-box. Crandle was in deep conversation with Two, who was probably enthusiastic about Derzan, but she didn't seem to mind. I wondered how much she'd had to drink to reach that state.

I slipped by them without a sound. I wasn't in the mood right now. There was just too much going on, my head a jumble of thoughts I didn't want. Zander's words echoed over and over. Could he be right? Could my exile from Earth be part of some greater fate?

Hell no. Sekai's advice was much more likely. The universe didn't give a rat's ass about me. Improbability was the currency of our world, ingrained in the base blocks of matter itself. We were constantly moving toward a more chaotic state.

I needed to find a place to calm down. If I knew how to meditate, I could have done that. But I didn't, and I wasn't sure there was a yogi on board, or whatever the alien equivalent of that was. Hell, I actually had time to sleep. I should probably take advantage. Sleep would make things better, the human equivalent of turning off and on again. That was the solution.

I applauded myself for my adult decisions. My therapist would have been proud.

I guessed no one would care if I caught some *Zs* in an officer's cabin. It's not like there were any officers on board right now. I tried doors, but, for the most part, they were locked. Maybe we needed those handy chip things to get in, which, of course, I did not have.

Of the doors that did open, none on this floor had any beds. I pushed one open on a vast library and closed that one quickly. The ability to sleep is inversely proportional to the number of books surrounding you, after all. No way was I going to get any rest with that amount of literature tempting me to read through.

This ship seemed to have everything except beds.

One door led to an Olympic-sized swimming pool. Another was to what looked like a dining hall straight out of a nineteenth-century Victorian mansion, along with drapes and thick carpet. The table could have sat at least fifty people. Impressive, but not a good place to sleep. Well, maybe on the plush carpet, if nothing else was available.

"You said the pulse would be undetectable, you imbecile."

I froze. There was a voice in the hallway, not one that I recognized. It was muffled, but the words were clear. A woman, fierce and furious. I stepped out of the dining room, closing the door behind me, and her voice disappeared.

I pushed it open again, and there it was—but the room was empty. By some strange rule of acoustics, the open door was magnifying her voice from somewhere else on the ship.

I didn't want to get in on this mess. I should have just turned and left, returned to the cafeteria and had a drink with the crew. But per usual, I screwed things up.

"It was undetectable," a man replied. "We just had a few ... variables ... that weren't taken into account."

"Someone sabotaged our sabotage?"

"Not exactly," he said. "Marcoli was supposed to do his rounds on that floor. He would have triggered the device much earlier if he hadn't stumbled on those fugitives. I had to set it off myself."

"Of course, you did," the woman sputtered. "So the film crew has you on camera."

"Which means if we reconnect, they'll have us arrested for sure."

"That's not going to happen. We're headed straight for the Consortium. They'll pick us up, and we'll be golden."

"Unless the other half of the crew overtake them," said the man.

"In that case, I hope you're right about the fugitives," she insisted. "If you turn them in, they'll probably overlook your involvement."

Shit. Her voice was getting louder, and I realized they were moving closer. In a spur of panic, I dashed into the dining room, throwing myself under the table, dropping the heavy tablecloth to cover my body.

Idiot.

I should have run up the hallway or something; I didn't want anything to do with this. And now, it looked like the two saboteurs had settled on this room to discuss their devious deeds in, actually closing the door and locking it behind them. They walked into the hall, and now, I was trapped.

So much for not getting involved.

I clutched my knees to my chest, hearing my breathing amplified tenfold. Could they hear me too? I focused on breathing quieter, not sure if I was loud or just paranoid. The latter made more sense and was probably rational when two people were discussing a devious plot not three feet away from you.

"What do you mean, my involvement? You want me to take the fucking fall for this? For you?"

I remained frozen in my stupid little hiding place. From here, all I could see were feet, wearing standard-issue Alliance military boots. The same one I wore.

In my head, I was already listing names, trying to

figure out who the voices belonged to. It wasn't hard; I knew who was stuck on this half of the ship with me. Ter. Crandle. Two. Kork, or Daniels, or whatever. Jurrah, who was sucking face with Blayde on the bridge. So this left ...

Doesso and Finch. Whoop-de-doo.

Which made sense, seeing as how totally useless they had been through this whole mess. I had barely given them a second thought.

"You're the one they have on camera, not me. You're the one who screwed up. If I have a chance to get out of this, I'm fucking taking it."

"Not if I have something to say about it."

"I'll deny all of it," she growled, "and who will they believe? The disgraced pretty boy, who only works here because he has a good face or the woman who will one day replace Crandle?"

"Like they'll ever promote you that far."

"Are you kidding me?" She laughed, her voice shrill, stifled only by the heavy velvet drapes on the wall, "They've been grooming me for this position for years!"

"Fuck you," Finch snapped. "Fuck you! Look, we screwed up. *We did.* We took the opportunity to prove ourselves to the Consortium, but now we have to pick up the pieces and you're in this as much as me. It was your idea, remember?"

"You're the one who fucked up," she said. "Not me. *You.* All I wanted was to get the crew out of the way for a little bit. The bridge cast would be no match for the Consortium, but because of your convoluted plan, we're drifting without an astrogator. And it's too late for Crandle."

"Shit," the man stepped back. "Shit. You were going to do it, weren't you?"

"Do what?"

"Kill her," he sputtered. "This wasn't about showing our worth to the brass! You were going to kill Crandle!"

"Of course I was," Doesso said, a hint of smugness in her voice. "Always have a plan B, right? You really think they would have promoted me over great crisis management that wasn't caught on card? I had it all planned out. It was going to happen away from the cameras, away from everyone. I *know* her. The second the ship disconnected, while you stood up to repair it, she was going to go back to her quarters for a stiff drink. A drink I would have time to spike. I would come in for some motherly advice or something. It would have worked perfectly, if you hadn't screwed up the ship's separation. Or murdered Xacrelf!"

"He saw me launch the program, and no, it would have worked perfectly if those felons hadn't showed up," he said. "Don't blame me for that. Blame the fucking siblings."

"The good news is, you can blame them, too. That'll get you out of the mess you created."

"Fuck you, Doesso," he spat. " If I go down, I'm taking you down with me."

"I'd like to see you try."

And then they were fighting. I watched from under the table as a leg went up to kick the other in the hip, and a feminine hand blocked it and twisted the kick in midair.

Both had military training. Both had spent years learning choreography for the show. And now they were going at it like a cage match. They were evenly matched, blocking the hits and sending them back quickly, professionally. They said nothing as they fought, all focus, like this was training. Grunts as they put effort into their blows, as they took punches. A small cry of pain as one found its mark.

Swing, miss, a fist against the curtain. A heavy fist against muffled velvet. Grab, throw; someone came down hard on the table. Good thing it wasn't set. Finch pushed Doesso back, but she deflected his blow and twisted his arm behind him. He shouted some insult my chip could not translate then threw a leg back and kicked her in the crotch. I winced, feeling sympathy pain for a woman I felt no sympathy for.

He threw her down on the table, and she let out a grunt, winded. And there was a pause; neither moved for a good minute. And then there wasn't much swinging going on. And not much fighting back. He had her pinned, but now her foot was running up the back of his leg, up and down the fabric of his uniform.

She pushed off her boot, using her other foot to brace herself, and removed the other with her bare foot. There was a deep intake of air.

"Damn, you're hot when you're pissed," Doesso said, as the sound of lips pushing against lips, of gentle moans, ended.

"Good thing I hate you," Finch replied.

Her pants came off. They fell in a pile right in front of me, crumpled. Oh shit. Of all the things.

I put my fingers in my ears, trying to ignore the grunts and moans above me. The table shook. They were yelling insults at each other, before locking lips again. Moan, moan, moan, deep breath, and insults. Repeat. I didn't need to see to know what was going on up there. They were practically narrating.

I plugged my ears deeper and tried to drown out the noise with music, wishing to high heaven I had my iPod. Then wishing I hadn't hidden under the table. Wishing I hadn't begged to visit this ship. Wishing I hadn't gone to space. Wishing that every decision I had ever made in my life hadn't added up to me being under a table while two alien saboteurs went at it above me.

They rolled off the table, landing with a loud thump on the thick carpet. Doesso was on top, her uniform open and hanging lopsided from her shoulders. Finch turned his head and locked eyes with me. There was a brief moment when they widened, but he didn't respond. He was too focused on something else to do anything. Doesso shouted louder, grabbing at Finch's chiseled chest as she lost herself in the moment. Probably not the right time to be discovered.

"Shit!" He shouted, then tried to get up, which was rather difficult with a woman propped on top of him. She struggled to find her balance then fell, making him scream when she landed wrong.

I dashed out from under the table, rushing to the door, grabbing the handle and hitting it repeatedly when it didn't open. I looked back. Finch was trying to get around the table, tripping with his pants still around his ankles. I had an extra second as he reached down to pull them up, but it wasn't enough; the lock would not budge. I jiggled the latch, but it was too late. A very nude Finch grabbed my neck, pinching hard, the pain forcing me to my knees.

"What the hell?" Doesso said, zipping her shirt closed and marching toward me. "What are you doing here?"

"I'm sorry!" I sputtered, my body shaking, the pain in my shoulder screamed in my brain. "I was ... I was just ..."

Finch finished pulling up his pants. Thank god. Alien junk was not what I wanted to see right now. Definitely not something I wanted to be the last thing I saw before dying.

They were going to kill me. That much, I knew for sure.

"How much did she hear?" he asked Doesso, who was searching for the rest of her uniform. She pulled up her pants, sitting her perfect ass on the table and slipping them back over her legs, covering the intricate tattoo.

She made eye contact with me, glaring. "How much did you hear?"

"Nothing. I swear, nothing." I trembled.

"What do you think, idiot?" Doesso hissed, pulling her hair into a messy bun. "The door was locked. She was here the whole time. She heard everything."

Come on, brain, think of a way out. But I couldn't make a run for it. I was surrounded, and I couldn't get the door to work for me. I could always lie, come up with some story that made it sound like they couldn't get rid of me. But I was terrified. Every course of action I could think of ended in darkness. I was trapped.

Lucky, lucky me.

"I heard nothing," I insisted, barely holding myself together. Playing innocent, playing patsy wasn't a performance.

"She could ruin everything," Finch insisted, throwing his hands up in anger. "Forget about having a way out. She would destroy all of that."

"I won't. I promise I won't!" I said. Yes, I am a coward. I just wanted to live. I wanted to survive. "I just want to go home. I won't say anything."

I didn't have to lie. I would have done anything.

"She's connected to the siblings," Finch pointed out, scowling at Doesso. "The main crew won't believe a word she says."

"Yeah, but Kork's got the hots for her," said Doesso. "He would vouch for her, and the crew listens to him over any of us."

"But I'm not going to say anything!" Tears streamed down my face. Come on, Sally, hold it together.

"We can't trust her." Doesso snarled. "We need to get rid of her— before we reconnect with the rest of the ship. Before the cameras come back online."

"We put her in the airlock," Finch said. "Then, when we meet back up with the rest of the crew, we pin it on her. She was working for the fugitives, after all. They wanted to take over this ship. They split it so they could pick us off one by one. They wanted the *Traveler* for themselves and were giving it up to the Consortium to turn the tide of the war. Blayde's relationship with the astrogator will just support our story."

"But no one would agree with that," said Doesso. "Kork, Crandle? They *love* the siblings. They wouldn't support our claims."

"Then fuck it, right?" Finch said, a sly look on his face. He threw his head back and laughed, a manic look in his eyes. I shivered. "Look, I'm not going down for any of this. And you still want Crandle dead, right?"

"Yeah. Where are you going with this?"

"We blow them all up," he said. "It's not that hard. I can overload the reactor, and I can fly us a shuttle out of here. Let's just blow this place and run. We come up with a sob story about Kork going crazy and trying to kill us all. Or we fly to the Consortium and hope they'll hold up their promise of asylum. Whatever. It doesn't matter; they wouldn't be able to prove anything, would they?"

"I love it," said Doesso, her mouth spreading into a wide grin, showing all her pearly white teeth. "Let's blow this place."

"Please, no," I stammered. "You don't have to do any of this! I won't—"

I didn't see it coming. I guessed that's what you get when you have two military-trained actors who want you out of the way. *Bam.* Probably going to get brain damage from this.

The knockout was brutal. Darkness was instantaneous.

CHAPTER TWENTY-THREE
SPACE TRAVEL TAKES MY BREATH AWAY

I opened my eyes and saw stars. Though it's very difficult, when in space, to tell which stars are real, and which are the product of your brain screwing you over.

Not to mention the ache in your head from where someone just kicked you. There's the dull memory of the act, a clench in your gut when you realize that you could have died. But no, you're alive, and there are stars, both real and fake, right in front of you.

Hang on. Why are there real stars in front of me?

I blinked. And again. There was, thankfully, a window between me and the void of space: I guess we weren't moving quickly, at least not enough to warrant closing the blinds. That was a relief.

What wasn't so reassuring was the fact that I was in

a small room, piled high with crates and scrap. Was I in a cell?

Or... I felt my heart sinking as the thought grew in my head. I was in the airlock. And soon, there wouldn't be a window between me and the stars outside.

There had to be a panic button. This ship, with all its fancy safety features, had to have something in place in case someone got stuck inside an airlock, right? I turned to face the large window that faced inwards to the ship. An empty room awaited me on the other side.

No one there to help save my life.

Which meant no one was there to see me fight my way out of this, or stop me from doing everything I possibly could to survive.

My hands ran over the walls, looking for a latch, a button, anything to release the door and let me back into the ship. My heart swelled as I found a plastic cover on the wall, protecting a big red button: My way out.

I opened the plastic, hit the button, and waited.

Nothing.

I hit it again.

Nada. Zilch. Nul points.

My fist came down on the button over and over again, until the skin of my hand was as red as the button itself. No. No, come on, please. But there was nothing to do: someone had shorted it. I was sure I knew who.

"One minute until airlock release, one minute..."

The gut wrenching terror came back at full force. Trembling hands, sweat on the brow, the urge to throw up, all back. I forced myself to take long, deep breaths. I knew myself, I knew my body, and I knew a panic attack was building. I needed to calm down, think this through, or I would die in awful terror, making everything worse and screwing myself over in my last minutes.

The voice counting down was not helping.

Fact. Space is big, and out to kill you. If I was going to get ejected from this airlock, my odds of survival were slim to none - maybe a passing Vogon ship would help, but that only worked for Arthur Dent. Me? I didn't quite believe in Vogons - yet.

The vacuum of space is lethal. I had seen enough science fiction to know that if I stepped out there without a suit, and without any air pressure to push back on my lungs, they would expand, possible to the point of tearing. Holding my breath would make it worse. I would have to fight my every instinct and relax.

No pressure. Which means the water in the soft tissues of the body would sublimate, vaporize, causing gross swelling. Lucky the skin is thick and elastic enough to keep me from bursting. Same for my eyes, they weren't going to explode but would dry up in an instant, same for the water in my mouth. This would suck - literally, with the difference of pressure pushing me out into the vastness of space the second that door opened.

Unless they emptied the oxygen from this room first... No, why would they? Nothing would get pushed out otherwise. It would be a forced ejection into space, no matter what.

The worst bit will be when the gasses in my veins formed bubbles. That could block blood flow, and if it reached my brain... I wouldn't die instantly, but I would be unconscious very quick.

I needed every second of functioning, oxygenated brain to get me through this.

"Forty seconds."

Crap, I was wasting time thinking. I needed to plan. All I had at my disposal was trash, but there had to be something useful in there. Anything.

Sheet metal. Broken tools. Painter's suits. Painters' suits?

Five suits, covered in paint. Flimsy fabric that only covered the body. Not a spacesuit, but strong enough to become a rope?

I tied them leg to sleeve, leg to sleeve, then tight around my waist. I tested the knots, praying to whoever was listening that they would hold. I tied the other end to the panel of the red button that had made me so angry up until now.

Maybe it could save my life though.

I didn't need the rope to hold forever, only long enough for the doors to close and for the air to return. Something to hold me as I passed out from lack of oxygen. A tether until the danger had passed. That was it.

Paint cans lined the walls, most empty and useless. But some had a bit of color left in them. White, black, grey, the colors of the *Traveler*, but it was all I had to work with. In my last remaining seconds, I pried the ones I could open, tossing their lids aside.

"Ten seconds. Nine... eight..."

Breathe, Sally, Breathe. I closed my eyes and pretended I didn't know what was coming. Breathing normally. This was just a normal day. Everything was normal. I was just going for a walk...

I felt it instantly, like the air had been sucked from my lungs and from the world all at once. I clutched the rope and was grabbed from behind, as if by an invisible hand. It was trying to drag me away, trying to throw me into the void.

There was no sound, not even a rushing of wind. Just emptiness, like the world had gone still. With my eyes closed, it could almost have been peaceful, if it wasn't for the full force of the universe pulling at my feet.

Which... didn't last long. The pressure equalized between the airlock and the void, and now, now I was just... floating.

But I couldn't breathe. I was choking, telling my body not to hold my breath, but I had none to hold anyways. I felt a cough come up and die stuck in my throat.

I pulled myself up, one hand at a time, to the big red button. My head hit the wall, gently, but enough to push me back again, and I clutched the makeshift rope for dear life.

And that's when the real darkness came.

I breathed.

Hands on my chest, pumping. Fingers pinching my nose, lips sealed against mine, forcing air into my lungs. And I breathed.

"Sally, oh good lord above..."

I gasped for air. Suddenly, there was a plastic around my nose, pumping slowly. There was enough air for days. I was breathing.

I was alive.

The hands were dark and gentle - Kork's. I couldn't think of him as anyone else but Kork, Matt's name thrown at him but not clinging. He was Kork. And he was holding me in his arms, smoothing my slick hair from my sweaty face, murmuring soft words as he urged me back to consciousness.

"Did... did you see my paint?" I croaked, smiling up at his face. In that moment, with the bright light of the ship's cargo bay hitting the back of his head just right, he looked radiant. An angel with a halo around his gorgeous head.

"Your what?" he asked, blinking.

"The paint," I said, "To catch your attention. It was supposed to explode and look all fancy and tell you I was in trouble."

"Oh, no, the ship told us," he said, letting out a laugh of relief, "When you hear there's lose material stuck in the airlock, causing it to not close completely, when there wasn't a dump scheduled for a week? You know something's off."

"You found me," I said, smiling - and coughing a little. Damn, everything burned. "You saved me."

"It was a group effort," he said. With a gentle hand, he guided me back to a sitting position, leaving his hand on the small of my back. I was thankful, oh so thankful.

Which is when I saw them all.

And when I say all, I mean all of them. Zander and Blayde; Jurrah and Ter and Crandle and Two and Nim. My team. My crew. All staring at me like I had woken from the dead.

"You're sure you're alright?" Zander asked, sitting

right across from Kork, reaching for my wrist to take my pulse, "someone should measure her tension. We need to run some tests, make sure her brain didn't receive any damage from the lack of oxygen - she was out there for over a minute."

"I should be dead," I said, more to myself than to anyone else. My mind was too numb to differentiate between what was said inside and outside of my brain. I shuddered. There would definitely be some damage.

"Who did this?" Zander asked the rest of the crew, eyes wide and eager, "What happened?"

"Doesso. Finch." I said, trying to push him away. I needed to breathe, and this many people, this close, it was almost feeling like the airlock again. "They're behind everything. And I mean, everything. They're the saboteurs."

"They can't be," said Kork, "Why—"

"They've been planning it for ages," I said, drawing on those blurry memories from the back of my head, "They were giving the actors to the Consortium, I think? But Doesso wanted to kill Crandle - sorry, Lieutenant - but we showed up and it messed things up and... They're going to blow up the ship!"

I jumped to my feet, much too quickly, making my head spin even more than it already was. Probably had a concussion on top of the possible brain damage. I felt the worst kind of hungover, wobbling on my unsteady legs. Kork grabbed my hand.

"Woah, take it slow," he said, standing and keeping me balanced. "You're alright now."

"I mean it. The two of them were going to clean up their mess and move on, but they've given up on that plan. They're blowing up the evidence—the ship."

"She's right," Nim pointed out, "One of your shuttles is missing."

We followed where he was pointing, and, sure enough, there was only the one hopper left in the bay. The two had been fast to make their escape. Which probably meant that whatever destruction they had put in place was already counting down.

"Shit!" called Kork, his eyes wide with fear, "we have to stop them!"

"Yeah, you said it," snarled Crandle, "try to murder me for my role? Doesso? That little bitch! Though, I have to say, she has drive. I was just like her at her age."

"Not now, Nolla," said Kork, "We need a plan of attack. Haln, you know the workings of this ship better than anyone. Take Jurrah and Two and find out just how this ship is going to blow up, and stop it. Thratra, Nolla, you're coming with me, we're getting on that hopper and retrieve those bastards. Think they can blow up our ship? Never in a million years. Jezeal can take Sally to the infirmary." He turned to me, his voice all sweetness, "We need to make sure your brain wasn't damaged, alright?"

"They tried to kill me!" I said, feeling my nails dig into the sweaty palms of my hands, "I can't let them get away with that!"

"You're right to be angry," said Kork, "but we can't have that kind of emotion on the job. You could get hurt, more than you are now. We've got this - trust us. By the time you recover, all this will be behind us. Alright, let's go!"

Like a well-oiled machine, they moved as one. Kork

gave me one last smile before dashing off after his small crew, and I wished them well. Finding a shuttle in the depths of space wouldn't be easy. But they had Blayde, and she looked like she would have them subdued and home by dinner, per usual.

Zander's team was already at a computer console, throwing technical terms at him and each other that I would never comprehend. I wanted to help. I had to help. But one step in their direction, and Ter blocked my way.

"Come on, Sally," he said, "this is for your own good."

"Look, can't we just do it after we're sure everyone is safe?" I begged, "I feel great. Well, not great, but I don't think I'm in immediate danger. I want to do my part. We can't let these two get away. I've... seen things."

I shuddered. Gross things. That, and I almost died again.

"You're not making your case anymore worth my while," said Ter, "I don't support revenge."

"You don't support a lot of anything, Ter," I pointed out.

"True. But I support your health. And as a fake medical doctor on a very real ship, it's my duty to make sure your brain is in tip top shape. Let me do my fake job, which is to point real instruments at your real brain and have the computer do the analysis. Okay?"

"Fine," I said, "do it quickly, and then I'm coming back down here to stop us all from blowing up."

"Great!" said Ter, extending a hairy hand. I took it and was surprised to find the hair to be soft, much more like silk than the terrier I was expecting.

"I could help repair the ship," said Nim as he

followed us towards the stairwell, "Seriously. I know what you're going to say..."

"What, that you're from an entirely different civilization that doesn't have the same technology as we do, and you'd waste their time if they have to explain everything to you first?"

"Yup, that," he said, "but if this ship is going to be my home, I'd much rather not have it blow up."

"What makes you think you're going to live here?" asked Ter, dragging me up three flights of stairs in a rush that probably wasn't good for a girl with possible brain damage.

"You took me in?" said Nim, "And I have nowhere else to go?"

"You're a minor," said Ter, as he pushed open the door to a floor I had not yet been to. He led us down a corridor and into a large room with cots on either side, all of them empty. "Which means the Alliance's child hire program will pick where you're stationed. Sally, take a seat anywhere. Just… don't sit too close to that wall."

I followed his gaze to a wall with multiple drawers. Oh. The morgue. Xacrelf's body would be in one chamber, waiting for the madness to end so we could give him a real goodbye. Ter's eyes lingered there, but only for a moment.

"What program?" Nim asked, this obviously being the first time he'd been told any of this, "Is that what Marcoli was in?"

"Yup," Ter nodded, placing a plastic bracelet around my wrist and sticking something black to my forehead, "Sally, lie back, please, this won't hurt a bit."

"But what if I don't want to joint that program?"

"Sorry kid, but you're a minor we picked up on a mission, even if it wasn't official," he said, "so you're going to have to go through processing. If the cameras had been rolling when we met you, it would be possible to have a bit of a story arc for you, but they weren't, so I doubt the film crew will care."

"Oh," said Nim, falling into a seat behind the doctor's desk. He stared at his hands, an empty look on his face, then shook his head, gazing instead out the window.

And said nothing more.

I didn't want that for the kid. We had taken him from his friends and family. He had no say in the matter, now even less so. From what Zander had told me, this child hire business wasn't all it it was cracked up to be. Nim deserved better. He deserved a chance.

"There," said Ter, pulling up a screen next to my seat, "all done."

"That was it?" I asked, following what he was looking at. Low and behold, there was my brain upon the wall, in full 3D glory. Ter rotated it expertly and looked around.

"This is, well, odd," he said, "but it looks like you don't have any damage at all."

I grinned at him. "So, can I go and help now?"

"But there should be some kind of damage," Ter continued. "I don't get it. Your brain is in tip top shape. But..."

"Sorry to interrupt," said Nim. He had been staring into space - literally - and now looked a little perplexed. "But I'm the exterior of this ship is supposed to be sleek, right?"

"Last I checked," I said.

"Except for where the ship took damage in the crash," added Ter.

"Then why is there an appendage that looks like a hopper?"

CHAPTER TWENTY-FOUR

IT SHOULDN'T BE THIS HARD TO SEARCH A SPACESHIP

"Shit," said Zander, staring out through the window. "Shit, shit, shit."

"You guys really should stop swearing," said Two. "It's unbecoming. Derzan does not approve of coarse language."

"Shut up. Please, just please shut up," said Zander. "I'm trying to think. Why in the universe would they be here?"

"It was a trap," said Nim.

We all turned to face him. Nim paced the room, back and forth, the gears turning in his head. We watched, waiting for more.

"They wanted to lure the best of us away from the

ship," he said. "It's logical. Who else but the best fighters would hunt them down, leaving the rest of the crew undefended? They wouldn't have to blow up the ship. All they need to do is pick us off, one by one, and then fly away who knows where, leaving the away team to die of starvation in their hopper."

"Makes a lot more sense than flying away and hoping to find a planet," said Zander, looking at Nim in awe. We were all impressed by this boy, who picked up languages as easily as a bad habit and thinking further ahead than even Zander. It was a little freaky, actually.

"So where are they now?" asked Ter, shaking.

"I don't know," said Nim, "but they want to kill us off. The ship is not in danger. We are. There's strength in numbers, so long as we stick together, they can't hurt us. I mean, *not as easily*."

"But we still need to find them."

Zander ran his hand through his hair, having a little nervous scratch. He didn't have much to work with: a droid, a kid, an actor, a woman who hadn't used her own legs for a century, and me. Not a dream team, but we were all he had to work with.

"Right. What we need now is accountability," he said. "We have to stay in contact every step of the way. Keep your coms open. I want you all to go to the bridge and keep an eye on the usual activity across the ship. Sally, you and I are going for a spacewalk."

"We are?"

"I promise you, it's a lot easier out there when you have a spacesuit." He winked.

"Great," I said, smiling as best I could. "You know how I feel about heights, right?"

"I'll be right there with you." The look in his eyes was begging me to trust him. Which I did, with my life. "We need to get the hopper back inside. It'll cut off their escape route."

"And shouldn't we call the captain back here?" asked Jurrah, her voice calm and smooth as honey. "He's flying into nothing, after nothing."

"They could be monitoring long-distance transmissions," said Zander. "Which reminds me, just in case, turn all your coms to channel five. They shouldn't be listening in there."

"Good luck out there," said Ter, nervously.

"Keep this place safe for when we get back."

"This suit should fit you fine." Zander handed me a bunch of bright orange rubber. I looked it over, feeling the stress in my gut, a fist coiled around my entrails.

"I'm not so sure about this," I said, but still, I took it from him.

"Trust me. We're just taking a walk to the shuttle, then we're flying it back into the cargo. Easy as pie."

"Pi the number or the pie you eat?"

"Whichever pie *you* find easiest, my dear," he said with a grin then grimaced at his choice of words and got back to taking off his shoes.

The suit fit right over my uniform. As I closed the last seal, the suit tightened around me. It squeezed, then released, finding a happy medium point. It was as if I wasn't wearing it at all.

"Your boots will connect with the hull of the ship," Zander informed me gaily, "so no worries. You'll need gloves—take any from the baskets over there—and a helmet. I'll help you with the last bit."

I did as I was told, trying not to panic. I had just been in space, and it had been the most unpleasant experience of my life. I wasn't looking forward to going back out there, suit or no suit.

I grabbed my gloves, sliding them over my trembling hands. They tightened to fit, too. My palms were sweaty underneath them.

"Are you ready to take a walk—*in space*?" asked Zander.

"I guess I am. If space can't hurt my brain, I don't know what will."

There was a harness to put on over our suit, the kind you wear while zip lining, only with extra straps over the arms. Zander helped me with mine, showing me what he was doing so I could help with his. I tightened the straps on his chest, and he pretended to wince, just to annoy me.

Almost like old times, joking around my apartment. Like the day I learned how to tie a tie on YouTube, so I could help him put it on for work because he always got it crooked. For a second, it was just like it used to be between us, two of my years ago.

With the added benefit of outer space.

"Now for the helmet." He grabbed one off the shelf and slipped it over my head. It was like wearing an inverted fishbowl. The last thing was to hook up my air, and I got to wear the canister on my back like a backpack. I snorted—which I regretted instantly, since the snot coated the front of my helmet.

Lights came on, on my shoulders, and I laughed louder.

"What's wrong?" he asked. "Seriously, breathe. No need to be nervous. Kids on Pyrina have fun parks for spacewalks. It's nothing to be afraid of."

"I'm not afraid," I scoffed. "Okay, fine, I am. The fantasy was to be in a starship, not in the void of space. This is surreal, you know? I feel like a cartoon character. How is this going to protect me?"

"You'll be fine," he insisted. " The stars are waiting for you!"

"You mean, two criminals and a space shuttle await."

"Yeah, that too."

I helped him get his helmet on, doing the clasps on his back and helping him hook up the canister, as he did with me. He coached me through the bits I hadn't seen, and soon, he, too, was ready to walk out into the void.

"And don't worry!" His voice coming crisp and clean through the speaker in the helmet, as if there weren't two glass bubbles between us. "I'm immortal, so if you screwed up, I'm not going to die on you."

"As reassuring as that it, you can seriously be grim, dude."

"You love me for it and you know it." He laughed.

And it was true. I loved him for it.

I loved him for a lot of things. Not romantically, no, I didn't think so. I couldn't think so. But being around him was effortless, even if there were two maniacs trying to kill us and we were about to walk on the hull of a spaceship. When he was around, I wasn't afraid. Not the way I knew I should be.

Actually, scratch that. I was terrified. None of that had changed. But when Zander was by my side, I didn't feel like that fear would hold me back. I knew I was afraid of going out there, but I still would follow that man out into the void.

He didn't take away my fear. He helped me be brave.

Or maybe he made me see how brave I already was.

"Ready?" he asked.

As I'll ever be. "Ready."

He opened the door into the small airlock, and I followed him in. The door slid shut behind us, releasing a loud hiss. I held onto one of the silver bars there as Zander worked out some details with the ship's computer.

"Hook yourself up." He pointed at one of the tethers that hung from the wall. I snapped it around my harness, watching as the metal fused with itself. The ultimate safety.

The hum of the ship disappeared. All I could hear now was Zander's breath in my ear, coming clear through the earpiece in the helmet. It was comforting.

"Here. I offered him a tether. "You need one too."

"Thanks." He strapped himself in with one hand while he typed a command with the other.

The door slid open, and we were standing in space.

Well, more precisely, we were standing on the hull of a spaceship traveling hundreds of thousands of miles per second. Living up to its name, I guessed. But you wouldn't see that now. We looked immobile under the stars, just ... hanging out, in outer space.

It was pretty darn cool.

"Just one step in front of the other," said Zander, demonstrating by walking out onto the hull. "Simple. Just tug twice on your tether if you want it to reel you back in."

"Easy peasy."

"Yup."

We walked out onto the hull together, just two friends out for a walk in outer space. And while my first experience in the vacuum had been a mortifying, death-defying disaster, this one was actually, well, pleasant.

"The ship's artificial gravity will still act on you while you're within range," Zander said, excitedly. "But if you get away from it ..."

He wrapped his tether cord around a hook in the hull, pushed himself up into the stars—holding his tether in one arm to keep from flying away—and did a quick pirouette, grinning ear to ear as he did so.

"You're having fun with this, aren't you?" I laughed.

"You're not having enough fun, Sally!" "Come on, join me!"

I tugged my tether so it looked like a seatbelt in a car and jumped right up, accidentally crashing into him. He laughed as I sent him spiraling like a pool ball smacked by a queue.

"Sorry!"

"Don't apologize!" He laughed. "Come on, let loose!"

I spun around, head over heels. The ship spun out of my vision, filling my eyes with stars, real stars, then filled my view once again. It was exhilarating.

"Oy, you two," said Ter. "You have a shuttle to find."

"Yes, true." Zander rolled his eyes in a *Can you believe*

this guy? kind of way. I stifled another laugh.

I was actually having fun in the midst of all this.

But back to business. Zander tugged his tether lightly, so it pulled him back to the artificial gravity of the ship. He reached a hand up to me, and I took it gladly, letting him lead me back to the safety of solid ground.

Well, as solid as we would get around here.

"Let's find this shuttle," Zander said.

It wasn't hard to find, what with the hull of the ship being all white and silver and the little hopper sticking out from the sleek exterior like a sore thumb. It was just sitting there, not even trying to remain concealed.

"This feels off," I said.

"It sure does," Zander agreed, "but most things have an eerie gloom when they're only lit by ship light. Interstellar space is pretty dark."

"That must be it," I agreed. "Right, can you get us in there?"

"Of course," he said, walking up to the shuttle and reaching down to hit the door's release. It slid open easily. "Shit!"

It was like a truck had slammed into me. In a split second, I had gone from staring at the shuttle to having my face smashed against the hull, a body heavy on top of me. I shouted and kicked, trying to get it off, certain it was Finch trying to kill me yet again.

But it was Zander.

And his helmet had blown clean off.

I screamed, but he was getting up as if nothing happened, as if half of his face hadn't been incinerated. Like a bad movie, the tendons and the muscles were visible and charred, showing off more teeth than you're supposed to see in a person.

He couldn't hear me scream—it was space, after all—but the ear near the speaker was gone, too. Very Van Gogh.

The shuttle was gone. Just gone. A trail of space junk spewed out from the spot where we'd just been. I looked around, dumbfounded, trying to make sense of what had happened.

"Are you two all right?" Ter's terrified voice buzzed through my ear. "One of your suits just registered as offline."

"We're fine," I said, speaking for both of us. Zander was opening and closing his jaw, like he was trying to pop a bubble in his ear. Already, the charred skin was looking pink and new, and a baby ear had popped up where his old one had been. Freaky.

"The shuttle was rigged to go off," I explained. "We're both okay. Zander caught it in time, and we're safe now. Any progress on your end?"

"Get back to the ship now!" Nim must have shoved Ter off the line, because there was a muffled thump in the background, "The ship is going to warp!"

"What, now?" I sputtered.

"We've reached the conduit. It's going to do that space-folding, faster-than-light thing," he said. "You have to get in here!"

"Got it." I mimed to Zander that we needed to get back to the ship. He nodded, wrapping an arm around me, and tugged twice on his tether. The rope spun and dragged us back in. I closed my eyes, not wanting to look at the mass of muscle his face had become, even though I knew it was going to be fine.

"Can you stop the warp?" I said, as Zander shut the outer airlock door and pressure filled the antechamber with a hiss. "If we leave without the away team, who knows if we'll be able to get them back."

"Trying to," said Jurrah from somewhere in the distance.

"This must be part of their plan—the diversion, blowing us up, leaving us on the ship, ready to be picked off. Zander, can you hear okay?" I asked, pointing at the tiny ear he had in the place of his regular one. He shrugged.

"I will in a second," he grimaced. "I think they're scrambling. They're trying to split us up, but eventually they'll have to get used to the fact that we're together on this. All of us. As a team. So, if they want to come at us ..."

He pushed the button to release the door into the ship, and I rushed into the suit room, pulling off my helmet and taking in a massive gulp of recycled air. Much better.

Zander ripped off his shattered suit, hurrying as fast as he could. I did the same, laying the helmet down on the bench and trying my hand at undoing all the clasps we had spent so much time putting on.

Until an arm grabbed me from behind, tightening around my neck.

I felt the burn of a crushing windpipe, the air hissing into my lungs, the pulse of terror filling my veins. My eyes widened, stinging at the edges. I couldn't see who had grabbed me; my field of vision was full of Zander, who had his hands up, watching me in shock.

Oh, and the gun that was pointed at him.

"Don't move an inch," said the voice—Doesso. The woman had me trapped once again, somehow catching me without warning. Suddenly, I was the scared girl being attacked in her hotel room; I was the terrified child who couldn't even put up a fight against a friend for practice.

Hello, panic, my old friend. Thanks for coming so quickly.

"I know you know who I am," said Zander, coolly. He took her command to the letter, freezing in place so completely he wasn't even blinking. "Put the gun down, Doesso. It's over. You're outnumbered."

"Oh, the gun's not for you," she said. I felt the cold metal press against my temple. Oh, crap.

I had to fight. I had to do something. I mean, come on, body, be useful for once! But I was petrified with fear. I was limp in my captor's arms, completely at her mercy.

Zander's eyes went even wider. Was that fear I saw there? The great Zander, afraid of something?

"Yes, I know who you are, Zander, the great enemy of the Alliance," she said. "You should be on my side, you know. I'm taking this ship from their hands and giving it to those who will use it wisely. Join me, Zander. The Consortium will give anything to have you."

"I'm not the Alliance's enemy," he said with a scowl, "nor am I their ally. I'm neutral in this. I'm only helping this crew because the rules of Space Law dictate—"

"Space Law," she spat, the spittle hitting my hair and drippling down. It was disgusting. "Like you care about Space Law. You want something; let me give it to you.

Let me introduce you to General Tasrath, and he'll give you anything your heart desires."

"Right now, I want you to let Sally go, unharmed. Can you do that?"

"Not until I know where you stand, no."

I wet my lips, which were drying in the artificial cool of the antechamber. My lips. I could move my lips.

"Why am I always the hostage?" I stammered, feeling my throat burn as I forced air past the tightness of Doesso's arm.

"Because he's immortal, dumbass," she said with more snark than was needed. "There's no point taking him hostage. You're the one I can kill."

"What makes"— her arm was getting tighter around my neck and I hissed, feeling the pain surge through my body—"what makes you think I'm mortal?"

She paused for a second. Even Zander seemed taken aback, but in the blink of an eye he regained his composure. He made eye contact, and maybe I was imagining this, but I thought I saw peace there. Acceptance.

"Think about it, Doesso," I said, calmly. I didn't know where the calm was coming from, but I let it wash over me. Whatever happened, I accepted it now.

"You've already tried to kill me," I said, gaining more confidence with every word. "Twice, in fact. Yet here I am, and I feel fine."

She laughed, a shrill laugh like the cackle of a witch, nothing like the powerful laugh she'd had in the dining room. "Why the hell won't you die?"

"I'm the siblings' secret weapon, Doesso," I said. "So secret that even the Alliance haven't heard of me. I'm

Sally Webber, and nothing you do will harm me."

She shoved the gun against my temple, and I pushed back, standing tall, standing strong. I could not fight with my arms or feet, but I could fight with words.

"Prove it," she hissed. I felt her trembling as she gripped me. "Prove what you say is true."

"Well, you could shoot me," I said nonchalantly, "but then Zander will have a window to bring you down. You sure you want to give it a try?"

There was a pause. She was hesitating; I was getting to her.

"You ever see a human head explode, Doesso?" I asked. Maybe I was pushing it too far, but I was fighting for my life here. "Shoot me here, now, and you'll be wiping gore off your face for months. And for what? I mean, look at Zander." I indicated him with a jut of my chin. The skin was growing back on his face as I spoke, and I knew she was watching. "You'd have shot me for nothing."

"Doesso, put the gun down," said Zander. "It'll go much better for you if you do."

"It's too late," she said, stammering now.

"Just stay calm," said Zander, stepping forward. This made her angry. She pulled me back with her, pushing the gun even harder. I gritted my teeth; I would not break. My body was steady.

She had tried to kill me twice and failed. I wasn't going to let her succeed.

I wasn't immortal, but I was starting to believe I might be. That maybe, just maybe, Zander was right: Maybe the Universe had a plan for me. Maybe the Universe wanted me right here, right now.

"What could possibly be worth all this?" asked Zander, his voice low and soothing. "You can't truly believe the Consortium will protect you. You're a defector, a traitor. They could never trust you."

"After everything I've done for them?"

"You mean, after you left in the ship you promised them and took it light years away? That's a very trustworthy move."

"A minor setback."

"Come on, Doesso, take it from me: It's over," Zander held out his hand, slowly.

She went silent but didn't give him the gun. No, she pulled it away from my head—thank the universe—and pointed it at the ceiling. Her grip around my neck loosened, and I tumbled to the floor, gasping for air.

I was alive. I was alive!

"Good to see you up and about," said Zander. I turned to look at him and took the gun from Doesso's hands, a smile brimming on his face.

And behind Doesso, a zombie. No, not a zombie. It dawned on me that maybe the man had never been dead. He put handcuffs on the woman, whose jaw was hanging so far to the floor I could have climbed right in.

"Did she notice how annoying her voice was?" asked the totally not dead Xacrelf. "No wonder they didn't make her lieutenant. You two all right? Damn, man, what happened to your ear?"

CHAPTER TWENTY-FIVE

BET YOU DIDN'T SEE ANY OF THIS COMING

One of the things I hate the most in television is when they pull a dead guy out of a hat and tell you he was never dead, that it was his evil twin who died or magic was involved. But in this moment, I didn't care how Xacrelf was back. I was just glad he was there to save my ass.

The crew convened in the brig, where two of the formerly empty cells were now occupied: one by Doesso, scowling in a corner, and the other by Finch.

Separate cells. Thank heavens.

Doesso had come after us when she realized we were still alive, leaving her partner to attack the bridge team. Thankfully, the away team had gotten the message and come back quickly enough to stop the two saboteurs, who were a little verbose for their own good and had rather stalled themselves. Finch had attacked a sick bay, but was no match for Two, who had distracted him with further talk of Derzan long enough for Blayde to knock him down.

Easy peasy.

It was nice, for once, to see everything fall into place. To have an actual victory. Have things wrap up in a bow—minus the annoying questions that would plague me for ages to come.

I couldn't stop thinking about that stupid hot air balloon. What else in my life didn't add up, apart from the fact that I was standing on a spaceship right now?

Oh, and that stupid alien fleet waiting for us to return. I kept forgetting about that. Maybe I just didn't want to remember.

No one was more shocked than Doesso to see Xacrelf alive, but the crew was making it a tough competition. Kork was hugging the man so tightly I wondered if he would kill him for real this time.

"Buddy, I'm so glad you're not dead," Kork said, his relief overwhelming his words. "What the hell happened?"

"Finch happened," said Xacrelf, pointing at the man in the cell. "You should probably let him out, you know."

"Let him out?" Kork stammered. "But he tried to kill us!"

"I was undercover, asshole!" said Finch, pushing the gag out of his mouth. "Why do you think I let Two go on that rant about murder? I'm not an idiot. Protocol has always been to shoot first."

"Wait, what? Finch was undercover?" asked Doesso.

She looked at Zander, as if somehow accusing him of all this. Zander threw up his hands and stood back—not his problem. This was the ship's affairs.

"The Alliance has known about the Consortium leak on the *Traveler* for years," he said. "They allowed it to continue, but only to give the enemy the information we wanted them to know. They sent me in undercover, fabricated a backstory about me being a rogue, and let the leak come to me. It took months to build up trust, but Doesso told me exactly what she was."

"You're a rat?"

Doesso seemed infused with energy all of a sudden. She flew to her feet, storming the force field that separated their two cells.

"I thought you were on my side," she spat. "I thought you understood! They took my name, Finch. They thought Aya Tri was too catchy for a mere co-star, so they changed it. Not to make me famous, but to make me *less* popular. I thought you knew what it felt like. I thought you understood me."

"You betrayed the Alliance." He turned his back on her. "I was doing my duty."

"You … you … you stupid conduit! I trusted you. I thought … I thought … I fucking loved you, Hunter."

"Sit down, Doesso. Don't get yourself in any more trouble than you already are."

She spat at him, the glob of saliva sticking to the force field, causing it to crackle blue as it dribbled down. He ignored it.

"So, will you let me out, or do I have to order you to."

"I'm captain of the ship," said Kork, coolly. "I give

the orders."

"I'm an agent of the Night division." Finch rolled his eyes wide, apparently bored by all this. "Not only do I give the orders, but if you stand in my way, I can have you wiped from existence."

That must have meant something to Kork because he let the force field down instantly.

"Hands," ordered Finch, and Two came over with the key to Finch's handcuffs. The agent rubbed his wrists, saying nothing.

"And Xacrelf?" asked Doesso. "What happened there?"

"The lieutenant caught me running the program under Crandle's so-called orders," said Finch. "I had to make sure he couldn't say anything. I dosed him with a sleeping agent and informed him about my intentions when he woke up. It also allowed me to prove myself to Doesso."

"I trusted you," she said again. "I trusted you."

"I spent the past day trying to get in contact with the Alliance," said Xacrelf, "but our long-range transmitters are down. I'm sorry to say we have no idea what to expect when we return to the other half of the ship. The Consortium is probably still lying in wait. A rescue mission would be suicide."

"But why let Doesso go as far as she did?" asked Kork, fuming. "What was the plan there? You tried to kill Sally, and you almost did!"

"Collateral damage," said Finch. "I couldn't blow my cover. Doesso promised the Consortium the crew of the *Adventures of the Traveler*. They watch the show, too. They know how much this crew means to the Alliance.

Kidnapping them would hurt the Alliance more than a blow to the ship, but we wanted this to happen. We believed that letting you be captured for real would be a rallying cry for the fleet and allow us to get enough momentum to strike the Consortium at its core."

"You wanted to sacrifice us," said Kork.

"No, we—"

"It sounds like they wanted to sacrifice us, Captain," said Crandle. A smirk grew on her face.

"It was for the greater good. Don't you understand that?"

"Oh, I understand, all right," said Kork. "I know how the Alliance sees us."

"As puppets," said Crandle, taking a step toward him.

"As sheep," agreed Ter.

"Disposable," added Xacrelf.

Before he knew what hit him, the crew had pushed Finch back into his cell and thrown up the force field. The agent staggered backward, shocked. He threw his hand against the energy that kept him in his cell, only for it to shock him as violently as the shocks he gave his child-hire.

"Let me out," he snarled. "Let me out! I order you to—"

"Come on, crew. We have someone's mess to clean up," said Kork, as calmly as anyone could.

"I am an agent of the Night Division! If you don't let me out of this cell, so help me."

"Do you hear something?" asked Crandle. "I thought I heard a voice. Oh well, no matter."

Doesso laughed from her own cell, watching Finch writhe in pain as he hit the force field repeatedly with his bare fists.

"Does that mean you're letting me out?" she asked.

"No, Doesso, we're not letting you out," said Kork. "You tried to give us up to the Consortium."

"Ah, true," she agreed.

"You threw Sally out an airlock."

"She survived, didn't she?"

"If you turn your life over to Derzan, then perhaps—"

"Shut up, Two!" snapped Kork. "Doesso, if we survive the Consortium, the Council of Justice will deal with you, which would make for quite a good filler episode, don't you think?"

"And if we don't survive?" she asked.

"Then you'll be too dead to care."

Doesso laughed, throwing her head backward and letting out a scream of manic joy. What she found funny, I would never know; we left her and Finch to deal with their own shit. We had much bigger fish to fry.

An alien army. Waiting for our return.

The Alliance, hoping they'd take us.

Our pilot, stuck in the brig with our chief engineer.

Our astrogator offline.

And a crew made up of actors. Somebody grab the popcorn.

"We're so screwed."

Crandle held her head in her hands as we sat around the conference table. It felt more official than sitting at the bridge where the warp shutters were down, a reminder that we were on our last warp before reaching the enemy. There was no way of knowing what would be waiting for us there.

"We still have time to go away, you know," said Xacrelf. "We don't have to reconnect with the other half of the ship. We know it's a trap; we don't have to go back."

"And go where?" asked Crandle. "We're the most recognizable ship in this arm of the galaxy. Even if we're missing half of it, people know who we are."

"Not to mention our faces are on every screen in the quadrant," added Ter. "We wouldn't be able to ask for help without someone recognizing us."

"So we're on our own," said Crandle. "More than ever."

"We're never alone," said Two.

"Two, so help me Derzan, if you're about to mention your gospel again, I'm going to—"

"I was not going to turn this solemn moment into a lesson about Derzan's great love," said Two, somewhat snippy for a droid. "Although yes, that is an entirely accurate assessment. I meant to say this ship is never alone because it has the love and admiration of the entire Alliance."

"Aww, Two, I never took you as the sentimental type," I said.

"I meant that quite literally. The cast is always being filmed."

"What?" Kork stood suddenly. "The cameras aren't off?"

"Most of the cameras are still rolling. The ones in the ship. The ones in the hopper. The ones in my eyes."

"Oh crap," I stammered. "So, they have everything we did on camera? Everything?"

"The good news is the Alliance can't use any of it," Kork said quickly. "They wouldn't want it to look like they were collaborating with the universe's most wanted criminals. Not to mention their own enemy."

All eyes fell on Zander and Blayde—some on me, but who am I kidding, a whole lot less.

"Raise your hand if you don't already know," asked Zander. All hands stayed on or below the table—except for Nim's, which he raised tentatively in the air. Zander could only stare at Kork. "Come on, man. I thought you were going to keep it to yourself."

"We all figured it out," said Crandle. "I mean, come on, we heard the rumors after the Da-Duhui catastrophe. The siblings are back."

"The Alliance simultaneously hates you and denies your existence," said Kork, "so we all know what you look like, but you're not real either. It's the dumbest paradox since the Bedford Sleep Loop."

"The what?" Blayde rolled her eyes. "Right, the secret is out: you know we're the Alliance's super, immortal rivals. Boom. Bye Thratra and Haln; hello Blayde and Zander."

"And Sally," I added for good measure. "Hi?"

"And Sally, yes," she agreed. "You going to turn us in once this is over?"

"Hell no," said Kork. "You stayed to help us, despite knowing the truth about us. We owe you our lives. We won't tell a soul."

"What about the cameras?" asked Zander. "Two just admitted he's recording everything. You'll be in trouble."

"The Alliance wanted to throw us to the enemy as a publicity stunt," the captain scoffed. "I really don't care what they think. Working with you makes this footage even more unusable."

"But you'll—"

"I'll take the consequences," he said, and the crew nodded in agreement.

"Beats being dead," added Crandle. "So, what's the plan?"

There was a pause. Silence fell over the room like a sheet, while all eyes went back to staring at the duo, intent. Blayde rolled her eyes.

"I get it," she said. "You won't turn us in because you think we have a plan."

"Don't you?"

"I don't. Zander?"

"Nope," he responded.

I cleared my throat. "Guys, I do."

"You do what?" asked Zander.

"I, um, have a plan," I said. I waited for the panic to rise in my chest, as it always did, but I was as calm as a meditating monk.

No one stopped me. No one stepped in. I actually had the floor, and these people's lives were in my hands. I swallowed my fear and clenched my fists.

"When you were filming, yesterday, I guess it was," I said, "that was the conclusion of a two-parter, wasn't it?"

"Yes," said Crandle, nodding vigorously. "But I don't see how—"

"Did the first part air already?"

"It should have," she said, "but…"

"What does the Consortium actually know about you guys?" I asked. "Do you think they know where to draw the line between reality and fiction?"

I was on a roll now. I tapped the table, pulling up a keyboard. I let my translator do its job of understanding the system, taking my seat once more, letting my fingers hover over the digital paper.

"Have I ever told any of you about my *Star Trek* fanfiction?"

Kork's smile was wide enough to fill the room, which was good because it eclipsed everybody's looks of confusion.

"I sure hope you're good at memorizing scripts."

CHAPTER TWENTY-SIX

THE SEASON FINALE TO END ALL FINALES

The ship burst out of warp in a blaze of light.

Light we couldn't see, of course, because the blinds were down, but no matter. We knew we had made an entrance.

"Places, everyone," said Kork, sitting proudly in his captain's chair. "Now let's put on a show."

Crandle nodded by his side, her own post lit up like a Christmas tree. She sat tall and steady, ready for action. Gone was the diva. In her place sat a soldier.

"Shields at one hundred percent and holding, Captain," said Xacrelf. "Shall I open the blinds?"

"Do it," Kork ordered. "Free the pods."

I hit the large red button at my side, letting the blinds roll up and away from the massive window. I was terrified of what I would see outside, but keeping composure was everything in this minute. I could not let an ounce of weakness show.

The little drones whizzed out of their cubbies, exploring the room with their little black eyes. With no one flying them—the control center still being in the other half of the ship—they dispatched randomly around the room, focusing on the captain and wide shots.

"And we're live," said Xacrelf. "The transmission is being sent in all directions on three popular frequencies. If no one hears us, it's because they've plugged their ears."

I gave a stiff nod. I had pulled my hair up in a tight ponytail, making myself look as non-Sally like as possible. If I was going to be part of the crew, I had to look the part.

"They're hailing us," said Kork. "Here it goes."

With the quick tap of his finger, he brought the video up on the screen. The window glazed over to show the face of…

A goat?

I didn't know what else to compare it to. The face before me was alien in more ways than I could count. The eyes were wide, round, and dark like a cave. Hair sprouted from the stranger's face, brown flecked with white, framed with wide nostrils on the bottom and long, curled horns on the top. Metal pendants hung haphazardly from the horns, displaying some kind of rank or insignia.

A red collar trimmed in gold peeked into the screen. A military uniform. Consortium colors.

Ooh boy. This was serious time.

I had to remind myself that this wasn't a show. That this wasn't a fun LARP back on Earth, at a con with friends. This was real life, and if our acting wasn't on point, we would be cadavers drifting in space.

Or worse.

"Ah, the *Traveler* has returned," said the stranger, bleating out a shrill laugh. "I didn't think you would be dumb enough for that."

"You took our crew hostage," snapped Kork, "and in the Alliance, we leave no man behind. Who am I speaking to?"

"You ran from us once, I fail to see—"

"Who am I speaking to?" Kork insisted, intertwining his fingers and leaning back in his chair, quite comfortable. I had to give it to him; his act was rather compelling.

"I am Grand Commander Morsul, Captain of the CSS Destroyer *Stamina*," he replied, "and you need not introduce yourself. I already know who you are."

"Ah, then you know that this battle is pointless," he said. "You watched the newsreel, I suspect."

"You mean your little… show?" Morsul bleated again. "Yes, yes, I have seen it."

"Have you caught up, yet? Last week's episode was quite exciting. Too bad you interrupted us just moments after we finished filming this week's segment. After we defeated Praedo."

"That mewling fiend?" Morsul shook his head. "Captain, I fail to see where this is going. Face the facts: You are surrounded, and we have half of your ship. The half with the weapons, I might add. You have no place to run. You have no place to hide. Surrender, and we might just let you live."

"You're not listening, Commander," snapped Kork. "We have the spoils of war. We have… the Alpha Box."

"The what?" Morsul scoffed, but if I could read a goat's face correctly, and I'm not saying I can, there was a hint of apprehension there. Maybe curiosity. "You mean that thing from last week where—"

"Commander, I forgot to tell you, as per Alliance protocol, this is currently being filmed for the people back home," interjected Kork, "and today, we're broadcasting live."

"This is an effort to increase transparency from the military to the civilians it serves to protect," added Crandle, "so they may see us confront the Alliance's sworn enemy in real time."

Morsul paused for a minute, as I hoped he would. Outright telling the world that this ship was a lie would defeat the purpose of his attack. They wanted the Alliance to lose hope over the loss of their heroes, not lose faith in them. Quite the opposite.

At least, I hoped. Any deviation from the plan at this point would ruin our chances of survival.

"Well, then, have you told your people that you are cowards?" asked the Consortium commander. "Do they know you left the battlefield at the first sight of danger? That our ships arrived just in time to see you run away?"

"Run away? You misunderstand, Morsul," said Kork. "We were getting reinforcements. Don't you see?"

Jurrah and Nim stood in unison, bald heads glistening in the white light of the bridge. They stared straight at the enemy's screen, letting him know they were here and to be feared.

"Is that… no." Morsul shook his head.

"Two astrogators?" Kork smirked. "Exactly. You injured our astrogator, Commander, and she's awake and angry. And by her side? The youngest graduate of the Academy. Together, they control not only this ship but the Alpha Box as well."

"You cannot possibly expect us to believe this," the commander insisted, but with less glee than he had earlier.

"Do you see any sign of the traitors here?" asked Kork, waving his arms wide over the bridge. "We apprehended them easily. The Alliance has no tolerance for treason."

"The Alpha Box is primed and ready," said Xacrelf, hands flying over his screen.

"Target has been selected," I added, pretending to hit buttons in front of me. *Beep beep boop.*

"Yes," said Nim and Jurrah as one. "Prepare to feel the pain you have caused us both."

"Now, hold on here," said Morsul. He glanced over his shoulder, frowned, and looked at us once again, the fur above his eyes furrowing. "Maybe we can talk."

"Maybe they need a demonstration of our power," said Crandle. "What do you think, Captain?"

"That sounds brilliant, Crandle," he agreed. "Maybe they need for us to show them what this baby can do."

"No, thank you," said Morsul, backpedaling quickly. "We believe you."

"Good choice," said Kork. "Now, leave our space. Return to your territories, and we shall return to ours. No one needs to die today."

"We are watching," said Nim and Jurrah, together in their eerie, creepy way. "We do not forget."

Morsul flickered off the screen. For a minute, I half-expected him to open fire on us, but our show was convincing. The ships began to leave, flickering into warp speed one by one until the only thing before us was the other half of the *Traveler*.

But things were not done yet. We were still broadcasting, after all.

The crew cheered and shook hands, all very professional. I shook one of Ter's hands. He had gone against Alliance protocol, cutting extra armholes in a new uniform rather than stuff his arms and legs into single sleeves.

I wondered how the Alliance would respond to that.

"Crew, we were lucky today," said the captain, standing before his chair. We made our way to stand at attention before him. He had a speech coming. "We won, but this was a victory only in that we all came out alive. No casualties on either side— now that's what I call a good day. But the Consortium will be back, and if we continue to fight over such trivial things as whose planet is whose, we'll never stop fighting. I hope that the next time we encounter the Consortium, it will be around a table of diplomacy and that the bloodshed will end. We've lost too many good people for this war to be the answer."

"We're being jammed, Captain," said Xacrelf suddenly, disturbing the moment.

"I'm amazed we got to say as much as we did," said Kork. "Shall we celebrate for real, now?"

There was nothing left in the mini fridge to eat or drink, but we still managed to have fun.

Ter broke out the military rations. Sometimes, you don't have the luxury of matching the right food for the right occasion, but, hey, we didn't blow up. Any food would work.

Blayde and Zander slipped out of hiding, bringing with them drinks they had found 'somewhere' on the ship. Judging by the look on Crandle's face, Doesso had intuited correctly about Crandle's secret stash.

I watched, slightly detached, as the crew joked and laughed together. They were no longer the actors on this stage. They had brought their performance to life, gone beyond their roles. They truly were the heroes they deserved to be.

I undid the tight pony, allowing my hair to fall back over my shoulders. It desperately needed a wash, and I wondered if I could slip away long enough to use one of the *Traveler*'s showers. They must have good ones here, what with so many actors around who needed to look picture-perfect.

"Sally."

His voice had come out of nowhere. With a start, I turned around. There he stood, the gorgeous starship captain with his hands clasped behind his back, the poised posture of a leading officer in an alien army.

Veesh, he was beautiful.

"May I have a word?" Kork asked, smiling sheepishly with only the corners of his mouth.

"Sure," I said, nodding toward the back of the bridge. He seemed to have been thinking the same thing. We walked side by side to the observation deck, leaving the festivities above.

It was amazing, yet again, to stare out into space. To think that barely a few hours ago, I had been out there. That I had experienced the vacuum of space first-hand and lived to tell the tale.

Add that to the list of things that did not add up.

"What's this about, Kork?" I asked, taking a seat on the bench. He sat but kept a polite distance, his skin not touching mine.

"It's ... difficult to know where to start," he said, exhaling heavily. "I'm sorry for earlier. I don't know what I said that sent you away, but I'm sorry. I hope I didn't—"

"Oh, no," I said, running a hand through my knotted hair. "I'm so sorry. My ex had the same name as you do, and he ... he recently passed away. It was just, tough, you know, to be reminded of him in such an intimate context."

"Oh," he said, and I had a feeling he thought I was making excuses. But if he didn't believe me, there wasn't much I could do. Thankfully, he said nothing about it. "I would have liked to know you more. To take you out for coffee, even though there isn't a great coffee equivalent here. You're amazing, Sally. But ..."

"But I'm leaving," I said, "and you know that, don't you?"

He nodded, slowly. "You're with the siblings. And as much as I'd like to stand for them in some kind of court, I don't think the Alliance would look fairly upon them. I'm pretty sure they know that, too. You'll leave the same way you came. You'll do that teleport thing."

"Jumping," I agreed. "We're already on camera. There are no secrets left to keep."

"The fact that you helped us against the Consortium will shine some light in your favor," he said, "but you need to get going. Before we reconnect with the rest of the crew. We'll play dumb, pretend we had no idea who you were. It's going to be a shit-storm, though."

"I'm sorry I can't help with that."

"I know," he said.

"What are you two lovebirds cooing about?"

Blayde strode down the ramp, Jurrah in tow. The two of them looked closer than ever. Jurrah's hand was tightly hidden in Blayde's.

"Ah, did we steal your spot?" I said, granting me a sneer from Blayde. By her standards, that was friendly repartee.

"I was just telling Sally that you should go before it's too late," said Kork. "We're incredibly thankful for your help today. I wish I could repay you somehow."

"Ah, it wasn't a big deal," said Blayde, slapping him hard on the back. I guessed she was back to liking him—though she wasn't going to keep him on that pedestal any longer. "For you? Any day."

"Us not turning you in might be as much payment as I can offer."

"Aw, it's sweet that you think you could actually turn us in." Blayde patted his hand gently. "But you're right, we'll get going. Sally, can you run up and get Zander?"

"Sure thing," I said, playing along to avoid any further dismissal from her. "Meet you back here."

"I'll walk with you," said Kork. "I'll be on the other end of the ship when you finally ..."

"Jump away," I said, offering him a warm smile. "Sure, walk with me."

We walked back up the ramp we had just come down, but together, it wasn't something that annoyed me. Kork let out another sigh, breathing as he took weight after weight off his chest.

"When you get back to Earth," he said, slowly, "do you mind looking up my mom? I think she needs to know what happened to me."

"Of course," I replied, not bringing up the fact that I was probably not going to find Earth for quite a long time. "What's her name?"

"Sydney," he replied, and I shuddered. The same as my Matt's mom. "Sydney Daniels. From Norwalk, Connecticut. Born 1953. I hope that's enough to go by."

"We have the Internet, I think it'll do just fine."

"The Internet? Wait, isn't that the…"

"Don't worry. You've got way cooler technology on your spaceship," I said, and he laughed. He put his hand on my shoulder then pulled it back just as quickly, like he had touched a hot stove. I wished he'd have let it stay.

But at the same time, he terrified me.

"Hey, Zander," I said, joining him. "It's time for us to go. Blayde's down on the observation deck."

"Right," he nodded, "let's get going. No goodbyes that way."

"Well, I would like one goodbye," said Kork, his eyes made contact with mine. The tug at my heart grew impossible to ignore, and I wrapped my arms around his neck, his lips finding mine before I could even begin to search for his, and he kissed me so wholly and entirely that I felt like I was going to melt in his arms.

When we pulled apart, the entire deck cheered. Well, minus Two, who was sulking about something or another. I wasn't sure what his religion consisted of, but it didn't seem to like people being happy.

"So much for leaving unnoticed," said Zander with a wide roll of his eyes. "Nice to have finally met you, Captain. I really do appreciate your work."

"Likewise," Kork said with a wink. "Sally, you take care of this man, you hear?"

"Yes sir, oh Captain, my captain," I replied.

He laughed again. "See? When I make that joke around here, everyone thinks I'm trying to come up with a new catchphrase. *Thank you.*"

"I'll see you around, Kork."

"You know it."

I walked away, feeling dizzy. There was a tingle on my lips from the electricity of our kiss. He made me want to stay.

"Well, that was a beautiful sight," said Zander.

"What was?"

"You"—he chuckled—"all pink and blushing and giddy. You were never like that on Earth."

"Oy, that's not for you to say," I sputtered. "There was a lot you weren't privy to."

"Fine, fine, I'll shut up," he said, winking at me. "But look at the great job we did. The crew is saved from two psycho cast members, we discovered a lost colony of humans, a robot started a religion."

"Yeah, but what about Nim?" I asked. "That poor

kid got rid of one chip only to be slotted for a new one. We haven't done anything about him."

"Seriously, Sally?" said Zander. "You helped save all these people, and you're worried about the kid?"

"Yeah," I said, "you didn't see him, Zander. The way his eyes—"

"I remember," said Zander, coolly, "and you're right. No good can come of it. The Alliance is wrong in many ways, but, of all their faults, their child-hire policy is probably the worst, stemming from the very best of intentions."

"So, what do we do about it?"

"Nothing."

"Nothing?" I spat, stopping in the hallway so I could glare at him. "We can't do nothing."

"We don't get involved with politics, even you reminded me of that," said Zander. "If we did, we'd be no better than totalitarian dictators—and immortal dictators at that. I'm pretty sure my ethics don't match up with a whole lot of systems out there."

"But—"

"We help out in times of crisis," he said sternly. "Like today. Space Law. We help. When it comes to policy, they might be bad, but we can't stop it. Unless it's criminal, in which case, fine. But we can't storm into the nearest government building and order them to stop their entire program for reintegrating abducted children. It will take time, and new solutions need to be offered."

"So, there's no way we can help?"

"Not in the immediate future. We can give a little push in the right direction here and there, from time to time." Zander smiled in what looked like an attempt to be reassuring, but I didn't buy it. "One day these things will be forgotten, or only told as stories to frighten children. It will be a thing of the past. I promise you."

"Marcoli's lucky to have gotten out, but Nim's not in the system yet. We can still help him. There's still time."

"To do what?"

"The kid's brilliant," I said. "He's smart. He picked up languages without having a translator in less than a day of knowing us. He figured out much of the plan to bring down this ship and helped thwart it. The Alliance is going to chip him all the same and put him into some menial job that's way below him, first contact with a lost colony or not. We need to get him out of here."

"I agree."

"Wait, you do?" I grinned. "I mean, great, but I thought you might need more convincing."

"I'm not the one who needs convincing," he said. "I like having company around. Blayde's not going to be so easy, though. I know exactly what she'll say: he's a kid; he could get hurt."

"And she would be right," Blayde said, popping out of nowhere. "We can't take a fifteen-year-old boy along with us. Sally's one thing, and look what happened to her."

"Thanks for that."

"No offense, Sally," Blayde insisted. "You are beginning to grow on me, like a benign tumor. But you're mortal and could die at any minute."

"I can take care of myself, thank you."

"Says the girl who got air locked into space a few hours ago."

"Says the girl who *survived* getting sucked out into the vacuum of space, with no brain damage," I said, proudly. "And got us out of the alien mess without making it look like you're choosing sides."

"Still," she said, ignoring me, "the kid's a liability. We can't bring him along. One mortal is enough."

"I'm not your pet," I snapped. "I can handle myself. I've proved that time and time again. And Nim might impress us all. It's not like I'm asking him to join some kind of team. I know it's always going to be you and Zander. I'm saying I want him to come with us. He can live on Earth, with me, or my parents, or something."

"Fine," she rolled her eyes. "If only because I'd rather not see his talent wasted on the Alliance. At least on Earth he could make something of himself. All right, Sally, we have a deal. You take care of him, and since Zander's in charge of you, he'll keep an eye on both of you. Grand-mentoring or whatever. I will not be held responsible. And the second we see your little rock of a planet, we're rid of you. Both of you. Agreed?"

"Agreed," I said, extending my hand to shake it. She slapped it, grabbed it, tugged it, punched it, and spat on it, all in that order. But our deal was sealed. Now all that was left was to figure out what to do with the spit on my hand.

"And he has to want it," she said. "We're not kidnapping this kid."

"Not a second time," Zander muttered under his breath.

"Cool," Blayde grinned. "I'm going to say my good-byes to Jurrah. Meet us downstairs."

I returned to the bridge once more, taking a last

look at the perfect set, at the gorgeous view, at the beautiful desks and the captain in his chair. I looked one last time upon the crew, who were chatting amicably together, laughing as if nothing had happened.

Nim, however, stood to the side, obviously sulking. I sidled up next to him.

"So," I said, "you don't really want to spend your life working for them, do you?"

"No," he replied, shaking his head.

"How would you like to explore the galaxy a bit?" I asked. "Just for a little while, and then, when we find my planet, you could live with me."

He spat up his drink.

"This isn't a joke?"

"No," I said, shaking my head, excited to speak these words. "Come with us, Nim. You won't ever have to work for the Alliance—or anyone you don't want to—ever again."

He took my hand. We said nothing as we walked to the observation deck, meeting our friends there without needing words to say what would happen next.

Zander took my hand. Blayde took Nim's. And with one last look at the astrogator, who smiled at us warmly, and one last look out that window, we closed our eyes and jumped into the unknown.

Sally's adventures continues with:

CELESTIAL

Book 4 of the Starstruck Saga

She wanted a holiday. They needed a chosen one.

Sally, Zander, and Blayde, accompanied by their new friend Nim, have only one request: no more bizarre distractions on their hunt for Earth.

But before their cells can complete a single jump, the team is shoved off course and crash into a dreary old temple. Worse yet, there seems to be some confusion over Sally's face, as it looks exactly like that the local deity, Selena, goddess of the moon and omniscient absentee. Sally's ticking every box on the ancient prophecies checklist.

Fresh off of her meds and riding the withdrawal, Sally must choose between embracing the role of Goddess to protect the planet from the mysterious Sky People, or being thrown in a Volcano. Not the best way to start a tropical vacation. It's not going to be easy uniting warring factions, dealing with excitable whispering forests, or fighting both literal and figurative demons. Not to mention keeping up the appearance of divinity when all Sally wants is a nap.

Armed only with some high school improv' classes and a basic knowledge of foreign pop songs, Sally must save the planet – before everything goes up in flames.

ACKNOWLEDGEMENTS

Wow, book three already! I never thought I would make it this far – I sure hopes I would, but it seemed like such an unreachable goal just a year ago. I have so many people to thank for helping me live this dream.

For starters, my amazing editor, Anna, who saw right through my weakest chapters and pushed me to my limits to make them better. If it wasn't for your tough love, *Traveler* would be a pale shadow of what it is now. You bring the best out of me and my work, and I can't wait to show you book Four! I always love your notes in the margins, and sharing a good laugh over everything bookish.

To my publisher, Michelle. This adventure has taken us into lands unknown, and I couldn't imagine braving the book world without you. You make every line sparkle and shine, and I know *Traveler* wouldn't be here without you.

To Cayleigh, for cleaning up my messes, and always making my books look spick and span. I always look forward to your notes too, and wish I could write faster to get my next books to you!

To Hugo, for always being here when I need him. Whether it's a mental breakdown about all the messes I've gotten myself into, or when I have a plot hole that needs a fix, you're there for me in ways you never know. Thank you for giving me the spark for the character of

Two, I can't ever thank you enough.

To the authors who have pushed me to keep writing: Madeline, Andrew, Ronnie, Dawn, Jeff, Kelly, Laura, Jess. To the artists who bring my characters to life off the page: Lloyd, Kelly, Emily. To the fans who became friends along the way – I'm looking at you, Cora! To my fellow Masters of Space, who always have my back when it comes to balancing my workload and my course load. To my family and to the family I've made along the way, you keep me sane and still writing.

Well, the sanity part is questionable. But thanks to you, I won't stop writing.

And finally, to Joanna. Always to Joanna. Thank you.

ABOUT THE AUTHOR

S.E. Anderson can't ever tell you where she's from. Not because she doesn't want to, but because it inevitably leads to a confusing conversation where she goes over where she was born (England) where she grew up (France) and where her family is from (USA) and it tends to make things very complicated.

She's lived pretty much her entire life in the South of France, except for a brief stint where she moved to Washington DC, or the eighty years she spent as a queen of Narnia before coming back home five minutes after she had left. Currently, she goes to university in Marseille, where she's starting her masters of Astrophysics.

When she's not writing, or trying to science, she's either reading, designing, crafting, or attempting to speak with various woodland creatures in an attempt to get them to do household chores for her. She could also be gaming, or pretending she's not watching anything on Netflix.

seandersonauthor.com
www.facebook.com/seandersonauthor
@sea_author

Printed in Great Britain
by Amazon

60494457R00208